Saving Dancer
Savage Brothers MC Book 2

Jordan Marie

Editors:
Twin Sisters Rockin' Book Reviews (TSRBR)
Promotions
Fran Owen & Carol Fling

Formatting:
Paul Salvette & BB eBooks

Copyright © 2015 Jordan Marie
Print Edition

All rights reserved. No part of this publication may be reproduced, distributed, or transmitted in any form or by any means, including photocopying, recording, or other electronic or mechanical methods, without the prior written permission of the author.

WARNING: The unauthorized reproduction or distribution of this copyrighted work is illegal. No part of this book may be scanned, uploaded or distributed via the internet or any other means, electronic or print, without the publisher's/author's permission. Criminal copyright infringement, including infringement without monetary gain, is investigated by the FBI and is punishable by up to 5 years in federal prison and a fine of 250,000.00 (http://www.fbi.gov/ipr/). Please purchase only authorized electronic or print editions and do not participate or encourage the electronic piracy of copyrighted material. Your respect of the author's rights is appreciated.

This book is a work of fiction and any resemblance to persons, living or dead, or places events or locales is purely coincidental. The characters are created from the author's imagination and used in a fictitious manner.

Cover:
Designer: Margreet Asselbergs – Rebel Edit Designs
Model: Justin Miller
Photographer: Shauna Kruse – KIP Models and Boudoir
Dollar Photo Club
(Photo used on the back of paperback only)

Trademarks:

Any brands, titles, artists used in this book were mentioned purely for artistic purposes and are either used as a product of the author's imagination or used fictitiously. None of the herein mentioned products, artists etc., endorse this book whatsoever and the author acknowledges their trademarked status which has been used in this work of fiction.

Author acknowledges trademarked status or owners of various products and further acknowledges that said use is not authorized or endorsed by said owners. While some places in this book might mention actual areas or places, author acknowledges that it was purely for entertainment purposes and not endorsed by owners or has nothing to do with actual place and was mentioned to further reader's enjoyment only.

This e-book is licensed for your personal enjoyment only. It is not to be re-sold or given away to others and doing so is a violation of the copyright.

Warning:

The Content in this book is intended for mature audiences only. 18+ and above. Contains sexual violence, sexual situations, violence, excessive profanity and death. Reader should please read with that knowledge.

Dedication

So much has happened between the publishing of this book and the last that my head spins. I've learned, I've loved and I've lost. Most of all I have lived. I lived a dream I've had my whole life. I've learned more about myself and more about the friend and person I want to be.

Sabrina Paige and Cora Brent, there are no words. None that I have. Helen Keller said

Life is either a daring adventure or nothing.

Thank you girls for encouraging me to continue my adventure.

Jenika Snow and Sam Crescent, I'm so proud to know you women. I'm not sure how it's possible that you can have as much talent as you have and still be the amazing people that you are. Thank you for sparing time to talk to me and support me. I love you.

Tammie Smith, rarely does someone come in your life that rocks your world with their loyalty and friendship. You are freaking amazing. Without you in my corner, Dancer would never have happened. I love you—BIG.

Jess Peterson, with so much on your plate you still find time to check on ones you care about. No matter where you are in life, may you always have one moment in the day where you realize you make a difference—always.

Tami Czenkus, you and I know so much about darkness. Thank you for helping me to make this story what it needed to be and not cop-out. Thank you most for sharing your heart with me. Without true friends in life, there would be no joy. Thank you for bringing me joy.

Mandie Nolan, few people surprise me, yet you continue to do so every damn day and always in good ways. I love you—always have, always will.

Jen Wildner, I am so proud of you for living your dreams. I'm even more proud that you are my friend. If the world had more of your kind and giving spirit, what an amazing world that would be.

Fran Owens, you were one of the first blogs to be good to a scared PA who didn't know what she was doing. You were one of the first women to give me support when I wanted to write and you have become a rock. Thank you so much. I love you.

Neringa Paulauskaitė, I don't think you grasp how much I love and appreciate everything you've done for me. You are totally freaking AMAZING.

Nicole Violino, thank you for the support, the smiles and laughter, when you probably didn't even feel like laughing. I have such a deep respect for you. Much FREAKING love.

Angel D., I freaking love the hell out of you. Thank you, doesn't cover it. Your friendship is so important to me.

Krissy Gentry, I am so proud to call you my friend.

Corry Parnese and Susan Garwood, it amazes that two wonderful women with so much on their plate, still give selflessly to author's they don't know. I'm so glad I've met you both. Love and respect women—love and respect.

Mindy McCray, have I mentioned that you're one of my favorite people ever? You give new meaning to the term BADASS BETA. Thank you so much.

Andrea Florkowski your heart is so big. You give when no able, encourage when you're tired and a friend always. You have my love, my support and my admiration.

Jennifer Mitchell, thank you for spending so much time going over Dancer and helping to make it better. You are a Godsend.

Thank you to the Badass Betas. You made me breathe and believe in my instincts when I found it hard to do so. **Melanie Cooper, Tamra Simons, Melony Bruce-Campbell, Erin Osborn, and Christy Armes**, much love women. Your feedback was so valuable and I LOVE EACH OF YOU. Here's hoping you stay around for book 3. I can beg, I'm so okay with that.

Shauna Kruse, thank you for holding my hand as I moved into the land of getting a model for my book cover. I appreciate you so much and I thank you.

AC Bextor, I love your face, have I mentioned?

NB Baker, I loved you from day one and that only grows with each day we add to our friendship. You are an amazing author, but you are a PHENOMENAL friend.

Freya Barker and RB Hilliard, I love you guys. Thank you for all the help and advice.

Mia Sheridan, thank you for being a light. A role model to every author and just an all-around amazing woman with extraordinary talent.

Kurt Gangluff and Leslie Wilder, your friendships are invaluable to me. Thank you, just thank you.

Kaylee Song, Mayra Stratham and Joanna Blake, thank you for your friendship, your sprinting partnership and just for being you.

Kayla McCoy and Dessure' Hutchins, you give me a smile every day. I love you woman.

Thank you to those in the Indie world who have welcomed me and to the online bloggers who have helped promote my books, have been so warm and giving and donate all their time to every author, we could do next to nothing without your support.

Thank you to my crazy **Street Team and Pimping Squad**, there are NO WORDS as to how awesome you are.

Finally thank you to these two crazy chicks **Glenna Maynard** and **Dawn Martens**, who gave me acceptance and laughter when I was a freaking mess. I LOVE YOU CRAZY BITCHES.

I promised this Dedication would be smaller, I think I failed. As my PA likes to say, Sorry, not sorry.

See you next book and we'll see if I succeed there.

Jordan

Table of Contents

Prologue	1
Chapter 1	3
Chapter 2	8
Chapter 3	14
Chapter 4	28
Chapter 5	35
Chapter 6	42
Chapter 7	53
Chapter 8	59
Chapter 9	64
Chapter 10	74
Chapter 11	78
Chapter 12	80
Chapter 13	85
Chapter 14	90
Chapter 15	100
Chapter 16	110
Chapter 17	118
Chapter 18	123
Chapter 19	128
Chapter 20	135
Chapter 21	142
Chapter 22	147
Chapter 23	153
Chapter 24	158
Chapter 25	165
Chapter 26	172
Chapter 27	176
Chapter 28	182
Chapter 29	190
Chapter 30	199
Chapter 31	204
Chapter 32	209

Chapter 33	215
Chapter 34	223
Chapter 35	227
Chapter 36	235
Chapter 37	239
Chapter 38	243
Chapter 39	251
Chapter 40	255
Claiming Crusher Excerpt	257
Etched in Stone Excerpt by Mayra Stratham	260
Playlist for Savage MC	268
Acknowledgments	269
Stalking Links	270

SAVING DANCER

Savage Brothers MC Series

Book 2

Jordan Marie

Prologue

'THE NIGHTMARE' DANCER

It's dark, pitch black. I can feel the hands holding me down. The laughter fades into the background as my heart accelerates and beats out of control. The sound drums in my ears and a fine sweat pops out over my body. I slam my head back with all of my might. I choke on the fear and I despise myself for it. The fear makes me feel weak and I have never been weak in my life.

The back of my head connects with some motherfucker and the feeling of blood smears against my bald head. I slam my head again hoping I can kill the son of a bitch.

I scream out as dirty hands try to clamp over my mouth. I twist and turn until I can get just enough of the hand in my mouth to bite down and tear. I do with an angry scream. There's a moment of disappointment that I can't manage to tear the finger off with just the force of my teeth.

Still, it's enough to get room. Some leeway so I can throw an elbow into the son of a bitch's stomach that has been helping to restrain me. There are four of the motherfuckers holding me, three now that the guy behind me let go. I hope I at least killed him. I will kill them all though. I will. I will tear them apart piece by piece. That is the last clear thought I have before a large silver flash comes at me.

I feel the impact of the pipe against the side of my head and at the same time a sensation of skin tearing down my side. The scent of blood mixes in with the dirty smell of my cell. Stabbed, I've been stabbed. Will I die here? Please let me die before they do what they are planning.

"Got something for you, pretty boy," the voice says as the darkness encloses around me.

It was six words. Six words that would destroy me and start me on my path through hell.

Chapter 1

DANCER

IT'S DARK, BUT not night, that much I know. The heavy, foam-backed curtains are pulled tight over the window and a small sliver of light is allowed to shine where the two panels meet. There is a pounding behind my eyes and a cold sweaty mist covers my body. My head is swimming as I close my eyes against the gut clenching nausea that slams through me.

Waking up like this is nothing new. It's the normal—my new fucked up normal. The room smells of smoke, cheap whiskey, perfumed whores, and sex. Hell, I've stuck my dick in so much loose pussy in the last week the damn thing smells like week old tuna.

I rub my hand over the short stubble on my head. In the week that I've been out of the joint, I've started letting it grow. I kept it shaved during my stint in jail. There are just too many fucking bugs in that damn hell-hole. I'm not sure if I'll cut it again. Anything different from what it was in there is automatically better.

I push bodies off of me and move to the edge of the bed. The two chicks in the bed should have left last night. One of them grumbles in complaint, but she rolls her ass over on her girlfriend and goes back out. When I look over at the lily-white ass sticking up in the air my hand automatically goes down to my dick and stretches it. Damn thing doesn't take the hint though. If anything, it seems to want to crawl inside of my balls and hide. It's a shame because it's a damn fine ass, but what the fuck ever. I stand up and the world spins as my body tilts too far to the left. I right myself and walk towards the bathroom, cursing when my bare feet kick one of the empty liquor bottles littering the floor.

Shit, that hurt. I lean over to pick the bottle up and the world tilts again. This time I overestimate my coordination and fall. I maneuver at the last minute and land on my side instead of my motherfucking head. I lay there a minute looking up in the darkness. It hurts to breathe, not really from the fall. Hell, it's hurt to breathe for so long I can't remember it being any other way. Why I can't swallow a bullet and get it over with? I'm tired of fighting it all. So fucking tired…

"Dancer! Open up, man!"

The old hotel door vibrates with the pounding it receives. My head goes down, both hands raking over it again. I don't want my brothers here. Why couldn't they just leave me alone? I told them to.

"Dancer, open this fucking door or I'm kicking it in!" Crusher yells as he pounds the damn door again. I wince at the pain the noise brings.

I struggle to stand. I may not have had shit to do with my brothers since I got out of the joint, but I know that he's not going to give up. Before I can fully pick my ass up out of the floor, the door slams open and bounces off the wall with a huge cracking noise. I wince in pain the noise brings and close my eyes against the glaring light that is now in the room.

"Fucking hell! Close the damn-motherfucking-son-of-a-bitching door!" I growl, not bothering to turn around and look at Crusher. It's better to keep my back against the light.

"Oh god."

I turn my head against my will when I hear that voice. I know that voice. That voice is imbedded in my brain, my motherfucking black soul. Carolina Grace, the woman who offered me heaven, and brought me hell.

I'm going to rip Crusher's head off. My eyes lock with the one person in this world that I never expected, nor wanted to lay eyes on again.

"What the fuck are you doing here?"

She jerks back like I just physically hit her. I've never hit a woman in my life, but I have so much anger stored up, she'd be smart to stay away from me.

"Hi, Jacob," she whispers into the room and it makes me want to scream and roar at her. I don't want her here. I don't want to see her, I don't want to deal with her and I sure as hell don't want to hear that sweet voice saying my name. She's poison; she's a fucking knife to the gut that repeatedly stabs. She's the reason my head is all messed up, that my life is all screwed up and most of all she is the reason I want to swallow a fucking bullet.

"GET THE FUCK OUT OF THIS ROOM!" I roar pulling myself up and charging towards her.

She gasps and backs up against the hotel door. I'm almost to her. I don't know what I'm going to do when I reach her. I really don't. I might even strangle the life out of her. I know I will push her out of my room, out of my space, out of my life. I know it. In the end the point is moot though because Crusher jumps in front of me and stops me from reaching her.

We're pretty evenly matched, but if I had been sober he wouldn't have stopped me. As it is, he contains me and looks over his shoulder.

"Red, wait for me by my bike, darlin'."

"Okay, Alexander," she whispers and gives me another tortured look.

Her green eyes are filled with tears, but I don't care. Her and her tears can rot in hell. Her auburn hair shines too bright in the dark room. It's like a beacon of hope, a memory of a better time, a better life. That pisses me off even more. Wait. Hold up! *Alexander?* What the hell?

"Are you sinking your dick in that cunt?" I ask in disgust, pushing away from Crusher.

"Jesus H. Christ, Dance! You smell like a damn gutter," Crusher says. His face is curled in disgust.

The bitches from last night are sitting up in bed looking at me and Crusher and it pisses me off. I told them to be gone by morning. I don't even know why I keep trying to bury myself in pussy. It's not working anyway and I sure as fuck don't want them around after.

"Get dressed and get the hell out," I growl, walking towards the small bath, intent on taking a shower.

"If you're going to wait around till I get out, make sure those bitches leave," I order Crusher.

"Dance man…"

"And you sure as fuck better keep that gash you came

with outside."

I make it to the door before a crash is heard. I turn to look and Crusher has taken one of the empty liquor bottles and smashed the old mirror hanging on the wall opposite of the bed. I look at my brother, his body is rigid with anger and the laid back country ol' shucks cocky vibe he normally has is gone.

"Dance, I'm warning you, lay off of Red. I know you're fucked up, but that woman doesn't deserve your wrath or insults."

"I've rotted in hell for two years because of that woman."

"Bullshit."

I want to argue, but truth is I don't give a fuck. The sooner I shower and talk to his ass the sooner he'll leave and I can find a new bottle.

"Whatever. Sorry I insulted your Twinkie of the month," I grumble and slam the door on his curse.

Chapter 2

CARRIE

I MAKE IT outside, stand by Alexander's bike, and drag air into my lungs. Almost two years and this isn't how I imagined seeing Jacob again. He's drunk, naked as the day he was born, and obviously has been in bed with two women...Two! At the same time! When Alexander told me he was going to stop by and check on Jacob, I couldn't resist coming in. It was a bad move. Still, even knowing I shouldn't go inside, I couldn't stop myself. It had been so long since I had seen him. The temptation was just too much. So, I caved.

I don't know what I expected, I really didn't. It wasn't pure hate. It really wasn't, but sadly that was exactly what Jacob radiated when he looked at me. I think he might want to kill me. I laugh hysterically. He'd have to get in line, wouldn't he?

The only reason I am in Kentucky is because someone killed my parents and is still after me. Dragon had ordered Alexander to come to Tennessee to get me after Jacob's mom called him. The next day I was packed up and heading to Kentucky with a man who called himself Crusher. It took me half the trip to get Alexander's real name out of him.

I have been here for four months now and for the most part I've loved it. The Savage MC has become my adopted family, with Dragon, Nicole and Alexander being some of the best friends I have ever had. That won't last though. The minute I heard Jacob was getting out, I knew it would end.

Don't get me wrong, I wanted him out. I really did. I just knew that once he was, I would have to leave. Jacob blames me for what happened to him and in a way he was right. It had been my stupidity to follow Jacob and his buddy to the club that night. I wanted to prove to him I was grown up. I wanted to show him that he needed to take me seriously, that I could be the woman for him. I was so stupid, so incredibly naïve. The only thing I accomplished was proving myself to be horribly immature and to ruin three lives.

"You're going to have to toughen up, Red, if Dance is the man you want to hang your hat on," Bull offers.

I hear Bull's voice and my body instantly stiffens. Bull makes me uncomfortable in ways I don't totally understand. I turn and see him standing in the shadow of the old hotel. He's leaning against the brick wall, wearing worn jeans, a faded red t-shirt and his Savage MC leather vest. He's got a black skull cap on and it looks good on him. I'm not sure there's much that could make him look bad though. The gold studs he wears in his ears sparkle as he walks to me.

"He's not," I say, as my eyes take him in. He stops in front of me and he overshadows everything, dominating. He's wearing these dark sunglasses and the silly girl in me mourns over the fact I can't see his eyes. Bull has the kind of eyes that sparkle with humor constantly, which is odd because he doesn't talk that often.

"Bullshit. Lie to yourself if you want, Red, but not to me."

"He's not," I insist. "Besides even if he was, Jacob hates me."

"Funny thing about love and hate, they tend to get all mixed up."

"If you had seen him a minute ago, you wouldn't say that," I explain, a little panicked at the way his eyes are pinned on me. I'm like a deer caught in the bright glare of headlights on a dark night. My heart even jumps in my chest.

"What's your name anyway?" I ask knowing it's pointless. Since I've been staying here, he has never given me his real name.

"Bull."

"No, I mean like Jacob and Alex...."

"I'm not him, Red."

"Him?"

"The one who folds to the promises on your lips. The name is Bull."

"I have no idea what you're talking about," I say honestly.

"I know; that's what makes you so fucking tempting."

"You're a confusing man, Mr... Bull," he busts out laughing and I'm drawn to the noise. It's husky and dark and it sends tingles of awareness through my body, not quite like they used to be when Jacob was around, but honestly it is the first time I've felt anything close to it.

Bull is dangerous. I'm drawn to him. If I hadn't been in love with Jacob my entire life, he would have been really dangerous. Something makes me keep trying to get Bull to talk to me; maybe I just appreciate the fact that he was one of the first men to ever notice me as a woman. I wish Jacob would do that.

"Red, I'm kind of hoping Dance remains a fool just so I can sample what you got."

"I don't know what you…" I stutter, but I don't get the sentence finished because his lips come down against mine. They're warm and soft. I can taste a hint of coffee on them. I'm in shock. I never expected to be kissed, not by Bull and not here. My body is frozen, but slowly things begin to register. Like the feel of his hand sliding up my back and the heat of his touch, even through my jacket. The woodsy outdoor smell of him is nice, and I take a deep breath through my nose wanting more.

"Open your mouth, Red," he mumbles against my lips. Would it surprise him to know that no man has ever kissed me before? I'm debating opening my mouth for him. Half of me really, really wants to and the other half fights against it. The other half wants to give all my firsts to Jacob. That's stupid. I know it is. Jacob wants nothing to do with me and certainly doesn't want my kisses. I have this amazing, good-looking, virile man wanting entry into my mouth and I'm thinking of another man. A man who hates me and can't stand me, and yet I can't stop wanting him. This would explain why I'm still a virgin at twenty.

My hands go to Bull's biceps to steady myself and to pull away, when I hear Jacob's voice.

"Don't look now *Alexander* but looks like your Twinkie has already moved on to another brother."

The contempt in Jacob's voice is so thick it physically wounds me. My body jerks from the thinly disguised blow. Of course he thinks I'm a whore. Why wouldn't he? I pull back and look up at Bull. His eyes are hidden behind his sunglasses. Can he tell how much Jacob's words cut me? Does it show on my face?

Bull's head moves down so his lips graze my ear and his finger slides along the side of my face. "Toughen up, Red. Anything good is worth fighting for."

I swallow as I try to concentrate on his words. They're good words. I would totally listen to them, if Jacob gave me anything to fight for. If we ever had anything between us, I would absolutely fight. We haven't though and I'm pretty sure Bull is wrong.

He steps away and walks back towards the hotel where he had first been standing. I watch him for a minute, wishing he had stayed. At least when he was here I didn't feel so vulnerable from all the hate pouring off of Jacob. I can feel it. He's doing nothing to hide it. How can a man stand in front of you with hate radiating from every single inch of him and yet still look so heart-stopping gorgeous? The color in his tattoos, the deep brown of his eyes, the short dark hair I crave to touch, the muscular build that makes me weak in the knees…There is so much to want, so much to crave.

"What are you looking at, bitch? You want to tangle with me too? I'd rather chop my dick off than have it anywhere near you," he growls and it hurts.

I look down at the ground so he won't see my face. I'm afraid I can't hold back the tears that want to fall. "Still, you seem to have Crush and Bull hot for you. I bet they'd tag team you if you asked nice enough."

I try to tune out his words. I stare at the cracked pavement at my feet. My eyes follow a jagged line to where it disappears under my shoe. I wish I could disappear. When I look up I see that Bull has returned and punched Jacob in the stomach. He's watching Jacob closely. Jacob is bent over rubbing his stomach and cursing.

"You're a fucking asshole Dance, but keep shooting your poison. I'll gladly take what you're giving away," Bull says over his shoulder as he grabs my hand and pulls me along with him.

"You're riding with me, Red."

I shuffle my feet and try to follow because he is tall as heck. It's hard for me to keep up and for some reason Bull is intent on pulling me with him, so I stumble.

"Where the hell is she going?" Jacob yells.

"If you had your head out of your ass, you'd know," Bull replies and I'm trying to decide which is more astounding. The fact that I'm in the same area with Jacob after all this time or the fact that Bull has said more words in the last twenty minutes than he probably has spoken all week.

He hops on his bike and I use my hands on his shoulder to brace myself as I get on behind him. I lay the side of my face against his back and wrap my arms around him tight. Bull pulls out and directs his bike towards where Alexander and Jacob are standing arguing. My eyes freeze on Jacob's. It seems like forever, but I know it's just mere seconds. It couldn't have been any longer than that but it's long enough that I have to close my eyes against the pain I see reflected back at me.

Chapter 3

DANCER

I WATCH AS Bull rides away with Carrie, it leaves me feeling unsettled. I don't know why. It shouldn't bother me to see Carrie on the back of Bull's bike. After the shit she pulled two years ago... Fuck, I know that's not fair, it wasn't her fault. It was me. I made the decision to gut the motherfucker who tried to rape her. I did that and I shouldn't hold her responsible. Hell, given the choice, I'd do it again. How screwed up is that?

She shouldn't have been at the bar. She was under-age; she had no business being there that night. I knew she was chasing me around like a little lost puppy and while it was cute, I made it clear that nothing would ever happen between us. She was—hell she still *is*—just too damn young. Instead of taking my rejection like the adult she claimed to be, she went outside with that slimy motherfucker and ruined all our lives.

My head is a dull roar even after the shower. I slip my shades on and get on my girl, without looking at Crush. I rub my hand over my stubby hair that's growing out.

My *girl* is a sleek black, Fatboy, Soft tail. She's smooth and shines like wet pussy and rides low with twin pipes.

She holds me close, her fat wheels grip the road better than any bike I've ever had. She's weighted perfect, just a slight movement by me and she knows where to go. She purrs when we ride and growls when I'm stuck in traffic or a light.

She's the only woman I need for sure and a fuck of a lot less headache than any bitch I've been mixed up with. Definitely less aggravation than that damn red-head who just ran off with Bull.

"I still don't know why the fuck I have to go to the club. I told you pricks that I'm not doing this shit anymore."

"Dragon wants you at the club and if I have to drag your fucking ass there, I'll do it."

"Like you could."

"Don't fuckin' try me, Dance," Crusher responds.

I ignore him and start my girl. I'll answer Drag's summons and that's it. I'm tired and I'm not getting into this shit anymore. The club was a life I had. A life from when I was a different person. I am not that person anymore. I never will be again.

We pull into the club about twenty minutes later. I look around the parking area, but I don't see Bull's piece of shit Triumph anywhere. I write off the disappointment of him and Carrie not being here as stupidity—caused by my hangover. I follow Crusher inside, refusing to ask where Bull is. It's not my business, but how fucked up is it that my club has brought in the woman who has caused me so much misery? She's nothing to them.

"Hey, Dance! Good to see you man!" Frog calls out as I walk through the door. He's talking to one of the newer members.

What was it Drag had said his name was? Fuck, not like I care anyway.

I nod my head in response and let my eyes adjust to the dim light of the room.

Dragon is in the back at his usual table. He has Nicole in his lap and he's biting on her neck, whispering in her ear and he's smiling. It's weird to see my brother smiling. I've known Dragon a long ass time and up until this woman came into his life, I'm not sure I had ever seen him smile. I sure as fuck hadn't heard him laughing before, like he is right now.

I've met Nicole a few times, she came with Dragon the day I got released and they took me out of hell (that's the best way to describe prison. It is *hell*). She was okay I guess. I never really bothered to find out. Still, seeing my brother like this, I'd have to say she must have a gold snatch. That's the only reason I can come up with as to why he would keep a ho' around permanently.

"Yo," I growl, letting Dragon know by the tone of my voice that I'm not happy with my summons.

Dragon looks up at me. His hand freezes on Nicole's breast and even I will admit the large globe would make a man beg for more. It fills my brother's hand and then some and the large nipple is dark through her white shirt. Oddly, I think of how Carrie's are much smaller, but they'd be perfect in my hand…I feel my dick jerk in reaction.

"Dance, you look at my woman's tit another minute and you and me got problems."

"You're the one playing with it for the world to enjoy," I respond.

Shit if he doesn't want other men to notice he needs to lock it up in his room, pious bastard.

"Mama, can you…"

"I'm gone, sweetheart. Six and Crush are taking me, Dani, and Lips to visit Carrie anyway," she says. Her voice is soft and loving and it amazes me that someone like that could be so wrapped up in my hard ass brother.

She gets up to leave and Dragon stops her.

"Be safe, Mama. Make sure you do what Crush and Six tells you," he orders, pulling her back to him. "Mine."

When the kiss is finished I hear her whisper, "Forever."

She turns and walks by me, giving me a slight nod. It is my brother though that draws my attention. He has the biggest fucking smile on his face I think I have ever seen.

He waits until Nicole gets to the bar and then calls out, "Hey, Mama?"

"Yeah, sweetheart?"

"Going to spank that ass later, don't think I didn't notice you're wearing those damned boots."

"I was counting on it, Dragon," she laughs.

Crusher follows her out of the room, yelling back out over his shoulder, "Lucky Bastard."

Dragon's eyes follow his woman until she leaves the room and then the easy going look on his face disappears. He kicks the seat out at the table across from him.

"Sit."

I rub my hand over my face. Fuck, this might be worse than I imagined. I take a seat though. There aren't many men I'd follow orders from. Dragon is one, and probably the only one.

"Drag," I say. My tone says I don't give a damn, and part of me doesn't. Still, Drag is a man I respect, a brother I love.

"You want to tell me why I haven't seen your fucking face around here, Dance. I got to tell you, I'm not happy."

"Drag, told you when you dropped me off, I'm done."

"You still got our brand on your sorry ass?"

My hand automatically rubs the back of my shoulder, where the Savage MC tattoo is. It was forged through me, not by the ink, but by the blood and tears my brothers and I shared.

"That's right, motherfucker. You're part of us, so you want to tell me why you're locking us out now, when we need each other?"

Fuck, he's going where I'm not ready to go. So I throw up some other shit that's bugging the hell out of me.

"What the fuck do you have Bull and Crush dragging that bitch around for?"

Dragon looks blank for a minute and then his face turns to stone. I've seen that look before and usually the person getting it, is about to die. I figure I'm at least safe from that, maybe.

"Watch your mouth. Red is family."

"You can see how having my brothers claim the bitch that got me in this mess as family might piss me the fuck off, right?"

"Red didn't do shit motherfucker. You got messy. You want to handle an asshole? You don't go off, in a town we don't own, with witnesses around. Dance, you've been around, you know how this shit works. You screwed the pooch here. That's on you. I couldn't get you out sooner and that shit? That's on me. Way I see it, Red is the only one here free and clear."

Fuck. He's right.

He's not saying anything I don't already know. It's not something I want to acknowledge.

"She shouldn't have…"

"Red was in love with you. For some fucking reason Nicole tells me the woman still is. I don't get women and this crap, but I do fucking know it makes women do shit they shouldn't," Dragon growls, looking away from me to stare out the window. "Nearly got my woman dead. You get lucky enough to get that from a good woman you don't mock that shit, Dance. You *embrace* it."

"I think claiming a woman has made you soft," I state the truth, ignoring the weird feeling his words send through me.

Love? Me? Fuck a duck.

"Fuck you," Dragon barks back at me, but at least his face is friendlier.

"Carr…Princess is too young to know what love is, fuck I'm thirty-five and I don't know what that shit is."

"Way I figure, women have a better handle on this crap. Red's just a few years younger than Nicole and I don't doubt my woman one fucking bit. Now if we're done with our Dr. Phil moment, we got shit to discuss, first being Red."

I sit watching him. I've got nothing to say to that. I shouldn't want to know. Anything and everything to do with this club and especially Carrie, has nothing to do with me. It doesn't bother or affect me in the least. At least that's what I tell myself. Still, here I am waiting for what he has to tell me.

Shit.

"Your mom asked us to pick up Carrie."

"No fucking way."

"Shut up and listen," Dragon returns. I bite my tongue to keep my retort from coming through. I don't know if I could take Dragon, we're pretty evenly matched. I do know he's my brother; I owe him everything. So, I shut the fuck up…for now.

"When you first…" Dragon pauses and I know he blames himself for everything. It's not his fault, but there is fuck-all I can say that he'd listen to and I don't really want to talk about that shit anyway. "When you first got put in the can," he continues, "Carrie came to see you. Do you remember?"

Fuck yeah, I did. I was pissed at the world, at her for causing this mess, at me for making the mistake, at the way I wanted to hold her and kill her at the same time…at everything. My head stays a fucked up mess. It's much worse around Carrie. I am NOT telling Dragon that, so I nod my agreement.

"You sent her away, but after that I guess, things started happening."

"Things?"

"Started small from what I understand. She'd get notes taunting her with things no one should know. There were a couple of break-ins. Her shit was tossed, notes left on her car, different kinds of shit."

My jaw tightens and that uneasy feeling in my gut gets worse.

"And," I prompt because I know there is more.

"There were accidents. At first it wasn't recognized. Don't know why, you would think even being fucking idiots, given the history of the case, that the cops would piece together what was going on. Some sick fuck definitely has it in for the girl."

"What accidents?" I ask, feeling even more on edge.

"A bus she was riding had a blowout, food poisoning, equipment short circuited at the library where she worked. She was nearly electrocuted. Each time something bigger, something more obvious would happen, until the night of the wreck."

"Wreck?"

"Yeah, some motherfucker ran her and her parents off the road. The car went off a mountain and down a cliff. Red was thrown out, escaped with a broken arm and a concussion. Her parents were trapped in the car. It caught on fire, she lost them both."

"Fuck," I said before I could stop it. Carrie came from money, and she never should have been friends with me or my little sister. Still, her parents were descent people. Hell, I don't know if I'm a good judge, but they had been kind and they loved Carrie.

"Dance, Red's been through the ringer. The last fucking thing she needs is your smart ass."

"Why did you and the club get involved?"

Dragon puts his hand over a plain manila folder and pushes it towards me. I look down at it, shore up my courage and open it. Instinctively, I know I will not like what I find.

I sift through it, pictures of Carrie's room with her

clothes scattered everywhere and her underwear laid neatly on the bed cut in pieces, pictures of notes threatening to rape her and kill her afterwards. Each picture is worse, each note more damning. Then there are pictures of the accident. Only these aren't police photos, these are pictures the sick pervert must have taken while Carrie lay unconscious. They are pictures of her parents burning alive.

I do my best to keep my hands from shaking, even with my anger and confusion I know that Carrie…is *special* to me. She always will be. The fact that she almost died while I was rotting away.

Christ.

"Your mom called when Carrie was released from the hospital and I put her under club protection," Dragon said.

Mary isn't my mom, not really. I grew up on the streets with Dragon. My life was shit, until I was placed in the care of Mary and her husband Walter. They were a nice, older couple who had always wanted a kid. For some reason, instead of adopting a baby or a young child, they took a chance on a wilder than hell teenage boy, who was mad at the world. I had been in their home for a year when Mary got pregnant with Jazz. Walter passed away shortly after Jazz's birth with a heart attack and I stayed around and helped out any way I could. When I went into the service, I sent money and always came home on leave to visit with them. Jazz was special. She was all sunshine and completely untainted by the world. I cherished my time with her. Had I known she would die so young, I would have cherished it more. Carrie was my last connection with Jazz, something pure and innocent in my world. I tried to take care of it and protect it too, just like I did with Jazz. Apparently, failure was all I managed with both.

I shake my head, trying to ignore the emptiness of not having Jazz and the memory of her death. I have enough on my plate, no sense in bringing even more ghosts to life. I take a deep breath and look at Dragon.

"I still don't understand why the club got involved."

"Dance, they're your family, whether you acknowledge it or not. That was why. Still, you haven't finished looking at the last picture."

I look back through the folder to find the photo in question. My body breaks out into a cold sweat and my breath stalls.

Fuck me. Why? What would be the point?

I pull it from the rest and look. It is a picture of me covered in the blood of the man I had killed. Carrie is crying and reaching for me as the police pull me away. I remember that night easily. It is engrained in my brain and frozen there in stark clarity.

I remember the feel of the knife in my hand, the breeze in the air, the stink of the dark alley, the way the moon shone down on Carrie's auburn curls, the lust in the fucker's eyes as he ripped the shirt off her shoulders and put his fat, dirty hands on her small, pale breasts. I remember everything. Every. Last. Thing.

Yet, there is one thing I had somehow forgotten. Maybe semi-forgotten, but just the same I didn't remember it as strongly—until right now. The dim memory of how it felt to have Carrie in my arms when I promised I would protect her. For a moment everything in my life had been…right. It hadn't lasted long, because minutes later men were tearing me away. I could do nothing but listen to her cry out my name.

I turn the picture over, read the writing on the back and my blood runs cold. My heart freezes.

Vengeance shall be mine. Phoenix.

"Who the fuck is Phoenix?"

"If you had been around here sooner, that would be one of the answers you would know. Dance, I told you the club needs you. We've got crap to take care of since the mess with the traitors."

Dragon never used Irish's name. He hadn't since the day it happened. When he came to the prison to tell me about it, he used the man's name once and after that it was never used again. I understood it, hell I felt the same. It was bitter shit to know that a brother we trusted as one of our own would do that shit. Twist wasn't that hard. Neither Dragon nor I had emotions tied up in the man. Irish had been a brother. If I had room for more nightmares, Irish might have been in them.

"I'm here now. Tell me who the fuck it is that's been coming after Carrie."

"I'd watch my tone, Dance."

"Bullshit, if some fucker was coming after your woman you'd be worse. Now tell me who the fuck I'm dealing with."

"Well don't that beat all," Dragon says and leans back in his chair, his eyes raking over me and instantly making me uncomfortable. Dragon sees more than the normal man, it is one of the things that makes him such a good leader.

"Drag…"

He holds up his hand to stop me from going on and then pulls himself close into the table.

"After the shit with Nic and her girl I went after Skull and his men full force. All roads led to them and I was ready for heads to roll. Only, it seems Tiny had just signed on with Skull's crew a month out. He came recommended by their parent charter."

I nod because while I figure this shit has nothing to do with me, it will eventually lead me to what I need to know.

"Skull swears he didn't know about Tiny and what the fucker did."

"You believe him?"

Dragon shrugs, but eases back in his chair.

"Skull's a smarmy son of a bitch, but he has a code and top of that code is no hurting women or children."

"So who is this fucker?"

"Some ass wipe having a ball toying with me and mine," Dragon growls.

"So you're saying we have no idea who this asshole is?"

"I didn't say that. Got to wonder though, if you're so done with the club and you hate Red so much, why you care?"

"Drag, psycho-analyze some other motherfucker, I'm not playing."

Dragon gives a half laugh, looks me over once more and rubs his chin and the side of his face, as if he's deciding something.

"The cop you gutted, turns out his dad has some pretty powerful connections."

"What's that mean?"

"This motherfucker is the father of the man you killed."

"If that's true, I could see him coming after me, after Carrie even, but why the club?"

"Because you are the club and it's not a secret I pulled in every marker I had to try and get your ass out of trouble."

"So why can't we just find this guy and put a bullet in him?"

"Damn, why the fuck didn't I think of that?" Dragon asks sarcastically and then flips me off. "Because, the man is like a fucking ghost. I can't find him. His bank accounts, his house, hell any of his assets haven't been touched since the shit with Twist and company. We've got surveillance in place; we've added someone in the bank to watch over things. Fuck, I've even had Freak mess around and freeze his account with a fake levy. We're coming up with nothing."

"All this over a sniveling piece of shit that didn't deserve to take his next breath of air."

"No, motherfucker. All this and more is because you went off half-cocked. Dance, I got your back man, but you have to be smart this time. This man wants you dead. Fuck, he wants all of us dead. We have to work to make sure at the end we're standing over the son of a bitch and spitting on his grave. You feel me?"

"So where's Carrie at now?" I ask before I can stop myself. It's fucked up, I admit it. I'm mad at her, I blame her…well mostly, but I'm not exactly crazy happy she's off somewhere with Bull either.

"Bull took her out to the safe house in Manchester."

"Is that necessary?"

"She has been staying at the club, but the girl is pretty innocent and I have the Atlanta Charter coming in tomorrow for a few days…a big party."

I don't know what to say to that. Several things run through my head, but none of them I want to voice so, I let it go.

"This fucker got a real name?"

"Francis Owsley."

"*Francis*? Jesus, no wonder the fucker is ripping off names from Greek mythology."

Dragon laughs and I almost do too, except all this talk of Carrie has me feeling like I'm crawling out of my skin.

"He hasn't made any moves since the day your woman was hurt?" It was tricky wording that question since bringing up Irish was bad, and saying Nicole and shot in the same sentence seemed to set Dragon off even more.

"Not a damn thing. He went underground as soon as we got his name. Something will give soon. I can feel it."

I don't roll my eyes, that shit would get *me* shot, plus I know from years of being in the service with Dragon that he has a pretty good sense for when things were about to get all fucked up. That means his surety that things are about to go to hell is bad, fucking bad.

"Well I better get back to the hotel," I say getting up to leave.

"I expect your ass here tomorrow night," Dragon orders and there's no doubt that it is an order.

I grunt and walk out without giving him a solid answer.

Chapter 4

CARRIE

I LISTEN TO Lips, Dani, and Nic laugh, and I have to smile. I love these women. I've never had sisters, but since the first time I walked through the doors of the Savage MC almost four months ago, these girls have made me feel part of them. Nic and Dani are best friends and as different as night and day. Nicole is head over heels in love with Dragon and a complete fool could see that from miles off. Dani is hilarious and she makes you laugh. She seems to flirt with everyone, but I get the feeling men are the last thing on her mind. Lips is a club Twinkie (a woman all the brothers seemed to share), but she is different from the rest. I don't really know how to explain it. She is just different. Of course the last month she has been dating Six exclusively. Six is a new member of the club. I'd heard the men refer to him as a prospect. He is funny and easy-going and he really seems to care for Lips. I'm hoping it works out for the two of them.

"I still don't see why you can't be at the party tomorrow," Dani complains while sitting on the couch beside me. Her legs are folded and crossed under her. Nicole and Lips are in chairs across from the couch. Alexander, Bull and Six are sitting at the kitchen table talking quietly to each other, but every time I glance up they are watching us. It is unnerving, but after having the club watch over me for the last two months, I am slowly getting used to it.

Dragon had his men come get me after the car accident. Nicole and Dani were hurt and recovering. Dragon seemed to think it was the same man after me. Maybe the three of us bonded over that, I don't know. I just appreciated the way they made me feel like part of a family instead of an outsider. After what I had lost, it was a welcomed feeling.

"She's not going," Bull speaks up and I turn to look at him.

We haven't talked since he kissed me. That wasn't unusual, Bull doesn't talk. This morning at the hotel was definitely not his norm.

"Why can't I go?" I ask confused. Maybe the club is tired of having me around?

"Red, some things are better not asked," Bull says and turns back to his brothers effectively dismissing me. I want to be assertive and demand to know the real reason, but I'm just not that person and it sucks.

"It's because of the Atlanta chapter. Last time they were here, the place was rowdy. They're protecting you," Nicole offers, putting her hand on mine.

I look up at her. She is beautiful. She has these blue eyes that just light up a room. Her hair is a golden blonde and has grown longer since I've met her. She is wearing these black leggings with matching high-heeled boots and a long burnt orange sweater. I almost feel dowdy next to her—to all of these women really. Dani is like a runway model, tall, skinny, perfect bone structure and this dark chestnut hair that is long, silky-smooth and gorgeous. Lips, whose name is actually Vida, is just as gorgeous. Her dark skin looks like warm, creamy coffee and her hair is long with purple color woven in. You'd think it was black until the light hits and you have to do a double take. They are all dressed kind of like Nicole, casual to be sure—but totally different from my faded blue jeans and baby pink t-shirt. My hair is pulled up high in a pony-tail and I spent the morning taming my curls and straightening them. Whereas, all the women around me have on makeup, I hadn't bothered. I seldom do. It just seems too much effort. If I made myself up and wore more stylish clothes, would Jacob notice me more then? I hold in my groan. It doesn't matter what I do, Jacob will never notice or care. Well, unless I died. He might notice then. At least long enough to celebrate.

"Earth to Carrie!" Lips says and I smile.

"Sorry, was just thinking."

"I mean it honey. It's not you. The men love you. They're trying to protect you from the party and everything that goes on," Nicole reiterates.

"I know," I say quietly, but out loud this time. "I don't understand why, I mean I know what sex is," I grumble and curse at the way my cheeks fill with heat.

"I'm with carrot top," Dani adds in. I hate that nickname, but I let her do it. Dani seems cold-hearted at times, but I think she has a lot going on inside of her. I'm horribly shy, so I've done a lot of people watching over the years. I honestly think that Dani uses being outspoken as a defense. I wonder if anyone has ever seen the real her? I'm not even sure she's shown Nicole.

"You're not going, Red."

I hear Bull over my shoulder and I screw up my face mocking his dour look I know he has right now. I don't need to look to know it's there. The girls automatically start laughing and I join in, but quieter.

"Have you and Dragon set a date yet?" I ask because I know they've been talking about it and I'm anxious to get the conversation off of me.

"We were hoping for Valentine's Day, but that's not going to happen," she says her face hid behind her hair. She's looking down at one of her nails like it holds the secrets of the universe.

"Why not?" I ask.

"Dragon's being a jerk," she grumbles.

"What do you mean?" I ask confused, because I've seen them together and he seems to dote on her.

"He won't ask his men to wear monkey suits," Dani explained.

"It's just for one day. I don't see what the big damn deal is! I mean really, I'm pledging my troth to the big dummy!" Nicole complains.

Dani busts out laughing and it's so hard that she's snorting. Eventually, we all join in.

"What the fuck is a troth anyways?" Dani asks wiping tears from her face when we finally stop.

"It's like you're pledging your loyalty," I explain with a grin.

"It sounds like something you hold for a pig to eat out of," Nicole says with a giggle.

"You could always let him eat you and get him to

agree to the suits while he's busy with other things on his mind," Dani says sagely.

"Um… if Dragon is going down on me the last thing I'm going to be thinking about is other fucking men and what they're wearing," Nicole explains.

"Maybe you can compromise," I suggest, blushing, because her words immediately bring to mind a picture, but it's not her and Dragon I see. No, it's me and Jacob and my body instantly reacts.

"Compromise?" Nicole asks and I look down because I'm afraid she can see the fact that I'm thinking of Jacob. Realistically I know she can't, but still…

"Yeah, have them wear black slacks or something with a dress shirt."

"I personally think a man looks sexy in a suit," Lips grins and her eyes lock over at the table. I look up and see Six giving her a knowing smile. It's a look a couple gives each other when they are close. I want that. I've only read about it in books and seen it between my parents and now among my new friends. I don't think I'll ever have that. I want it, but being totally real, I can't see me getting it with Jacob and I can't see myself opening up to anyone else. Maybe someday, but I am starting to really doubt that. If a man can hate you and you still want him, there's not much else you can do.

I must have sighed aloud, I don't know but I sense the change of vibe with the girls around me.

"Carrot, he's not worth it," Dani speaks up.

"He might be to her," Lips defends.

"He has a lot of stuff he needs to work through," Nicole adds quietly and I don't know why, maybe I am wrong, but it seems like she knows more than the rest of us.

"He hates me," I say the simple truth that everyone is avoiding. Secretly, I'm hoping they will argue. They don't.

"There's other fish in the sea," Lips says. I look at her and she still watching Six, but this time I can tell Bull is also in her line of vision. I swallow feeling out of sorts. I like Bull. I really do and a girl would be crazy not to return whatever feelings he had for her. He is an amazing man. Only thing is, I don't like Bull that way and even if I might someday? It would never work out, because of Jacob. They are as close as brothers, they even call themselves brothers.

"Maybe I could just refuse to give him sex until he caves and gives me the wedding of my dreams," Nicole says changing the subject and I'm thankful. She leans back over to hold my hand in support.

"Bitch please, all that man has to do is say Mama and your panties catch on fire," Dani replies.

"He's started letting you wear panties again?" Lips ask, with a drawl.

Nicole flips her off and more laughter ensues.

"Alright women, we better be heading back. Drag will flip if Nicole is out after dark," Crusher announces.

"He ain't wrong," Lips adds. Nicole just shakes her head, but I notice she doesn't argue.

They pack up and I follow them to the door.

"Ladies first," Dani speaks up trying to walk out the door in front of Crusher who has already started out.

"Don't see a lady around," Crusher replies, making sure he goes through the door first.

"You're such an ass," Dani complains following him.

"You love my ass."

"You think all women love your ass. Later, Carrot!" She calls over her shoulder. Lips gives me a hug and follows her.

Nicole stops at the door and turns around and hugs me tight.

"If you want him, you're going to have to throw caution to the wind and go after him," she whispers in my ear. She pulls away slightly, each of her hands holding my arms and looks into my eyes. "He's broken baby, but if your heart is set on him then try to reach him. Take it from me, if it works out it will all be worth it."

I give her a weak smile because while I know what she is saying, I really think it's hopeless. She smiles back, pats my arm and walks out the door with Six following behind her. I stand there staring as Bull closes the door, feeling lost in the quiet. At the club something is always going on or happening. The quiet just makes me feel more alone.

"You hungry?"

"I'll fix us something."

"I'll cook," I say, turning away from him.

"I said I will," he grumbles.

"Okay then. I'll just go take a shower I guess."

"Okay, Red."

Chapter 5
DANCER

I DO NOT want to be here. I'm standing outside of the club's safe house in Manchester. It's a small four-room house on a side street off the main town. You wouldn't know it was there unless you were looking for it. Yet, it is close enough to the main drag that too much shit would bring down the cops. That way even if rival clubs finds it, we still have an advantage.

What am I doing here? Fuck that is another question all together. I left the club with the intention of getting drunk, getting laid and forgetting Carrie was even around. What I did instead was call Mary. I hadn't talked to her since the day they pulled her away from me at the Courthouse. I made it known I did not want her visiting me at the prison. It was a fucked up thing not to check on her when I got out. I know that, but I just cannot deal with people. I spent the night feeling guilt at the pain I heard in Mary's voice and drinking myself into a stupor with a bottle of vodka. I woke up a couple hours later, just like always—covered in sweat, my heart pounding out of my chest and screaming.

I rub my forehead with the palm of my hand and fight

the memories that are always there demanding to come to the forefront. Fuck, I may never be ready to deal with people again.

I know I can't deal with the party going on at the club tonight. That is going to piss Dragon off, but the way I figure it, he might as well get used to the feeling when it comes to me. I pull my hand down and stare. It trembles and shakes, mocking me. What the fuck has happened to me? What happened to the man who walked in the world with a one finger salute, not giving a fuck? What happened to the man who went to war and faced anything without fear? I'm a coward. I can't even live with myself. I haven't got my revenge yet, because I can't bring up the courage to even see the ones I would have to face. I haven't even helped the club exact revenge against a man who is only fucking with them because of me. I am a waste of breath and I know I've said it a million times over, but I'm so tired. So fucking tired that deep down inside it feels as if I am literally drowning. It takes all the energy I can muster to get out of bed every day. What the fuck does that make me? I am rotting from the inside out.

I take an unsteady breath and walk up to the door. I close my eyes and bite my tongue to let the pain focus me. I'm a pansy-ass-sorry-mother-fucker. I knock once…twice…then bring my hand back and push them both into my jean's pockets. I don't want Bull to see them shake. Fuck, *I* don't want to see them shake.

Bull opens the door, the gold studs in his ears shining under the glare of the porch light.

"Dance," his voice is dark and even more pissed off than normal. It doesn't take a rocket scientist to know why. Sorry, Fucker, you're not going to get pussy tonight—at least not from Carrie.

"You going to let me in?"

"What the fuck are you doing here?"

"Come to relieve you."

"Hell no."

"Just fact man, Drag needs his enforcer at the club tonight with the Atlanta Chapter in. He doesn't want Carrie to be alone. So, I am here," I say, lying through my damned teeth.

I'm not even sure why I'm here. Yes, I am avoiding the party, but I could have done that from my room at the hotel. Something inside of me is pushing me towards Carrie. Maybe it is because of all the shit she has gone through; maybe it is the anger I have towards her. Maybe I've drunk so much that my brain cells have completely left me. I did not the-fuck-know. All I do know? I am standing here in front of this damn safe house at seven o'clock at night, lying to my brother and planning on spending the night with a woman I…shit, it's a woman I want—I've always wanted. It's also a woman I blame, whether she deserves it or not.

"I'll call and have him send Six out."

"Six is working the bar tonight with Lips. Just get going man, I think I can babysit for one damned night."

"And give you the chance to spew more of your poison at Red? I don't think so brother."

"Oh for Christ's sake, I won't bother the bitch. I'm going to lock the doors, grab a bite to eat and sleep. I won't say two damn words to her. Now quit being a prick and let me in."

He backs up to give me room to get in. I walk by him and scan the combined living and kitchen area. It's separated by a small half wall and then open where the table and chairs are. Carrie is sitting there and her face goes pale and white when she sees me. I know it makes me a sadistic fuck, but I can't help but enjoy seeing how uncomfortable I make her.

"Looks like I missed dinner," I say my eyes locking on Carrie's. She holds my look for about half a beat and then looks back down. Why does that make me feel like I've won something? I could almost smile.

Bull grunts. "I'll call Nailer."

He takes out his phone and it pisses me off. Obviously I'm twisted up even more than I realized.

"Knock it off, Bull. I'm not going to say shit to her. Go back up our boy."

"Red? You gonna be okay?" Bull asks ignoring me.

This fucker is obviously pussy-whipped. Maybe it's the younger pussy?

"I'm fine, Bull. I'm getting ready to go to bed anyway," she says. Her voice has always been quieter than others. Almost meek and soothing, it's like a lullaby. I used to love to listen to her and Jazz chatter for hours. The memory of that rings clear before I lock it down.

"I still think I should call Drag first," Bull obstinately continues.

For a second my chest gets a punch of adrenaline. If Bull does that he'll know I'm lying my ass off and Carrie will know it too. I don't even know why the hell I'm doing it myself, I'm not ready to try and explain it to anyone else.

"Bull, please? I don't' want to make a scene and tonight is important to Dragon. Just go, I'll be fine. Jacob… He won't hurt me."

"Red? You call me if you need me for anything."

"I'll be fine," she says with a smile, while Bull puts on his cut. I can see the fear in her eyes. It's fucked up, but I like it. It's like my body has come alive, as if I'm a hunter and oh yeah, I'm definitely smelling blood now.

Bull turns to me as he opens the door.

"Motherfucker, one wrong move and I'll make you sorry you were ever born," he growls.

I thought about telling him he's about thirty-five years too late. At the very least, he's a little over two years too late. I don't though. I shrug and watch as he slams the door behind him.

I wait the space of a heartbeat and then turn my attention to Carrie. Her big green eyes are caught in mine and her skin is definitely lily white now.

"Having fun playing house with the bad boy biker, Princess?"

She closes her eyes and looks down at her lap. My eyes follow and I see she's wringing her hands tight. My lips jerk a little, not quite a smile but definitely a hint of one.

"I don't remember you being so timid around me before, Princess," I say, lounging against the door now, my arms crossed at my chest.

"You didn't hate me in the past. I'm going to go take a bath and call it a night. Sorry you got stuck with me," she says, without bothering to look up. She gets up from the table, still looking at the ground.

"I don't hate you Carrie, not most of the time. You shouldn't have been there that night," I confess, a dose of honesty pushing its way through my lips.

"I know. If I could take it back, I would, Jacob."

"All of it?" I ask before I can stop myself.

"Would it matter?" She asks instead of answering and the anger that is coiled tight in my stomach heats.

I resent her not giving me an answer. I want to know what exactly she would change. Why? Fuck if I know. I want to know if she still has those feelings though, if what Dragon says is true. I want her to admit it.

I should let her go. It'd be better for both of us. I don't.

"I'm hungry. What's for dinner?" I ask, wondering if she'll tell me to get it myself.

"I made a casserole," she says finally looking up at me. Were her green eyes always so deep in color?

"Sounds good. You got beer too?" I ask, walking over to the table and sitting down. It's a dick move and I think I see a flare of irritation in her eyes, but she doesn't tell me to go fuck myself. I almost find it disappointing. She takes a few minutes and brings me a plate and a beer.

She starts to walk out of the room when I stop her.

"Always did hate eating alone."

"Jacob, we both know you don't want me anywhere around you," she answers. She doesn't sit down, but she doesn't immediately leave the room either.

I take a bite of the casserole. Chicken. It's pretty good actually.

"Where'd you learn to cook?"

"I've always cooked, my mother taught me how," she responds, and the blush on her face is kind of cute, even if I am getting ready to be a dick to her.

"Why bother when you had chefs to do that shit?"

"We never had chefs, Jacob. We never had any servants."

"Who was Velma?"

She looks confused for a minute.

"She is family."

"Did your parents pay her?" I question, knowing the answer.

"Well yes, of course…"

"Then she was a servant."

Her face goes pale white as she looks at me.

"You really are a horse's ass," she says and then turns and walks out of the room.

I grin because I got to her. It almost feels like a victory. I ignore the emptiness that invades the room when she leaves.

Chapter 6

CARRIE

IT TAKES ME a good hour to calm down after leaving Jacob. I hate that I let him get to me. I knew from the minute he acted like he wanted me around, what his game was. I wish I could be more like Nicole. She'd kick Jacob in the balls or something. I jump in the shower and decide to just go to bed. It is early, but sleep sounds better than taking more of Jacob's abuse.

I slip on a long t-shirt that Bull gave me to sleep in. It's soft and worn and lands at my knees. It has short sleeves and is half way to my elbows. Did I mention Bull towers over me?

I prefer my pajamas, but I accidentally left them at the club. I crawl under the covers with a sigh. Maybe I could move to Georgia, my friend Tammie lives there. Surely whoever it is that is after me won't follow me down there? That's the last thought I have before I'm out for the night.

I AWAKE WITH a jerk. I can't tell how long I've been sleeping, but now the room is dark and the house is silent.

At first I'm confused. I'm not sure what woke me. I yawn, thinking it was nothing and close my eyes. Then I hear it again. Yelling.

I worry that I've been discovered. Did I get Jacob in trouble? Oh god, I can't have him get hurt in any way because of me. I've already been responsible for robbing him of two years of his life.

"NO!!!!"

I hear again and there is so much pain in Jacob's voice. It feels like something grabs my heart and chokes it. I wipe the sleep out of my eyes and jump up out of the bed. I use my hand on the mattress to guide me as my eyes become adjusted to the darkness. I walk blindly, feel the wall with my hand, and find the light switch. I turn it on but leave the light behind, just thankful it illuminates enough so I can follow the sound of Jacob's moans.

"Oh god, get away from me! I don't want this! I'll kill all you fuckers! Every fucking one of you!"

I freeze as he says the words. The words register and they paint a scene, I might not see clearly, but it's clear enough that my brain rejects it.

"No!" The wounded sound comes out and it's so full of misery of pain.

No…just oh god, no. His words are beginning to paint a picture, and I don't want to see it. I come out of my trance and rush to get to him, hoping I can somehow stop him from saying more. I don't want to know. That's selfish, but he wouldn't want me to know. I'm the last person he would talk to.

I find him in the room Bull has been using. There's an old floor model television sitting catty-cornered, which offers pale, flickering light. Jacob is sitting in a chair and the darkness feels…ominous. The TV screen casts a dim light in the room, hiding Jacob in the darkness. All that is visible is his form. His shape absorbs just enough light to look eerie. It sends chills running up my back. The TV has been muted so the only sound in the room is the low, aching moan of misery that comes from Jacob intermittently.

I lick my lips nervously, my throat feeling closed off. I'm not sure I'm equipped to deal with this. He's sleeping, but obviously in the thrall of a nightmare. I realize it's more than that, but I can't deal with the implications right now. Now I must concentrate on helping, somehow. Would Jacob know who I was if I wake him? Would he wonder why I came into the room?

The television switches scenes and the brightness infiltrates harshly in the room. That's when I see it—the gun in Jacob's hand. My heart stops, my blood runs cold. Then, it jumps back to life, pounding so hard it hurts to breathe. He has the gun half way up his chest, pointing towards his face in a haphazard manner that speaks volumes.

His head jerks, and his eyes open half-way.

"Fuck, not again," he moans out and my heart clenches. It's said in a way that I understand instantly he's used to waking up from this nightmare.

In his other hand there's an almost finished bottle of whiskey. I watch as he brings it up to his mouth and swallows the last of it down in one gulp. He moans again. It's the sound I imagine an animal would make if it is caught in a trap.

Somehow the painful noises coming from him are worse now that he is awake. This doesn't just haunt him when he can't help it. It's constant. Is this my fault? Is this why he hates me so much now? Dear God, I think I hate myself more.

The light flickers again and this time it is bright enough it reflects off his face. Had it not been so hauntingly sad, it would have weakened my knees from the sheer beauty.

I take another hesitate step into the room. Unsure at this point of what to do or say, only knowing I have come too far to turn back.

The bottle falls from his hand, or rather he drops it. The carpet softens the fall and you can't hear it drop—not really. Still, I think the thud echoes in my heart. Nicole's words come back into my head.

He's broken, baby.

Oh god, I don't think I had any idea of just how broken.

"Jacob," I whisper, my voice unsteady. I have heard you don't sneak up on a wounded bear. If anyone is wounded, it is this man, that much is clear, now more than ever. Yet, this is beyond my scope of experience. All I know is I just can't leave him alone.

His head moves to the side as if in a daze. My first instincts are to turn on a light and try to connect with him. Still, if I do that I won't get the chance to help him further. He'll throw me out. Heck, he might anyway.

"Care Bear?"

The old nickname rolls from his tongue. It delights and wounds at the same time. The only people to ever use it were Jacob and Jazz. Besides my parents they are the only two people to own my heart. Completely own it. My life has been so empty without them. If Jazz was still alive, she'd know how to reach Jacob, she'd know how to make everything better. Never have I missed my best friend more than I miss her right at this moment.

"It's me, Jacob. I wanted to check on you," I say cautiously, walking a few more steps towards him.

"Why?" He asks, his voice is slurred and full of confusion.

"I wanted to see you. I thought you might need me," I respond honestly.

"Care Bear always wearing your heart on your sleeve, world will eat you alive someday."

I wish I could argue with him, but that has pretty much happened.

"Let's get you in bed. You're tired," I say, standing in front of him, praying I am distracting him enough.

"I'm fucking tired of it all," he says, as his eyes close. A grimace of pain bathes his face and it breaks me. The pain seems so huge, so engrained in him I want to curl myself around him and cry.

"I know, Jacob. I want to help you. Let's get you in bed. It'll look better in the morning," I lie, wishing it was the truth.

"It'll never be better."

I slide my hand around the gun gently, hoping he doesn't notice.

"Someday it will. You just have to hold on, Jacob. Isn't that what you told me all those years ago?" I ask. I pull on the gun, thanking God that he seems to be concentrating on my words. He doesn't realize he is giving it to me.

The weapon feels weird and heavy in my hands. I don't like it, anything about it really. I want it far out of his reach, but I can't do that just yet. I back up to put the gun on top of the television. I don't want to turn my back on him. I'm afraid if I lose eye contact with him that he might sober up enough to know I'm really here. I'm pretty sure he doesn't register the fact right now. If he did, he'd be screaming for me to leave…or using the gun on me.

"You shouldn't be here," he says, sounding even more confused.

"I know," I agree walking over to the bed and turning it down. Finally, I make it back in front of him. His eyes look so dark and bleak. I wish it was a trick of bad lighting, but I know better.

"I told you to leave me alone."

"I know that too," I agree and take his hand into mine. It's big and rough. The feel of it is like coming home. I wish I could freeze the way my heart feels when his hand grasps mine. Freeze it and hold it with me forever, because I know this will be all he ever gives me. This is it and I'm only getting it now because he doesn't realize it.

"Come on let's lie down for a bit. When you wake up in the morning, I'll be gone."

Instead of letting me pull him up, he yanks me down onto his lap. I gasp and brace myself on his chest.

"What…what are you doing?"

"Giving you a taste of what you've been wanting for years," He growls and then his lips are on mine.

At the first touch of our lips, sensation flames through my body. His tongue runs over my bottom lip and his teeth nibble against it and he slowly sucks it inside his mouth. I should hate it, the taste of alcohol is heavy on him and the flavor isn't what I have dreamed of all these years. Yet, instead of pushing him away, my hand moves up to his head. The short hair teases against my fingers. It's one more sensation to add to a million, as he releases my lip and then pushes his tongue inside my mouth.

I'm twenty years old. By that age most women have slept with a man, or more than one. They have been in relationships, they have held hands, they have been kissed and they have been in some type of love. I have never had any of that, save the last.

I have been in love with Jacob since the moment my little five year-old-self laid eyes upon him. I know that sounds stupid. I know that others wouldn't understand. The thing is, even knowing that, it doesn't make it any less true. I love Jacob Blake completely. I always have.

That makes sitting here in his lap, feeling his arms around me, pulling me down against him, feeling his erection ground against my ass…surreal. There are so many things bombarding me. I can't even begin to decipher them.

All of these thoughts are flowing through my brain, but not registering. Nothing registers, because the dark whiskey soaked taste of Jacob is invading my body. His tongue forges into my mouth and claims it as his. Investigating every inch he can, he devours and drinks from me. There is nothing I can do, but accept it. Tentatively my tongue follows his lead and dances in tandem with his.

His hand wraps around my hair and pulls me harder

into him. Our teeth clash, and I try to pull away, unsure if I am doing this right. He won't let me. He takes the kiss further. He takes my mouth harder, demanding more. I am unsure of what to give but I try, nothing has ever felt this wonderful in my life.

"God Care, you taste so fucking good, so clean. I need more."

I hear his words and my heart fills. After so long of not hearing that nickname, Jacob is giving it to me. He's saying the name he gave me and kissing me. Even better, hearing Jacob say it with his voice so full of hunger and need…there are no words, just dreams coming true.

My heart is beating out of my chest. The last time Jacob called me Care Bear was that horrible night over two years ago. The night that I have cursed and wished I could erase for both of us. I was so stupid, so very stupid.

The only thing good from that entire night was the moment Jacob took my shaking body into his arms and held me. He kissed the top of my head and whispered the sweetest words I have ever heard in my life.

It'll be okay, Care Bear. I got you. I'll never let anyone hurt you.

Ever since, especially after my parents died, I would lie in bed thinking of Jacob. I would hear those words, those exact words with Jacob's voice in a soft loving timber and I wouldn't feel alone.

He pulls the shirt I am wearing over my head in one swoop. My arms go up to help because honest to God, I want more of whatever he will give me. I have wanted this since I was old enough to know what two people could do together.

He grasps my breast, covering it completely, kneading it and stealing my breath all at the same time.

"So perfect."

I hear his voice as if it is somewhere in the distance and through a great fog. I have so many new feelings and sensations it feels almost as if I'm sailing away.

"Jacob," I moan as his lips leave mine. I take in some much needed oxygen. His mouth goes down my neck, his teeth nipping along the skin with just enough pressure that I can't tell if it is pain...it is just exquisite. My hands are biting into the arms of the chair we are in. My body starts rocking against him without me even realizing it. I push my ass against his hard erection. His jeans are in the way, I want more. I need more. My movements are out of rhythm, but it feels like I am on fire.

He stands up with me, one hand on my breast, the other around my stomach holding my back tight against his front. I push my head against his shoulder as he continues his assault. There will be marks on my neck...I want them. I want anything he will give me.

"I'm going to fuck you, Carrie. I'm going to fuck you so hard you won't be able to walk tomorrow," he groans in my ear, his breath hot against my skin.

His hand moves down my stomach, sliding underneath my panties. I feel his fingers fan out and caress the outer lips of my pussy. My hips thrust out to try and force his hand to move where I want. He increases the pressure of his touch and stills my movements.

"Don't worry I'll give you what you need."

His voice grates against my skin, as his fingers slide between my folds. I gasp at the way he immediately begins caressing my clit. Lightly grazing, never giving it enough pressure. Over and over he continues, slowly destroying me. I can feel the blood surging in my body. I'm twenty years old and though I have never been with a man, I have given myself orgasms. None of them have felt like this. Intense, consuming, I can literally feel it building with a force that scares me. It's nothing like the lukewarm emotions I've had before.

My hands move behind me, I grab his thighs, needing a connection with him. His fingers push inside me, not all the way but enough that my legs threaten to give out on me. I'm so close, if he would just move his finger over....

"Take me, Jacob!" I call out, knowing the explosion is about two seconds away. My nails bite into the cheeks of his ass so deeply, so hard, I know I'm marking him too. I want too. I want my mark on him so I …

He thrusts me away abruptly, pushing me from him with such force, I stumble. I try to catch myself on the bed before I go all the way down, but I can't. The metal of the bed frame tears into the skin on my lower leg. I pull myself up and turn around to look at Jacob.

"What…"

"Get the fuck out of here! I told you I'd rather chop my dick off than have anything to do with you."

"But Jacob…you…I…"

"I was teaching you a lesson," he growls and picks up my shirt off the floor and throws it at me.

With everything going on, I didn't realize I was naked. Before, it felt beautiful, now I feel exposed and dirty. I hold the shirt tight to me, covering my front from him.

"Think my brother would like knowing you wear his

clothes to come and fuck me, Princess? You really are just begging for any man's cock, aren't you? Did you tease that bastard two years ago like you just did me? Did you only cry wolf when you noticed me there? Is that how you play your games?"

His words are full of venom and hate and as I listen to them, I realize he fully believes them. Tears start falling before I can stop them.

"Oh, poor little rich girl. Turning on the waterworks, get the fuck out of here!"

That sounds like a great idea. There's so much I need to digest, so much pain, mine and his. Worse is the fact he called me Princess. It is more hurtful now. For a small space in time I had everything I wanted, when he called me Care Bear. Being called Princess now? A knife couldn't cut sharper.

I turn and hobble from the room, my leg hurting and slowing me down. I don't even care that my ass is hanging out. I just want away from him. I'll get dressed when I am out of his sight.

Chapter 7
DANCER

I WATCH CARRIE run from me and the disgust curls and foams inside of me. I push my hand hard into my forehead wishing I could stop the memories and the words swimming in my head.

"FUCK!!!" I yell and start grabbing shit off the table by the chair, throwing it across the room.

I fall back into the chair holding my head, so fucking exhausted. I lied through my teeth. I want Carrie. I've always wanted Carrie in some form or another. She was always a cute little freckle faced girl that my sister adored. As she grew, she was a sweet kid who I looked out for. Then, she became the last real connection I had with Jazz. We helped each other grieve. When she told me at seventeen she loved me, I laughed it off and told her I didn't think of her that way. Again, I was lying. I seem to do that to Carrie often.

I had noticed the changes in her body. I would have been a fool not too. She is beautiful and her beauty goes beneath the skin. She has this kindness and gentleness I've never found in life—except with her. I've always pushed her away because I'm fifteen years older. That's too damn much and even before the shit of the last two years, I was a twisted fuck. I don't deserve her. I don't want any of my darkness to touch her, but I am weakening.

The night when she showed up at the nightclub I was pissed as hell. She shouldn't have been there. The bouncer had no business letting her through the front door. She was wearing this sexy little green silk dress that moved with her body and turned every fucking man's head in the place, something an eighteen year old shouldn't do. When she stood in front of me asking me to dance, I followed like a lamb to its slaughter.

It's been years. My brain is fucked up, I'm half drunk and yet I can still remember how it felt to hold her in my arms that night. How it felt inside when she told me she loved me…when she asked for my kiss. It took everything I had to tell her to go home.

The minute I saw the tears in her eyes and watched her run from the room, I had to follow her. I fought it for five minutes or so but in the end, I didn't have a choice. I would rather try and be what she deserved, to ignore all the reasons why I wasn't the man for her. I would rather try, than cause her pain.

I thought I missed her. I stood outside the main club doors, looked around and didn't see her or her car anywhere. I was about to go back in when I heard her scream. I don't know how I knew it was her, but I did. I ran, my heart filling with fear. I made it to the corner of the building in time to see that fucker backhand Carrie.

The blow was so hard her head jerked back and blood sprang from the corner of her lip. He ripped the strap of her dress and it separated, leaving her bare breast open to his assault. Before I could move, his hand covered her pale, small white breast. It seemed unreal and froze me in my tracks. She began screaming again and he slammed her against the brick, his hand around her throat, applying so much pressure her voice instantly stopped.

I lost it, completely and utterly lost it. I know what Dragon said was true because if it had been anyone other than Carrie, I would have done things differently. It was Carrie though. I knew how innocent she was. I knew how precious she was. Seeing someone abuse her, touch her... fucking put his hands on her? I completely lost it.

I charged in grabbing the knife from inside my cut and I don't even remember ending the fucker, I just reacted.

I rub the back of my neck and walk into the living room. I feel strangely sober now, which is a shame because I would rather be lost in a haze of alcohol. It always seems like things are easier to deal with that way. Maybe there's a bottle I've overlooked in the kitchen.

I was almost in front of the table when Bull throws the door open. It slams against the wall with a loud bang. He stands there glaring at me, catching the door as it comes back toward him. He takes a step in and gives it a push. The door slams behind him.

A lesser man would have been intimidated. I was probably still fucked up from the alcohol, because strangely I'm not.

"RED!" Bull calls out.

I give him a shit-eating grin that I would have gladly knocked off a motherfucker's face, if I had been on the receiving end. Then, I lean back in the cockiest pose I can muster.

"RED!" Bull calls out again.

It is a few minutes before she walks into the living room. She is limping and I feel guilt hit me. I want to help her to the chair and see what's wrong.

"What the fuck happened?" Bull barks going over to Carrie and doing that before I can get my alcohol soaked brain to function. He gets down on his knee to look at the damage. It annoys me how protective he is over her.

"I...I fell," she says and she looks so innocent and frail sitting at the table. Her hair is mussed up, her lips are swollen from my kiss and my dick jerks in reaction. I can't see her neck for her hair. It takes all I've got not to go over to her and see if I had marked that pale sweet skin. I want Bull to see it.

"How?" Bull asks, pushing his shirt up to look along her leg.

Carrie grabs the shirt and holds it tight to her thigh so Bull won't show more skin and her eyes lock with mine. Bull looks up and he sees Carrie staring over his shoulder. He turns to follow her line of sight, which of course is me.

"You son of a bitch! I warned you!" Bull growls and drops Carrie's leg, coming at me in one big movement.

"Bull!" Carrie yells, but my brother grabs my collar and then throws a punch. I feel the impact of his solid fist cover the top of my hand that I throw up in defense, twisting it away and then coming down to my jaw at an angle. The force is strong and my head jerks with the impact.

I immediately step back, and deliver a return hit to his gut. I feel him connect again, this time I drop down so he just hits my shoulder. I deliver another blow and he steps back to refocus. We trade a few more hits back and forth. I finally get a good one connecting under his chin. It sends his body backwards, making him fall against the sofa. I'm not even sure how we made it from the table area to the living room. I'm kind of shocked. I back up thinking that it is over. My brother may be mad at me, but I don't really want to fight with him.

I don't have time to say anything, because Bull recovers quickly and charges with his head down, aiming straight for my solar plexus. I'm pushed back a good five feet or better. We fall from the force of the hit. I slam against the kitchen table. It tilts under my weight and I hear a crash and feel a jarring, as the table tips over. Chairs fall in every direction around us as we land. I grab him in a head-lock while he's trying to deliver a kidney punch.

We stop when a loud scream draws both our attention.
"STOP IT!"

We look up at the same time. Her auburn hair is gorgeous in waves around her face and those wide green eyes are filled with tears. I have the strangest urge to reach out and stop them before they have a chance to fall.

"Just stop it," she cries. Bull shoots me another death glare and pulls away.

"Sit down, Red," He orders softly and helps her to the chair in the living room. I lay against the upturned table watching them and I feel physically ill.

He cares about her. You can see it in everything he does and in the way he wants to take my head off. I can do nothing but watch as he sits her down. His large dark hand caresses her. It stands out against her milk white skin. It's odd watching his large thumb wipe away the tears falling from her eyes. It makes the breath lodge in my throat. How could this happen? How can my brother fall for Carrie? She's mine.

"Damn it Red, tell me what happened," Bull demands, his hand moving along her calf muscle. There's a bruise and obviously a good size cut that is no longer bleeding, but looks hateful and swollen. It's ugly against her perfection. More guilt pummels me.

"It was an accident," she whispers her hands twist together on her lap, her face down.

"Dance…"

"I fell Bull, Jacob didn't do anything," she whispers, looking at me. I expect to see hate or disgust. Heck, even mocking would have been preferable, yet all she does is spare a quick glance at me.

"I'm going to go back to bed," she mumbles and Bull stands instantly. He bends down to lift Carrie up in his arms.

"Bull!" Carrie gasps.

"Red, hush. I'm going to doctor your leg and then you can rest."

"But…"

"Stop arguing. I'm doing it."

She looks over Bull's shoulder, her eyes connect with mine. There's so much sadness in her eyes. It shames me. This time, I'm the one who has to look away.

"Dragon wants you at the club. I suggest you don't keep him waiting," Bull calls out.

Well fuck a duck.

Chapter 8

DANCER

I KNOW I should have gone back to the club and answered Dragon's page. That would have been the smart thing to do. These days it seems, I don't do smart. Hell, if you looked back on my life, maybe I never have.

The truth is, I'm reeling. Reeling from the fact that a man I truly like and respect has feelings for Carrie. Fuck, I'm not an expert, but I think it could easily be said that he is in love with her. I don't know how to react to that. I've always labeled Carrie off limits because she was fifteen years younger than me. Damn, Bull is older than I am, not by much, but still.

It is enough to fuck me up even more. I am already dealing with the taste of Carrie, the feeling of her in my arms, the eager way she ground against me, silently begging for more. I have wanted Carrie for years, dreamed of her, and wished I could have just one taste of her. The reality of it was more than I imagined.

It has only been an hour, but I already want to charge back and claim her, just from that one taste. I can't. The minute she touched me, those damn memories came back. Her sweet voice demanding I take her wasn't what I heard.

It had been replaced by a darker voice.

My hand shakes as I bring the bottle up to my mouth. Fuck. I can't stand to be touched. I can't. I don't allow the whores I've been fucking to touch me. I make sure their hands are busy with a friend or I take them from behind. I don't want their hands anywhere on me. I got nervous when Carrie touched my head, but I managed to drown out the memories with her taste, but fuck, she grabbed me. She said words that were burned into my brain. I lost it. I never meant to hurt her and I know she thinks I did. I didn't. Hell, as much as I want her I'm not sure I can ever allow myself to actually have her. I'm so tired of living like this.

If I hear one more time about how what doesn't kill you makes you stronger, I may scream. People who say that shit have never been so deep into a hole that they can't find a way out. They've never sat by the window and prayed that the sun would hurry and go down because the night seemed safer. People didn't move around so much in the nighttime, things weren't done. The world was at rest. At night the fear that clenched around my heart and held on, eased up—never a lot, but enough so I could pretend to be normal on the outside.

You don't go through shit and get stronger. That is a lie. You go through shit and lose parts of yourself. Whole fucking pieces, which leave holes so big, so mind-blowingly huge that for people to even say you'll be stronger? It is complete and utter bullshit.

So that's where I find myself tonight. Sitting in my car, perched on the edge of a dam. Letting the darkness surround me, letting it cover me and the only friend I have in the world. I look at the empty bottle in my hand. Well scratch that, just me. Seems I've drank the last of my friend.

If I were stronger, I would have driven off the edge of this concrete monster and sunk to the bottom of Laurel Lake. This is not the first time I've been here. It's not the first time I've thought of ending it all, it's more like the millionth time. This is something that I have faced every day since I stepped out of the doors of the Federal Prison in West Liberty.

It's not something that ever leaves my brain. It's always here. I'll be driving down the road on my bike enjoying the feel of the cool air on my body when bam, a memory hits. A memory so dark it chokes me. Another vehicle, or even better a coal truck will go by and my hand shakes with the need to cut in front of it.

It would be deemed an accident. Everyone would write it off as if there was a vehicle malfunction or if I had fallen asleep…no one would know I was just another coward too tired to keep moving, too worn out to keep fighting against the current.

What has stopped me up to this point is fear. I am scared. Scared that I'd somehow fuck this up too. Somehow it wouldn't kill me, I'd be stuck a vegetable and trapped with nothing but my memories for the rest of my life.

I lean back against the seat of the SUV I'm driving. How long have I been here now? An hour? Two? Time doesn't really register when you're this far down into hell and the Devil is calling your name. I keep seeing Carrie and her face when I pushed her away, when I hurt her.

The fear, the pain and even worse than both of those, was the love. I could always see the love in her eyes. Even before she told me how she felt. It was fucked up that I wanted it, needed it. It was even more fucked up that I kept running away from it and every time I did, bad things happened.

It would be better for her if I wasn't here. She'd be able to forget me and with the way my brother seems to care about her, they'd be happy. Bull would give her everything I wanted to, but couldn't. She'd be happy. I want her happy. If I do this it'd give her peace.

I've tried blaming her for what happened to me. Truthfully there is no one to blame but myself. I did this. I did it all. Dragon is right. I should have kept my head. I knew better. Fuck, I should have never turned Carrie down to begin with. If I had held her, given her the kiss she wanted, kept her in my arms, then none of this would have happened. It's all on me. I'm the maker of my own demons. I'm the sole party responsible. I can't keep lashing out at her, at any one. At the same time, I can't be the man I once was. That man is dead. He died that night in prison when he was held down and violated against his will. He is not me. Me? I'm just left over residue—the scum that's left in the strainer when you let the water out of the sink.

I start the vehicle and stare over the water. Laurel Lake brings back so many good memories. Memories of when life was simpler, quieter and happier. Memories of when Jazz was alive and my days were spent watching over her and Carrie, memories of parties with my brothers and just being free.

It seems a good place to let it all go, to let it all just fade away. That's the last thought I have before I release the park break, jam it into drive and lay on the gas.

Chapter 9

CARRIE

A GAIN I ASK myself why I can't be attracted to Bull. Jacob is an ass. Bull played doctor with my leg, and then he demanded I watch television with him. After popping popcorn, we sit down and watch a Rock Hudson and Doris Day movie. Now I'm sure Bull hates every minute of the movie, but old movies make me giggle and it makes me happy.

"You doing okay, Red?"

I look over to find him staring at me. Bull may not talk much, but I get the feeling he sees a lot more than most do.

"It's just been a rough day."

"I should teach him a lesson. You should have let me."

I sighed. I didn't want to get started on that again.

"Just let it go. I told you it was an accident."

"And I told you I didn't believe it."

"Tough noodles."

"Noodles?" Bull asks with a grin.

I shrug, "They can be pretty tough if you don't cook them, or you know don't cook them enough."

He shakes his head and turns back to the television.

"I think I was born in the wrong decade," I say without meaning to really. It's just that the silence is a little strained.

"How so?"

"The fifties look so much better. Man wanted woman. Man got woman. Happy ever after."

"Life isn't like the movies, Red."

"Maybe it was in the fifties," I insist, knowing I am being silly.

"In that case we're all screwed."

"Why's that?"

"Have you watched *The Thing*? *Invasion of the Body Snatchers*? *War of the Worlds*? *The Blob*?"

I start laughing, I can't help it.

"Okay, well maybe you have a small point," I concede.

"Of course I'm kind of bummed now," he adds and he gets this cocky look in his pretty brown eyes and they sparkle with laughter. A girl could just sigh. Why can't I want him instead of Jacob?

"Bummed?"

"Yeah, I mean it might be good to be attacked by a fifty foot woman."

I throw popcorn at him as he tosses his head back in laughter. It's a nice sound, full of life, robust and rich sounding. The smile I give him this time is completely sincere.

We start our second movie when Bull's phone rings.

"Speak."

I watch as he listens to whoever is on the other side. It must have been bad news because this cold look comes over his face.

"What about Red? I can't leave her alone…Yeah…Okay…no I'll be there, but I'm going to kick his ass for pulling this shit," he barks and hangs up.

"Red, there's been an accident."

Bull barely gets the words out and the room starts swimming.

"Fuck! Breathe, Red," Bull says kneeling down in front of me. I'm just glad I am sitting on the couch, or I would have fallen.

"I'm sorry. Red, I didn't think."

"It's stupid I know, it's just…"

"It's just that I'm an idiot and forgot about your parents and your past. It's okay though. I promise you everyone is okay."

"Dragon? Nicole?"

Bull grimaces and the strain on his face makes my heart stumble again.

"Oh no, please tell me that Nic…"

"It wasn't Nicole, it was Dancer."

"Jacob?" I close my eyes as fear washes over me.

"He's okay, just banged up, but I need to…"

"I'm going with you," I whisper trying to stand up.

"You can't. It's too dangerous. I won't be long, keep the doors locked. Dragon is sending a prospect over to guard the house while I'm gone."

"Bull, I'm going with you. I need to see Jacob. I need to make sure he is okay."

"You are supposed to stay here. Dragon is sending Frog to watch over you," Bull says getting his coat.

I ignore him and make my way to the door.

"Where are you going? Damn it, Red."

I hear him growl as I hurry out the door. I'm climbing into the passenger seat when I hear the screen door slam. He gets in with more door-slamming and shoots me an evil glare. He throws my sweater at me.

"At least put this on," he demands.

It feels like it takes us forever to get to the hospital. Realistically, I know that's not true. It's about a twenty minute drive. Still, the minutes tick by and it feels like I can hear every one of them echo inside of me.

Bull barely has the car in park before I'm jumping out. My hands are sweaty and my mouth feels so dry. I haven't been inside a hospital since the night I lost my parents. It's funny what you remember after something like that happens. The sterile smell, the sound of the sliding doors whooshing as people go in and out, the annoying sound of laughter from the employees, the memories all comes rushing back. There is just so much, it bombards me. I ignore it, going to the big reception desk that's marked with the sign REGISTRATION above it.

"I'm looking for Jacob Blake?" I ask the rather bored looking woman sitting at the front desk in the emergency room. Before she can answer I hear Bull's name being called out.

"Yo, Bull!" Alexander hollers and I start running towards him.

"Carrie darlin', what happened to you?" Alexander asks and I have no idea what he's talking about. Me? I need to know about Jacob!

"How's Jacob?" I ask. He looks over at Bull instead of answering me and if I was a different person I would have grabbed him, made him focus on me and answer my question!

Bull puts his arm around my shoulder when he gets to us and gives Alexander a bored expression. "She fell and hurt her leg."

Oh...okay so that's what he meant. Like that even matters! I mean I'm limping! I'm not in the hospital! Jacob could be...

"Then she should have her ass at home like Dragon ordered," Alexander says and okay that's it. I've had it. I stomp my foot, which really was a stupid thing to do because it was my bad leg and it hurt like freaking Hades!

"HOW IS JACOB!?!?!?"

Bull and Alexander both look at me like I have three heads. I push my hair off my face wondering if I should go back to the nurse, I turn to try and do that but Bull stops me by putting pressure on my shoulder and keeps me at his side.

"Damn...where do the brothers keep finding them?" Alexander asks and heaven help me if he doesn't start making sense soon I may have to kill him.

"Fuck if I know brother. How is Dance?"

The easy-going attitude slowly slides off Alexander's face and my stomach turns. *It's bad.* I can see it written all over him. *If something happens to Jacob...I can't take it...I just wouldn't be able to...I* sway a little at the thought of losing the only man I ever loved. He may have hated me, but at least he was still alive.

The thought of a world without Jacob is so physically painful the tears I have been trying to hold in break free. Bull pulls me tighter to him and I go because honestly I don't think my feet can remain under me.

"He's…"

"He's going to be just fine," Nicole interrupts Alexander as she comes out of a door behind us.

My eyes lock on hers to see if she is lying to me. Since I've been at the Savage MC, I have learned several things and one of those Nicole can't lie. Her eyes give her away every time. When she looks at me dead on, I can see she truly believes that. It's the first time I've taken an easy breath since Bull's phone rang.

"See, Red? Now you need to let Crusher take you…"

"I'm staying."

"Red…"

"I know if it was Dragon in there, I wouldn't leave. Leave her alone Bull, Dance needs her," Nicole interrupts as she pats my shoulder. "Let me take you back to where his room is."

Bull and Alexander give us strange looks but they let us go. I follow Nicole through a door and we start walking down a hallway.

"How bad is it?" I ask because the silence and our echoing footsteps are driving me crazy.

"He'll be fine. There are some things that you need to know. Things these stupid men in their effort to protect Dancer, won't tell you," She says, turning in front of me and stopping our progress.

I nod once and freeze, because she doesn't know what I overheard earlier. *Will she hate me too? As much as I hate myself?*

"Carrie, while Dancer was unconscious tonight…he had this dream…" Nicole starts and her voice is quiet and full of sadness and my heart stalls. I mean I know. I had probably heard the same things, but a part of me is in denial. I want to pretend I hadn't heard it. Something like that was just too horrible to happen to Jacob.

I swallow, trying to find my voice.

"Carrie, I think he was hurt, while in prison. I think maybe he was raped…"

I stop her immediately. I do *not* want to hear that word. I do *not* want her to say that word. I do *not* want her to know that dark secret. That secret should be Jacob's. It should be Jacob's and he should be allowed to bury it so deep that it never reaches the outside world again.

"I know," I say my voice is full of pain and panic and it sounds harsh.

Nicole looks at me questioningly.

"I uh… he was at the house while Bull was gone. He…the dream…he had it then."

Nicole nods.

"Do you love him? I mean really love him?"

"Yes," I answer instantly.

"You're going to have to swallow a lot of crap to get to him, Carrie. Honey, it's so bad. I'm not sure you will be able to get through to him."

"You've dealt with this before?" I ask.

"That's not my story to tell, Carrie. Let me just say, I love someone who has that same darkness in them. It changes who they are, in ways you can't explain."

I nod.

"Dancer is at rock bottom, Carrie. If any man needed a woman to stand by him—It's him."

I nod again. I don't think I can find my voice at this

point.

"Dragon and the boys they aren't going to tell you this. They think they are protecting Dancer. I can't say they're completely wrong. What I can say, is that if you love him? If you are going to fight for him? Fight to stay with him?"

"I am."

I don't know where that answer came from. It pops out of my mouth but as it does, it feels right. I put Jacob in the mess he is in. It is because of me he was in jail. It is because of me he was vulnerable. I owe it to him to try and help now. I want to help.

Nicole smiles a sad smile, as if she knew what my answer would be all along, and she probably did. She loves Dragon. She knows how I feel about Jacob. I don't have a choice, other than to try and help him.

"The accident tonight, I mean it wasn't—an accident. Jacob drove off the Laurel Lake Dam."

"I…"

"He drove off of it all on his own and he didn't try to get out of the car."

"Oh god," I cry out my legs giving out and I sink onto the floor as my eyes fill with tears.

"If it wasn't for a person walking on the lakefront, watching, and rescuing him, Dancer would have died tonight, Carrie. I'm pretty sure he'll be upset he's not dead. You need to know that if you're going to stay around, honey."

I nod, my knees cradling my head. Nicole bends down in front of me and her hand touches the side of my face. I look up at her.

"It will get worse before it gets better. He will never be the man you remember, Carrie. You need to know that."

Those words cut me open inside. Can you die from bleeding internally from emotional wounds? It feels like I am.

"But, the man you love. There are pieces of him in there; there are new parts of him to love. If you are strong, you can help him come out the other side, you just have to be able to love the new him too."

"You seem to know a lot about this, but Jacob and I...I mean he's never let me inside, we've never had a real relationship. Nicole, what if I'm the wrong person to do this? What if I fail?"

"It's a horrible thing to see happen to someone you love, Carrie. I don't know what to tell you. I just know Dancer has a history with you. I also know that you're the only one who has a chance of getting close to him right now."

"Dragon and the men at the club they'd be better...they know him..."

"No. Something like that makes a victim feel powerless. Dancer wouldn't let his brothers in enough. He won't let them see. You, he might allow in. You, he might let help."

I nod. I don't know how she knows this. What I do know is, I can hear the truth in her voice. She believes what she is saying and something makes me believe it too.

She gives me a weak smile.

"Then suck it up, dry those tears and go in there and fight tooth and nail for your man because you will have to fight."

I wipe my face and slowly rise back to my feet. She points me to Dancer's room and turns to go.

"Nicole?"

"Yeah?"

"The person you helped…did you get them back?" I ask, her answer is important.

She walks to the first door and holds her head down.

"It's a work in progress Carrie, but I'm glad I never gave up."

It's not at all what I wanted to hear, but I will have to take it. I don't have a choice.

"Crusher dear, seems you're taking me home. My master has spoken," she calls out as the door closes behind her.

I take a deep breath, close my eyes and try to get a handle on my emotions. Just as I'm walking into Dancer's room, Bull comes up behind me. Damn he moves quickly. He looks at my face and I'm sure he can tell that I have been crying, but he doesn't say anything. He kisses my forehead and opens the door for me.

Chapter 10

DANCER

I'M LYING IN the bed feeling as if I'm floating. At first I figure I'm dead. I can almost feel relief. Slowly I start recognizing the voices, Dragon and Nicole talking. Their voices are low, but I can hear them. Maybe this is my hell? Listening to two people obviously in love talk about their poor pathetic friend like he's not around?

"I need you," I hear Dragon say in a tone I have *never* heard from my brother.

"You'll always have me," She whispers back.

What would that be like to know that the woman you wanted would be there beside you no matter what? Carrie would have given that to me. I know it. I've always known it. She's young and she's been protected from the world, but she's strong and she never waivers in supporting those she cares about. She would have given me exactly what Nicole is giving Dragon and probably more. She still would. At least I think she would try. What would she do though? How would she feel if she knew the man she loves, the man who she thinks can protect her from the world was so weak, *is* so fucking pitiful that he couldn't even protect himself?

The thought of Carrie finding out about the attack, of finding out what I was too weak to prevent fills me with dread. How can she love someone like that? Someone like me?

"Red, I told you…"

I try to open my eyes, but can't. I manage to open them just enough to see blurry images, but that effort takes too much. I hear Dragon's words but it's Carrie's scent that slams into me. It reaches me even over the antiseptic smell of the hospital room. It is the scent of sweet flowers and summer. It is Carrie. I take it in. I've dreamed of that scent for so long. It calms me, it tortures me, and it haunts me.

"I thought I gave an order," Dragon says again.

"I ignored them. How is Jacob?" Carrie asks and then I feel her fingers wrap around my hand. I feel a little less cold hearing her voice and having her touch.

She's here after I hurt her. She's here holding my hand and worried about me, despite everything.

"Doctor says he's doing fine, he just hasn't regained consciousness yet."

"What happened?" Carrie asks and my heart stops. I don't want her to know. I don't want her to have proof of how weak I am. I need her to see me as she always has.

"Car accident," Dragon answers. My brother has my back, even after everything.

"It happened down by the dam? I know I'm new, but there's not usually a lot of traffic by a dam this late at night. Was there another party involved? Was there other people hurt?" She questions and I can feel her smoothing out the covers over my chest. I want her to let it go, to stop the questioning. I don't want her to know. I need her to remain clueless. I can't see the disappointment in her face, or worse the disgust if she knows the whole story.

"I'm going to get some coffee," Bull speaks up. I shouldn't feel this way, but I'm glad he's leaving. I want him as far away from Carrie as he can get. That's just further proof that I'm a bastard, and that she deserves better.

"What aren't you telling me?"

"Carrie, all due respect, but Dance wouldn't want you here and he wouldn't appreciate you knowing his business. Let me take you home."

Fuck. I can't hear this shit. I did this. I put my brother in this position. Worse I'm responsible for others hurting Carrie now.

"I'm not leaving."

"I have to think of my brother…and this may hurt you Carrie, but you have to know the minute he wakes he's going to tell you to leave."

"Then when he wakes up and tells me to leave, I'll go."

The room goes quiet and I'm thankful. Hearing them discuss me, discuss how hateful I've been to this woman who even now cares about what happens to me? *Fuck, I am in hell.*

She still has hold of my hand, but now I can feel her fingers feather gently across my face. How long has it been since someone has touched me in a way that I can tell they care? Carrie touched me that night two years ago. Her hand had gently touched my face, much like now. She had looked at me with those damn green eyes of hers, so full of dreams and told me she loved me. I can still remember the panic I felt. Hell, I feel it now.

Maybe if I have Carrie, the darkness won't swallow me. Maybe if I let her, she could save me. Because, I'm dying a little more every damned day. Inside I'm rotting away and I can't stop it. I'm desperate, and when her hands are on me, it's the first time I've been able to draw a breath that feels even half way clean.

Can she take away all of the darkness?

Sleep begins to drag me back under. I want to fight it, but I'm just too tired. I concentrate on Carrie's touch. If she's here, maybe the nightmares will stay away.

Chapter 11

CARRIE

MY FINGERS MOVE over Jacob's face, tracing the cuts and scrapes that mar his beauty. He seems to be resting better now. Was it my imagination that I felt his hand weakly squeeze mine?

"Carrie, you might hear...well there are just things that Dancer might say while he's sleeping that he would not want you to hear," Dragon says.

I swallow. He wouldn't want Dragon to hear it either.

"I already know," I whisper the words like a guilty secret. I check Jacob over trying to find everywhere he has been hurt. I'm not doing it stay busy. The fact that Dragon knows Jacob's secret has rattled me. I haven't given myself time to process it yet. Dragon and I discussing it now seems like I'm betraying Jacob somehow.

I move his gown to the side and find an ugly scar on Jacob's side. It is old, there's no way it came from the accident. It's healed over and ugly to look at. It's at least a couple of months old... maybe more.

I bite my lip, but not before a whimper of noise escapes. Jacob has endured so much pain. I close my eyes and try to get control. I cover him back up. It's another secret that Jacob should be allowed to keep. Another secret, that Jacob would hate Dragon or me knowing.

"Did he tell you?" Dragon asks, and I sigh. It would be easier if he had. I'd feel less like I am trespassing where I shouldn't.

"No, I found out like you did. You heard him in his sleep right?" I add when I worry about if he'll get mad if he knows Nicole told me. She trusted me, I owe her.

Dragon nods once, "Some demons haunt the loudest when we can't fight them."

"Amen."

"You need to get home to Nicole. Let me stay with Jacob."

"I don't think…"

"If nothing else Dragon, it will give him someone to direct all his rage on."

Dragon walks towards the door.

He has almost left the room when he stops and asks, "You care for my brother?"

"I love him. I always have."

"Being lost doesn't make you weak."

"I never thought it did."

"The strongest motherfucker still gets tired," he adds.

My heart feels like a tight fist has grabbed it and is slowly choking the life out of me.

"You'll get them?" I ask, knowing he will understand. If he isn't planning on it, so help me God, I will find some way to do it myself.

"Every last fucking one."

"Make it hurt," I order, sitting back down as the tears fall because I can't hold them back any longer. I grab Jacob's hand. I need to touch him to hold onto him as long as I can.

Chapter 12

DANCER

CARRIE HAS A unique scent that is all her. I'm not a man who knows these things, but she reminds me of the morning air after a thunderstorm. I could get drunk on that smell. Every time I breathe it in, even when I am at my most angry, I feel this surge of *rightness* come over me. I've pushed and pushed her away but she keeps coming back and if she stopped…I'm pretty sure I wouldn't have to worry about finding the courage to end it all. No, without the hope she gives me, I'd already be dead.

I'm sore all over. When I made the decision to drive off the dam into the lake, I accepted that it was over. I wanted it to be over. The problem was that I hadn't picked a big enough dam to drive off of. The car hit the water with a splat. Nothing happened like I thought it would. No air bags released, no bright lights shown through the dark pointing the way to a better place. I got none of the things my brain had envisioned. Most of all, there was no instant relief for me. Instead, the car began filling with water. I was groggy, dazed even. I think my head hit the side of the door. I can't really recall. I just remember feeling the water rising on my legs and silence so thick I could almost taste it.

Then, I felt hands on me, pulling. I couldn't get awake enough to fight them off. The next thing I knew, I was on the side of the bank, coughing up lake water with the sound of an ambulance's siren in the background.

Which brings me to the here and now and the fact that Carrie has her head on my stomach. I open my eyes slowly to see her gorgeous red hair fanned out over me. I love the color of her hair. It's always been like a beacon to me. So bright and deep in color with these long twists and curls that I instantly need to bury my hands in it.

Hell, I could have made a living from making Carrie off limits. Her small hand is clutching mine. It's warm—so damned warm it feels like her touch has invaded my bloodstream. I angle my head to look at her soft face. She's sleeping. She still looks the same in sleep, but somehow even more innocent. Worse, Carrie looks so damn young. I feel ancient next to her. My large hand has signs of age that hers don't. The sane thing to do is to keep pushing her away, to feed the anger that has festered inside of me. I should continue to blame her for it all….at least on the outside. Doing so will mean she is far away from me and that's better for her. I'm on the edge of doing it. It's not that I'm a selfless man. It's just that Carrie deserves more than some dirty, bastard ex-con in her life. She always has. She is made for a white picket fence, for a three bedroom home in the suburbs, with children running around at her feet. That's the kind of life she is made for and deserves to have. I am not that man. I wasn't that man before my stint in jail, before the demons lodged themselves inside of me. Now? I am definitely not that man. I should leave her to a world, far away from me.

My decision is almost made when Bull opens the door. He looks at Carrie first. I can see a small shudder in his body. I know he cares for her, so I know what that tell-tale movement means. I'm a bastard. I fully admit it, but that makes up my mind.

I am not giving Carrie to a brother, a man I have to see constantly. I cannot handle the thought of Carrie falling in love with Bull and sharing her life with him. That shit is *not* happening.

I flex my hand in Carrie's. Not that much, to be honest even if I wanted to I couldn't. My body feels heavy and thick. Those beautiful green eyes open up, looking at me in confusion. I watch her blink a few times before she focuses on my face. That familiar kick in my stomach hits me.

God, she really is beautiful. She licks her pale pink lips and I'm mesmerized by her tongue sliding along the flesh. I want to taste them. It's a move as old as time. Something women have used to tempt and lure men for years. Thing is, I know that with Carrie it is completely innocent and that makes it even sexier. I see trepidation flash in her eyes and I hate the wariness on her face. It's what I've conditioned in her. She expects me to lash out at her now.

"Hey, Princess," my voice breaks and sounds hoarse and wrong. She jerks. Her eyes go large. She tries to pull up and let go of my hand. I don't let her, instead I tighten my grip. She looks at our joined hands and then back at me.

"Sorry, Jacob. I'll just…"

"Kiss me."

"I didn't mean…what did you say?" She asks, the shock echoing in her voice and I have to grin. This is going to be more fun than I imagined.

"You said you wanted me, so kiss me."

"Kiss you?" She asks.

"Care Bear, this isn't going to work if you repeat everything I say. Now bring those lips down here and kiss me."

Damn it hurts to talk that much. Part of my throat feels like it has been cut by glass. Still, the minute I use her childhood nickname, I can feel some of the tension in her body slowly evaporates. Delicious.

"Jacob, I…are you okay?"

"I'll be fine as soon as I get your lips, Princess."

Sadness flashes in her eyes. It seems odd how I can read every emotion she feels. I think I always have.

"I'll call a nurse and get her to…"

"I don't need a nurse. I need you."

"Jacob…"

I pull her hand and bring her lips closer to me, her eyes never leave mine, until she's so close that you can't put a piece of paper between us. Her eyes flutter close, her long eyelashes fan out. They are even more beautiful close up. Her lips briefly touch mine. It's a peck, not a kiss and I might let her get away with that, except for one thing. Bull is standing at the door watching us. I mentioned I'm a bastard. So I wrap my good hand, the one without the IV, into her hair and grip it hard. She gasps at the small bite of pain and I push my tongue in.

It's not a deep kiss, it's not long, hard and devouring like I'm longing to give her. I'm not able right now, plus my mouth and throat don't feel like my own. Still it's a good kiss. It's a kiss that delivers a message—two actually. One, it lets Carrie know that I'm through pushing her away. Second, Bull can see up close and personal that I own this woman and she's mine. Whenever and wherever I say, Carrie is mine. Maybe that's what drives me to hold her close after our lips break apart. Carrie thinks I'm hugging her, and I am. She thinks I did it so I could talk in her ear. I didn't. My lips are close to her ear because I like the idea of my breath fanning her exposed neck. Still, that's not the reason for this embrace. *I'm a bastard.*

"No more running. I'm going to take that pussy you offered me earlier, and this time I'm not stopping with just touching it."

Can she tell I'm not bothering to whisper? Can she hear the extra crack in my voice, as I actually speak louder than I should?

"We...Jacob, we should talk," she says pulling back slightly so she can look at me. I worry she's had enough and that I have burned too many bridges with her.

"Do you still want me? Care Bear, do you love me?"

She looks at me like she is trying to unravel a mystery. Good luck with that baby, I can't even fucking figure out my own self.

"Yes, Jacob...but..."

"Then we'll work it out baby. Together."

Silence for a few beats and I beat down the fear. I need her to help me survive.

"Together," she whispers and I smile. I smile because as I pull her close again to hug her and place a small kiss on her shoulder? My eyes lock with Bull's and I grin at the way the words obviously hurt him.

That's right fucker, I win.

Chapter 13

CARRIE

IS IT WRONG if you lie to yourself? *I know.* I'm not stupid. I look into Jacob's eyes and I know beyond a shadow of a doubt that he is playing me. I don't know why. I don't understand. I want to yell and scream at him. I want to slap his face and demand he treat me like I have a few brain cells. I don't. Instead I remember what Nicole said. I swallow down the need to scream, the need to demand. I remember that I love this man and I want to fight for him, not with him.

So I let him kiss me. It's not like that's a big hardship. I want his kiss. I crave his kiss. The fact that I can count the hours from the last time I had his lips? It just makes me want his kiss that much more. So I take his kiss and I let him lie. Does that make me weak? I don't know. I need to try and reach him and if he pushes me away that can't happen. So I make a decision. A decision to tread lightly and see where it goes. God I hope I'm doing the right thing and not making it all worse.

As Jacob slowly lets go of me, I hear a noise. I look over my shoulder towards the door figuring Dragon has come back. The door is clicking closed. Maybe it was just a nurse peeking in to check on Jacob?

"Get me a drink of water will you?"

I walk over to the other side of the bed and grab the cup that was sitting there. I angle the straw to his lips and help him get a drink. I'm about to go back to my chair, but as I put the glass down on the table, I feel Jacob's hand on my hip.

"What?"

"Come here, Princess."

I shake my head no. I may have made the decision to try, but I need to try and keep a clear head and I *cannot* do that with Jacob's lips anywhere near me.

I turn, his hand digs into my hip and he pulls me down to the bed. I reach out to catch myself, bracing awkwardly with one hand on the mattress, the other on his shoulder.

"Jacob, stop you'll hurt yourself."

"I know you're upset with me. You have every right to be, but you've got to believe me. Care Bear, I'm tired of running."

His hand moves under my hair and cups the side of my face.

"I need you, Carrie. I need you."

I'm hoping my body doesn't betray the emotions swimming around inside of me. This man will be the death of me. Would he turn his back on me if he knew what secrets I'm holding? Would he push me away, if he knew how much I love him? I think he knows already, I haven't exactly been playing hard to get with him. The question is what has changed with him?

"I want you lying on the bed beside me," he says again.

"There's not much room and you are hurt…"

"You're so small, there's plenty of room. I need this. In fact I think it's essential to my recovery," he says as his hands move to my sides.

He pulls me further down and I curl into his rock hard thigh, being more careful around this ribs and abdomen. I shouldn't, but I can't bring myself to say no. I angle myself and put my head on his shoulder. I feel his lips kiss the top of my head and I close my eyes, soaking this moment in.

"I thought you would order me out of here," I say honestly.

He doesn't answer for a minute, but his body is still relaxed against me. I am about to give up hope that he is going to talk to me when his voice whispers out.

"I should for your sake, Carrie…obviously you know by now that I have things I need to work through…"

"There wasn't another car involved tonight, was there, Jacob?" I ask the question that I already know the answer too. I don't want to bring it up, but I'm desperate. I need him to at least talk to me. I need to try. If I don't I think I'll hate myself.

"Carrie, I…I don't think I can talk about this yet. Not now. Just let me be here with you for now? I'll try and work through it all later, okay?"

"We can work through it together, Jacob."

"I can't…"

"I mean it, Jacob. You aren't alone I'm here and I am not going anywhere as long as you want me."

"Carrie, I want you. I do…but some things a man has to deal with on his own."

"And some he doesn't."

"I…"

"Don't send me away. Not now, Jacob. Please. Let me in, let me help?"

We lie there on the bed in silence. Me, because I don't really know what to say. I'm not sure about Jacob. Maybe he is already regretting me being here? Maybe Nicole is wrong? Maybe I should give him an out? I can't bring myself to do it. I just can't.

I am however, starting to feel self-conscious. I'm not sure how long I've been lying here without talking. I figure at least twenty minutes or longer. I slowly pull myself away from Jacob. He's been quiet for so long, I figure he's sleeping.

"Where are you going?" Jacob asks, his hand on my hip tightening to keep me from pulling further away.

"I thought I'd let you sleep."

"I want you here," I think I'm lying to myself, but I choose to believe he's referring to our earlier conversation. If I allow myself time to think about it? I would acknowledge that the tone of his voice, and how he refuses to look directly in my eyes, disagrees completely with what his lips are saying. I choose to ignore it. It's weak, I know. Sometimes, love makes you weak.

"If you're sure."

His fingers are combing through my hair. It's nice so I settle down against him and close my eyes.

"How come you don't have a man?" He asks and his fingers continue to sift through my hair. It relaxes me and with my eyes closed, Jacob filling my lungs and his arms around me…I let my guard down and answer honestly.

"I told you the last time we had this conversation Jacob, you're it for me."

"It's been over two years since that discussion, Carrie."

I kiss his chest, through the hospital gown, to still his words. It's not like I haven't heard them before. I'm used to people thinking I'm too young to know my own mind. It seems unreal to me. If I had slept with the entire state of Kentucky people would take me more seriously. I may only be twenty years old. I may have never had sex before. All this is completely true. What isn't true however, is that I am not adult enough to decide who I want in my life or who I want to take my virginity. Was I stupid to wait around for Jacob to give me a shot? Yes. I can admit that. It is the very definition of stupidity to pine over a man who has spent years pushing you away. That however, doesn't change the fact that the only person my body responds to, the only person I want it to respond to, is Jacob. I'm not naive. I do **not** see happy ever after in Jacob's arms. In fact, I know that I will probably have my heart ripped out and stomped on. I'm still moving forward with Jacob. I want to try and help him. I need to try. Some rides are worth the pain. If I run from this chance, I will regret it my entire life.

"Don't Jacob, just don't. Whatever happens, happens," I answer, fully meaning it.

The rest of my visit with Jacob is spent talking about incidental things, silly things. The conversation is purposely navigated away from anything heavy. Jacob has enough of that on his plate.

Chapter 14

DANCER

I HAD TO stay in the hospital for three days. Worse, they wouldn't let me out of the damned place until I agreed to outpatient therapy. It was a bunch of crap, but I agreed to it. Hell, I would have agreed to anything if it got me the fuck out of there.

My brothers are trying really hard not to ask questions about the accident. It would be comical really, if we weren't dealing with my life. Well, all of them except for Dragon are avoiding it. Dragon has been really quiet. I find him watching me at times with this look on his face and I have a feeling he knows more than the rest. I'm not sure how that makes me feel. In the end, I guess I'm not much better than my brothers, because I'm ignoring the issue with Dragon. Fuck, I don't even know what I would say to him anyway.

The next problem is Carrie. I made the decision to grab her up without thinking it through. She spent every day with me in the hospital. It was both heaven and hell. I loved having her close. I loved touching her, kissing her and having my brothers know she's mine. A sad part of me figures I look a lot less pathetic in their eyes having

Carrie as my old lady.

That's where the good part ends. The thought of any type of relationship with Carrie scares the fuck out of me. Once I got out of the hospital the touching, kissing and fuck just everything has gone to hell.

My brothers moved my stuff into the small house with Carrie. I thought that was good. Yet, now that we're here together, basically living together as a couple? It feels anything but good. It feels like the walls are holding me in? How fucked up is it to want someone, but panic constantly once you have them. I can't even understand my own mind these days.

I think I'm doing better at hiding my reactions from Carrie. I don't want to hurt her and the thought of her leaving me, sends me into a deeper panic. My brain feels like it never shuts off anymore. I didn't mind playing house when I thought Bull would be here. I liked the idea of flaunting Carrie's need for me in my brother's face. It gives me a perverse thrill. Only, Bull isn't here. So for the last week I've found myself playing house with a woman I want in my bed, but afraid to touch. We're living some kind of sad, perverse, platonic relationship. Something is going to have to give soon, I realize it.

I should walk away, a huge part of me is even demanding it. My brain just keeps playing Russian roulette with my memories and sooner or later the wrong one will escape and take…everything.

I've been sitting in my room for the last hour, alone, listening to the silence and hating every last minute of it. I lied to Carrie and told her I had a headache. She thinks I'm just turning in early. Lying to her is so easy. I guess because I do it daily. She thinks I'm seeing a therapist the hospital set me up with. I'm not. She thinks I'm suffering from side effects of almost drowning, I'm not. The list goes on and on. The biggest lie of all is that I'm just not able to make love with her. That's what she calls it, making love. I do not do *love*. I have sex. Sex that is down and dirty, hard and raw, and not made for a virgin.

I was stupid thinking I could do this. I can't. I am not what Carrie needs. It is time I face the facts, as much as I want Carrie, I will never be the type of man she needs or wants.

Decision made I walk in the living room, intent on going out finding a bottle and maybe pussy. I haven't gone this long without pussy since I got out of hell. This is the best decision for all of us. Carrie needs more than I can give her.

I find her lying on the sofa, sound asleep.

"Jacob?" She questions, her voice full of sleep and sounding so fucking sweet my teeth hurt.

"Hey."

"What are you doing?" She asks with a yawn sitting up. I watch as she yawns again and subtly shifts her body in a stretch. My dick instantly stands up and takes notice. Son of a bitch.

"Thinking about heading down to the club for a beer," I say and it's the truth absolutely, I'm just not mentioning what else I'll be looking for when I get there.

This strange looks comes over Carrie's face. Her green eyes flash at me and her face pales. Apparently I didn't need to tell her what else I'd be looking for, I'm getting the impression she definitely knows.

"I see," she says quietly, not looking at me.

I swallow the excuses that want breath. I resent that I'm feeling guilty about going out and getting laid. When did I become a man who answers to a woman I haven't even had my hands on in a week?

"Where are you going?" I ask when she walks from the room.

She doesn't answer. I follow her into her bedroom. I watch as she goes to the closet and pulls out a duffle bag. Placing it on the bed, she takes clothes from the old wooden chest across from the bed and puts them in it.

"What the hell are you doing?" I ask and I'm trying to ignore the panic that I feel.

"I'm going to leave."

This should make me feel better right? It doesn't. Fuck, it fills me with terror.

"You can't. Drag said someone was trying to kill you."

"Haven't heard anything in way over a couple of months. I can't keep putting my life on hold. I'm going to move in with my friend Tammie. No one knows her, I doubt whoever it is will find me."

"I've never met a Tammie," I say trying to breathe because it feels like my heart is beating so fast I'm going to stroke out.

"That's because she lives in another state."

Just like that, the panic increases. Carrie moving out is bad. Carrie somewhere I don't know? Carrie somewhere without protection? *Oh hell no. No. Just, no.*

"Since we have no idea who the hell is after you, you could be playing right into their hands," I say trying to direct the conversation back to why she shouldn't leave.

"Yeah well, living like this isn't changing anything either and I'm tired."

I walk over and dump her clothes back on the bed, because with each thing she adds I feel fear course through me stronger. She can't go.

"What the hell do you think you are doing?" She asks and the anger in her voice is sexy. Fuck, it is sexy as hell.

"You're not leaving."

She's not. Fuck, I can't handle this. I need to call Dragon. He'll talk some sense into her. I have no idea how to deal with women.

"I am. I don't know what kind of game you are playing, but I'm done."

"What are you talking about?"

"Don't play stupid Jacob, I might be younger than you, but I'm not an idiot."

"I have no idea…"

"Then you're a liar to yourself and me," she growls and throws her clothes back in the case.

Her red hair is bouncing along her shoulders, her voice is filled with anger, her face is flushed and I have the strongest urge to get on my knees and beg her to help me. Beg her to stay and not give up.

"What has crawled up your ass?"

"What has? Oh my god! You know Jacob, I'll take a lot from you. I have actually. That never made me feel stupid, until right now!"

"I don't know what you're talking…" I end with an umpf noise as I catch the bag of clothes she throws at my stomach.

"STOP LYING TO ME!"

I freeze. I've never seen Carrie this animated, this angry and outspoken.

"WHY? WHY, JACOB!?!?!?"

I drop the bag and stare at her.

"I am not cut out to be a monk."

Her mouth opens and then this look of confusion goes over her face and she crosses her arms in front of her chest.

"Gee I would have never guessed that," she says sarcastically. Somehow this new side of Carrie is just as sexy, if not sexier, than the old one. She's not getting it though, so I soldier on.

"Right now, it's taking all of the energy I have not to grab you and take the promise you have in your eyes and make it a reality. It is killing me. *Killing* me. We're not sharing a bed, we're not kissing, we're not…fuck, we're doing nothing. We're not even holding hands. Living with you is requiring sainthood from me, Princess. I'm not a fucking saint.

"Who asked you to be, Jacob? It sure as heck wasn't me!"

"See? Right there that's what I'm saying. You can't even cuss. You say the word heck for Christ's sake! You're too damned innocent for me."

"Oh my god, Jacob! Everyone is a virgin at some point! Even you were!"

"Yeah, but it's been a fuck of a long time, Carrie. It happened in a dirty alley with a hooker who was high enough not to mind giving a street kid a freebie."

She jerks back and it is that moment I figure I have shown her just how wrong for her I am.

"What does that have to do with anything?" She asks, and now she just sounds thoroughly confused.

"You're a virgin! A damned virgin, with stars in her eyes and what you want Princess, I'm not capable of giving you."

"Fine then! I'll just go out, get laid and then you can feel better about touching me? Would that work for you, Jacob Blake?"

"Damn it, Carrie…"

"Just save it. I wouldn't believe anything you said at this point anyway."

She delivers that last sentence and bends down to pick her bag back up. My hands go sweaty. Shit I don't know how I feel about this. I don't want her to leave. I'm terrified about what will happen if she stays. Fuck.

I make a split second decision. It may be a decision I live to regret. I just don't know. I'm going completely by instinct and what I do know is that she can't leave. If she leaves she'll be in danger. I can't deal with that. If she leaves I won't even have the chance to touch her and I don't want that. If she leaves there's a very big chance that Bull will run after her and I can't handle that at all.

"Wait…"

She stops, turns and looks at me. Her green eyes scan my face and I worry that she can see the doubt and indecision I'm feeling. Worse, will she see that a large part of me does not want to go there with her? What the fuck is wrong with me? Why is this so hard?

Because it's Carrie.

Carrie means something. She always has.

When she doesn't say anything, I force myself to try

again.

"Carrie…"

"I am not anyone's responsibility and I sure don't want to be that to you," her soft voice interrupts me.

She reminds me of a girl playing at being a woman. She is standing there telling me how she feels, but her posture is unsure, her voice way too soft for her words. I'm too old, too dark, too damned jaded to be anywhere around her. I want her, I want her in ways I've never wanted a woman. Fuck, I'm trying to do the right thing here, but I don't want her to leave. The thought of her leaving fills me with this overwhelming emptiness.

"Damn it all Carrie, I do want you. Hell, I've always wanted you."

I watch as her face lifts and her eyes seek mine yet again. I can see the hope flare before she taps it down. She's so innocent and pure staring at me. Does she realize that her eyes are pure seduction? Does she have any clue the things I want to do to her sweet body? Maybe…. maybe I should show her.

"Jacob, I need you too," she argues like she doesn't understand why I keep pushing her away. She acts like it should be just so damned simple.

It's not. It is anything but simple. The fact that she thinks it should be easy pisses me off.

"I should take what you keep offering. You owe me your innocence. You have no idea the fucking hell I have lived the last two years because of your naïve ass. You waltz into my life again after nearly destroying me and you think it should be easy to give you a piece of me? Fuck, I've had so many pieces of me torn away and it's all your fucking fault, Princess."

I regret instantly what I say. Apparently I haven't got a good enough lock on my anger. I'm going back and forth so much, I am getting dizzy. Fuck. I swallow, because I know my words have wounded her. I know I shouldn't have said it. I don't even truly believe it. There's just this huge rabid animal in me and I have no control over when it strikes out.

She looks at me with so much sadness, it seems to surround her. If there has been a more beautiful woman, I have not seen her. Her eyes look almost liquid.

Any minute now she is going to turn and run. I can't even blame her. I wish I could gather my words back up and keep them from touching her, but I know that is impossible too. So I wait for her next move. Part of me is already feeling relief, but a larger part is grieving, it's just further proof that my head is completely messed up.

What she says next? It shocks the hell out of me. I didn't expect it.

"Then take my innocence. Take whatever you want. It's yours, Jacob. It has always been yours, so take it. I'm yours."

Carrie's wearing a pale yellow sundress, looking young and untouched. This is who Carrie is. I love the dress on her. It reminds me of how innocent she is, while at the same time making me wonder what will happen once I dirty her up, and I do want to dirty her up. As confused as I am about taking this next step with Carrie, I at least know that.

I watch as she slides her dress off. She stands in front of me so fucking perfect, I want to scream.

I made a decision when I was in the hospital. I tried to go back on it, but there's not a man strong enough to turn down what is before me right now. I'm not even sure why I've fought it this long. I haven't been a better man in over two years.

Her words are brave, but her eyes falter and her arms cover her bra and breasts from my sight. I know I am in fact the biggest bastard ever born because I take pleasure in the way her hands shake.

I swallow, swearing I can taste her. Suddenly my mind clears, all I can see is Carrie and all I want is to touch her…to brand her. I want to fuck her so hard, for so long that anyone who comes after me will be a pale comparison. It's all kinds of fucked-up, but it is how I feel.

"The bra now, Princess," I say, my voice hoarse with need.

She fumbles with the clasp on the front of her bra and another thrill moves through me at seeing her hands shake. I like that she's new to this, that her moves aren't practiced. I especially like that I will be the first to taste her. The bra falls to the floor as her hand fumbles to keep her breasts hid. Even though she is shielding them from me, I can still see those pale creamy globes and I breathe easier. We've gone too far to turn back now. She will be mine.

Mine.

Chapter 15

CARRIE

I CAN'T BELIEVE this is happening. I mean, I'm glad it's happening. I've been dying for it to happen. This last week has been driving me crazy. I knew instantly what he had planned tonight and I couldn't handle it. I can't be around him now, if he slept with other women. It might have been saner to leave. I know that. I just keep remembering my talk with Nicole. I keep seeing the hopelessness in Jacob's eyes and I need to keep pushing forward. Maybe eventually I will give up, I just know I can't right now.

I turn to fully face him with a deep, calming breath.

Yeah, that didn't work.

"Drop your arms. I want to see you."

Drop your arms he says, like that's so easy. I swear if my heart beats any faster I will probably have a stroke. I'll keel over and stroke out and be naked when the freaking paramedics get here.

"Princess?" Jacob asks again and I close my eyes, but manage to slowly remove my arms.

I'm standing in front of Jacob Blake wearing nothing but a pair of panties. They're not even sexy panties. They're boy-cut green satin at least and there is lace—not a lot, but a passable amount. *That's good, right?* I mean they could be granny panties and I would die a horrible death.

"Damn. Care Bear, you're gorgeous," Jacob says. I can feel his breath so I know he has moved closer while my eyes are closed.

I smile at the use of my favorite nickname. I don't think he realizes when he uses it. It seems to be when his guard is down the most and it always gives me hope.

I jump when he palms one of my breasts. His touch feels heavenly. I feel him do the other breast in the same fashion. His thumbs rake over the skin, skirting close to my areola, but not quite touching it. Just that alone sends chills up my body.

I've made out with a few boys before, but nothing has ever felt this fantastic. I knew it would be different with Jacob. I knew in my heart that he was the man I was supposed to give my virginity to. This here. This feeling, these emotions…this is why I waited to have my V-card punched.

I open my eyes just as Jacob's head goes down and he kisses my breast. He's so close to my heart. Can he feel how hard and fast it is beating? I'm afraid to breathe, afraid to do anything that might stop him.

My hands come up without thought. One rests on his shoulder, with the other, I dig my fingers into his hair. The short strands tease my fingers. I wish he'd let it grow out longer. I could fast become addicted to the feel of it and….

His tongue slides along my nipple and I can't stop the whimper that escapes. His tongue is warm….wet…. an instrument of torture. He licks, twirling his tongue around it. My breasts aren't large, but they're not horribly small so I've never thought about it. I always worried though because my nipples seemed overly large. So, when I feel how amazing it is to have Jacob's tongue on them...I send up a thank you. Large nipples are awesome, I...

"Yes," I whisper.

The word slips out as he begins sucking my nipple so hard that the heels of my feet pull off the floor. I can't help it I have to follow, to get closer. At the same time, he pinches the other nipple with his fingers and my head goes back on a gasp. Can you come from breast play alone? I hear Jacob's grunt of approval as I tighten my fingers in his hair and pull him harder into my body, wanting more. To reward my eagerness he bites down on the nipple and flicks his tongue over it simultaneously.

"Yes...Jacob...that feels so good," I moan as both of my hands push his head closer to me, demanding he not stop. I never want him to stop.

He switches breasts now, devouring the other one and my legs are starting to grow weak. You think you know. You research, you study, you ask your girlfriends (Okay at least I did) and you think you know what to expect, what sex will be like and you think you are prepared. I had no clue. No clue at all, there's no way to describe this.

All at once, I'm moving. I'm moving fast, because Jacob is pushing us in the direction of the wall. We were at the bed, that makes more sense to me, but I don't have time to question it. My back connects with the wall and I hear the ripping noise echo in the room over our breathing. Cool air hits me as my panties are torn away. Jacob looks at me and his eyes are wild. They are this deep brown color that is so deep, so intense. I doubt anything from this moment on will live up to the beauty that is Jacob Blake.

"I can't wait to be inside of you, Princess. I'm going to fuck you so hard that your pussy is shaped for my dick and my dick alone."

I move my hands to his hips, trying to grab his shirt and pull it over his head. I want to feel his skin against mine.

"Keep your hands on my shoulders, Princess. Don't move them."

"I want to feel you...please Jacob take your shirt off," I beg and make no mistake I am begging. Right now, I would do anything just to feel him...feel more of him.

Jacob groans but pulls back enough so that between the two of us we manage to pull his shirt off.

I can't wait. I want to trace my fingers along the outline of his tats and follow that with my tongue. Jacob doesn't let me though. I whimper out in disappointment as he grabs my hands and puts them over my head imprisoning them with one of his against the wall.

"Jacob, please..."

"Not on your life Princess, you touch me and this will be over. There's only so much a man can take," he responds and then I give up worrying about it because his lips are back on my breasts, sucking and worrying the nipple at the exact same time I feel his fingers moving over my clit.

Oh my god.

That's the only thought I can have. No one has ever touched me before except well...me, and nothing I've ever done has felt this freaking good.

Jacob's mouth comes up kissing and licking above my breast and along my collarbone, giving little nips with his teeth and driving me crazy. I push against his hand, wishing I was free so I could touch more of him. He won't let go. I grieve the loss somewhere in the back of my mind. That's all I can do, because I feel Jacob's finger sliding against the lips of my pussy and then slowly move inside.

"Princess, you're dripping for me. Do you want my cock, baby?"

Yes!!!!

I want to scream out, but I don't. I'm a little afraid of what is to come, but that's not it. I've dreamed of making love to Jacob forever, but as intense as this is, it is not like I imagined. It is not what I dreamed. I'm afraid to say that though, if I do he will stop and I don't want that.

His finger pushes inside of me and I groan. It feels full and uncomfortable, but at the same time amazing. His thumb grazes my clit over and over, faster and faster and my hips begin to rock before I realize it.

"That's it, Princess. Get out of that head of yours and just let your body feel," He whispers as his tongue pushes into my ear and I feel yet another finger slide inside of me, stretching my passage.

I can't stop a moan that breaks free. I am beyond full. I am stretched so much it's almost painful.

"Shhh… I got you, Care Bear. I got you."

I hear his voice and feel his breath against my face. I hear my old nickname and my body relaxes slowly, he lets go of my hands and I open my eyes that I didn't remember closing.

He slides down to his knees and my vision is hazy because I'm so excited. Still, the sight of him on his knees in front of me, steals my breath. My hands move down to tease through his hair again, but he looks up at me and traps me with his eyes.

"Keep your hands flat against the wall, Carrie," his order is quiet but full of demand.

"Jacob..."

"Do it."

I swallow at the command in his voice, but flatten my hands against the wall and wait.

"Good girl. You want to be my good girl don't you?"

I lick my lips, almost afraid of this new Jacob. I nod yes, because I'm not a fool. I want more. Heck at this point, I need more.

He smiles and that smile is full of cocky male and promises bad things. I apparently am a lover of bad things, because I feel myself getting even wetter and his fingers slide in a little further. *How far can he go?*

He uses one of his hands to open my pussy to him. Cool air hits my clit. It is in direct contrast to the heat that flushes and travels through my body as Jacob's studies me.

"Damn Princess, you have the prettiest pussy I've ever seen. Look at all these pretty red curls trying to hide you from me. We're going to have to shave that. Later though, right now I'm way too hungry for you."

I bite my lip to keep from crying out as he flattens his tongue and licks my clit, pushing against it.

"Oh god..." Not very intelligent but all I can manage at this point. It only gets better when Jacob somehow captures my clit between his teeth and flicks his tongue back and forth. It's similar to what he did to my breasts, only better... like a thousand times better.

All the while, he continues to move his fingers very gently back and forth inside of me. With each thrust his fingers sink further inside of me.

"Jacob, I think... I'm going..."

I'm gasping trying to figure out what I want to say, but unable to be coherent enough to put the words together.

He growls. He literally growls against my pussy and once again sucks my clit into his mouth, humming against it. His fingers pick up speed. Faster he slides in and out of me and I can hear the sound of him plunging through my wetness. His fingers become harder, relentless as they drive into me. My hips rock, following him with each withdrawal before he plunges back in. I'm riding his hand, trying to take in every touch, every feeling. I can feel a climax building, and I try to fight it off. I don't want this to end.

"Let go, Carrie. Let it go for me. I want to hear you as you come all over my face."

His words combined with the way he is working me, send me over the edge. I scream out his name in one long, broken cry.

My head goes back hard against the wall, but I barely notice it as my body quakes in release.

It feels as if all the bones in my body have melted. I can only moan and tremble while Jacob picks me up and carries me to the bed. He lays me down and I open my eyes to smile, there is so much I want to say to him. So many words come to mind. Three certain words are the ones I long to say.

I love you.

I can't say that. I know I can't. Luckily, all thought stops when Jacob pulls off the gray sweats he is wearing.

I have never seen a man naked before. Well okay, I've seen pictures, but as far as seeing a live, naked man standing in front of me? That has never happened. The fact that the man is Jacob, along with the fact that he is oh-my-god-holy-smokes-flat-out-gorgeous, fries what little brain receptors I have. All I would be able to do is babble some unintelligible words, so I bite my tongue to stop them.

I do reach out though, I can't help it. Finally, I get to touch him, to feel him. My hands collide with the warm skin of his abdomen. I flex my fingers wanting to feel more…to dig in and never let go.

I don't get the chance though because Jacob grabs my hands and pushes me back completely against the mattress.

"Princess, I told you, no touching."

"Please Jacob, I want to feel you…"

"Not now, I need to concentrate on you. I know this is your first time and if you touch me, I won't be able to make it good for you. Do you trust me?"

Make it good for me? Can it get any better than what we just shared? That has already blown every preconception I had of what an orgasm feels like. His dark brown eyes are right in front of mine. Until this moment, I thought I knew everything about Jacob, but his eyes are not brown. Well they are, they're like a dark brown but they have these flecks of green and gold in them...Hazel...the most beautiful shade of Hazel I could ever imagine, so deep and drugging. I swallow at the darkness I see in them. I know, well I have always known that Jacob has demons that threatened to consume him, but now? Now, I can feel them radiating off of him and I want to fix him, I want to *save* him. I just don't know how. So, even though I want to argue? Even though, I want to scream that it is my first time and because it is, I want to be able to wrap my arms around him and hold him to me? I don't. I don't do any of that. I nod yes.

He rummages until he finds a scarf I had in the clothes he dumped out. I try to get up again. I'm not sure why, to be honest. Jacob is naked, it's a really good show and it just feels like I should be closer.

He doesn't let me though. He pulls my hands above my head and wraps the scarf around my wrists. I should panic, but Jacob is on his knees beside me, he's bent over wrapping my wrists up and his penis is jutted out in front of my face. I've never seen a penis this close up...umm...okay I've never seen a real live penis! More importantly, I've never seen Jacob's penis!

My first instinct is to touch it. It's large, thick and I guess I can't judge, but beautiful. The head is glistening with moisture and I'm dying to run my thumb over it. My hands pull against the restraint of the scarves, but I get nowhere. He's secured me to one of the metal spindles on the headboard.

"Jacob, I want to touch...it."

"It?" He asks looking at me now that he has finished securing the scarf.

"Your...you know."

Jacob laughs and it is a really good sound, but since it is me he is laughing at? Kind of embarrassing.

"Princess, I'm about to make you real familiar with my *'you know'*. I think the least you could do is say the word, don't you?"

"I want to touch your…penis."

He laughs again, but this time the look on his face is worth it. He reminds me of the old Jacob like this. His face relaxed, almost happy and the sound of his laughter is free and easy. This gift alone makes me forget my embarrassment. I don't have time to dwell on it however. He moves to lay beside me, his hand rough and callused, moves down and rests against my stomach. His head tilts over me and his lips slide briefly against mine.

"I like having you completely at my mercy, Princess. You're mine to do whatever I want," he whispers against my lips and I can't stop my tongue from reaching out to gently stroke his lips and taste him.

Chapter 16

DANCER

HER TONGUE SHYLY slides between my lips and just that simple movement makes me feel like I've won a war. Which is completely false since I'm being a major dick. She wants to touch me and she deserves to. I'm not stupid. I know this will be Carrie's first time and it should be special. I can't let my guard down enough—not now. If she touches me the wrong way, or does something to remind me like she did before? I could accidentally hurt her and I can't handle the thought of that, not again. So for both our sakes, I need to restrain her. I will just have to make sure I make up for it in other ways. She's a virgin and completely innocent. Maybe she won't notice that something is off—maybe I can make sure she doesn't notice?

I take over the kiss, devouring her as I've wanted to do since the beginning. The taste of her is drugging. My tongue keeps plunging back in needing more. I feel her moan break free as I finally release her mouth, only to kiss down her neck. Her skin is salty-sweet and unlike anything I've had before.

I kiss every inch of her I can reach, while using my

hands to touch her, and praise her. Her skin is so smooth, so warm and soft that I could spend hours doing nothing but touching...worshipping her.

I slide one of my hands into that wet as fuck pussy. When she had ridden my hand earlier, I nearly came in my damn pants. I watched her eyes the entire time and when I felt her cream slide out against my fingers it took all I had not to join her.

I let my fingers dance along her clit, petting it and slowly bringing her where I need her to be, her hips thrust out and she moans at my intrusion.

"Jacob, it's...tender..."

"It's fucking perfect. You're perfect. I can't wait to be inside of you," I answer bringing my lips to her ear. I use my other hand to play with her hair and hold her head as I continue torturing her clit.

"Oh god... I can't stand it," she gasps, her hips bucking wildly against my hand as she clamps down trying to ride. Her moves are out of rhythm and unpracticed and damn, it excites me.

I own this, no one else...just me.

Me.

No other bastard has got this from her. I'll kill any motherfucker who tries.

"It's time for our first lesson, Princess," I whisper close to her ear, before stretching over her to suck her nipple into my mouth. I suck so hard, I know my mark will be there in the morning. Hell, I'm going to mark her entire body, just because I fucking can.

"Lesson?" She questions, her hips rocking faster. She's bearing down so tight against my hand, I'm amazed with the force she's using to ride.

"Carrie, you're my woman, aren't you?"

"Yes."

She answers immediately, no denying it, playing coy or bargaining—just straight out admitting it. I feel something inside of me lighten with her agreement.

"My woman doesn't use the word penis."

"Jacob!"

She screams out my name as I push two of my fingers inside of her. She's so wet they slide in further than before and I can feel the barrier of her virginity.

I've fucked a lot of women, but this is new ground to me. I hope like hell I can make it good for her. I promise myself that I won't let her out of bed the whole day so I can make sure sex is something she wants…fuck that, to make sure sex with me is something she craves. That's my goal.

"Jacob, I'm going… I'm going to orgasm again."

"You're going to come, Carrie. Say it."

Her head is thrown back against the mattress. That gorgeous hair is strung all over her pillow. Her eyes are closed, her lips swollen, wet and open and her body is moving to a pace I am setting. Magnificent.

"Say it, Carrie. Tell me you're going to come. I want to hear that dirty little word from your lips."

"I'm going to come…" She cries out, the word comes echoing out in the room.

I smile. I smile like a fucking loon at her words.

"That's good, Princess. You deserve a reward," I say, biting along the corded muscle in her neck.

"I do?" She asks her voice soft and breathless.

"Yeah baby, you do. Do you want my cock?"

"I...Jacob..." She cries, as I push my thumb hard against her clit and fuck her with my fingers, stretching her passage and curling them to get her ready. God, she's so tight. She's going to squeeze the hell out of my dick. I take my hand away from her pussy and sit up. She moans out her displeasure.

"What, baby?" I ask moving so I'm sitting in between her legs. I pull her legs further apart and push so her knees are bent close to her chest.

She's exposed completely, her hungry pussy pulsating, so slick it's glossy with her need. I thrust my fingers back in at the same time flattening my tongue out and licking that clit which is so engorged, I know she's about to explode.

"I... oh...yes...that... Jacob, keep doing that."

I smile. That doesn't sound like a shy virgin at all. Breaking her in is going to be fun. She's going to be a wildcat, I can feel it. The anticipation is almost as good as the taste of her on my tongue... almost.

"I can't, Princess. I'm going to give you my cock. You want my big fat cock in this pussy don't you? You want me inside of you, right?" I ask moving my tongue teasingly over her clit, lapping at it like it's the last taste of my favorite ice cream.

"Yes..." She whimpers, clenching against my fingers which I've thrust back into her pussy and just leave there, refusing to move. She's tightening up and trying to ride them, but can't. I refuse to let her close her legs to get the traction she needs.

"Jacob please, stop torturing me!" She cries out.

"Aw baby, I'm sorry. I just love the taste of you so much I can't seem to stop. You taste like fucking nectar of the gods. I could eat out this sweet little pussy for days on end and never get enough," I explain taking my fingers out, smiling at her disappointed moan.

"Oh… please, I need to…"

"Say it."

"I need to come."

"Good girl. Just for that, I'm going to be nice."

I lift her ass, sliding a pillow under it. I slam my fingers back in her pussy curling them upward and fuck her hard with them while eating out this sweet little cunt with all I've got. It doesn't take long. She detonates, riding my face, bathing me with her sweet cum. I growl with hunger, because it's not enough—not by a long shot. I want more. I'm going to have more.

I position myself at her opening and stretch over the top of her perfect body.

"Princess, you have the sweetest tasting pussy I've ever had."

"Jacob…" she moans, her body moving restlessly and still quaking from her release.

I use my hand to slide my cock back and forth over her throbbing clit, teasing both of us.

"Eyes on me, Carrie."

She slowly opens her eyes, the green color glows back at me. Her pupils are so dilated they could swallow a man in their depths.

"Untie me now, Jacob… please. Please, let me touch you."

Motherfucker!

"Taste how sweet you are, Carrie," I say to divert her, slamming my lips against hers and thrusting my tongue in her mouth. I rest my cock in between the lips of her pussy and just glide there gently while she kisses me back, her tongue fighting with mine.

"You taste good don't you, Princess? Do you see why I need more and more? Soon, I'm going to spend hours, doing nothing but eating your pussy until you pass out from the pleasure."

I pull back now, once again positioning my cock. I'm dying to be inside of her.

"Carrie. Eyes. Now," I order.

She instantly opens them again and locks onto me.

"Don't take them off of me, Princess. Not once. I want to see it all."

She bites her lip nervously, but nods.

"It may hurt, but I promise I'll make it feel good soon."

She gives another slight nod. I don't want to hurt her. To be honest I don't know anything about taking a virgin. I figure I've given her enough pleasure to make up for the pain and this sure isn't the end of it. I caved because I wasn't going to let Bull claim her. With this taste of her I know it's not going to stop—not now. Fuck, maybe never. I've not felt alive in so long and with Carrie I feel way more than just alive.

I take a breath and then brace myself on top of her and plunge inside. I feel a barrier, but she's so slick and with just a small thrust I push through and suddenly I'm completely inside. It sounds stupid. It sounds ridiculous, but I'm home. I fucking like being the only one to have been here.

Carrie cries out at the intrusion and those beautiful green eyes water. It takes all I have, but I hold myself still—letting her become accustomed to me.

"I'm in now, baby. Tell me when it starts to feel better."

"It burns," She confesses and one lone tear rolls down her cheek.

I lean down and kiss away the tear and then kiss down her neck making a path down to her breast. I capture a nipple between my teeth and worry it with my tongue. Teasing gently, but never stopping. I'm trying to get her back to the point I need her. I put all my weight on one arm while sliding my hand down between us. I tease her clit.

"Jacob…" She gasps and I can feel the moisture gathering around my cock and slide a little further in.

"That's it, Care Bear, you feel so good baby. There's never been anything better."

"Jacob…."

"You're fucking amazing, Care. Amazing," I praise.

"I need more," She gasps her hips trying to move under my weight."

"I got you baby, now comes the good part."

I pull almost all the way out and then push back in. Slowly at first, but when she starts to follow my rhythm, I pick up speed.

"Fuck yeah. Lock your legs around me and hold on."

I know she's a virgin, I know the importance of what I just took from her. Yet, I can't slow down. It is beyond me. I'm too far gone.

I have the presence of mind to manipulate her clit, bringing her to the edge again. I can feel my balls tighten and I know I'm going to blow.

"Come for me, Princess. One more time, let me feel you come all over my cock," she moans as I pull up on her hip and sink down to my balls.

Fuck, it can't get any better.

That's my last sane thought as she calls out my name. It blends with my groans. Her walls ripple against my dick and takes every drop of cum I have to give her.

I was wrong, it can get better. It just did.

Chapter 17

CARRIE

Wow.

I should probably think of something more profound, but I'm pretty sure my brain is mush. All I got is… wow. Jacob is lying beside me, one hand across my stomach. I feel the other against my side. His fingers moving up and down along my thigh. I'm trying to process everything. I don't think I was prepared for sex, not sex this intense. It is everything and more than I thought it would be with Jacob. It was perfect. Except, *it wasn't*, not really.

Now there is silence. All you can hear in the room is our breathing slowly coming back down to normal. There are no soft words of love. No laughter, no playing, none of that. Worse, there are no soft touches being exchanged, no holding each other close. None of the stuff I dreamed of is happening in the aftermath. Instead, I'm lying in a bed with Jacob's hands on me, willing myself to be quiet because he's not talking and I'm afraid of saying the wrong thing. I can't touch him or hold him close or do the million and one things I want to do. Why? Because my hands are still tied. My lips feel dry, my throat feels raw…but then I did scream out that last time. When I can't stand it any longer, I take a chance to shatter the silence.

"Jacob can you untie me now? I need to go to the restroom."

"I don't want you to go yet, Care Bear."

My heart aches at the use of his nickname. Not because it's not beautiful, wonderful and amazing—no. It's because those are the words I want to hear. The words I need to hear, but yet it seems…not quite right.

"I'm sticky…"

He smiles and those hazel eyes sparkle. Somehow with that smile, he reminds me of the old Jacob and that knot in my stomach loosens its hold, if only slightly.

He kisses my lips gently almost reverently. This…this is what I want.

"I like the idea of you being overfilled with me—of you dripping with my cum."

I blush at his description, but secretly I'm jumping for joy too. I like the idea. I like everything about it and I *love* that he likes it.

"I need to stretch my arms though."

He looks up at the binding above my head and something flashes in his eyes. I don't get the time to decipher it. He reaches up and in just a few seconds I'm free. I bite my lip to keep from moaning out loud. I kind of understand what is going on, even if it does confuse me. I wish Jacob could be completely open with me. I keep thinking back to the first time I saw Jacob in the hotel room. He had been in bed with two women. Neither of those women were tied. Why were they allowed to touch him, if I can't? Is there something wrong with me?

I don't ask, I suck in the hurt. I don't want to push him away. Whatever this is, it is new. I've never been in a relationship before. What I do know is I love him and I need this to last. If it doesn't, I'm going to lose such a large piece of myself, I will never recover. Again, my conversation with Nicole flashes in my mind. I signed on to fight, not quit.

Jacob has my hands, rubbing them gently. Slowly, he brings the circulation back in them.

"Better?"

I smile and nod, which makes me feel stupid, but I can't seem to find my voice.

He places small kisses on my hands and when he's done I feel even more awkward. Maybe I should have allowed him to keep me tied? Because right now? I'm afraid to touch him, so my hands are just clumsily lying at my side.

Oh god, shoot me now.

"Hey, what's wrong?" Jacob asks and I want to tell him, let it all out and tell him. I don't. I'm afraid. This might not be everything I want, but it's already more than I thought I would get. It's a start.

"This is new to me…" Not a lie.

"Oh I noticed that Princess, believe me." He pulls me on top of him, so I am now straddling him. I can feel him hard against me and I instantly feel my insides quiver in want and need.

"What…what are you doing?" I ask, wondering if he can feel the way I rocked against him.

"I want you to ask for my cock and if you convince

me? I'm going to let you ride me until you make both of us come."

"I…like this?" I ask, not because the position is so new to me, but more because maybe I can touch him now and that thought excites me even more than knowing I will have him inside me again.

"Exactly like this," he confirms and I might be squealing like a little girl on the inside.

"Are you too sore for me this soon, Care?"

I blush at his words. I shake my head no. I'm totally lying, I feel really tender and sore there, but nothing will stop me from having him again.

"Thank fuck," He says and I have to concur. "Do you want my cock?"

"Yes…"

"Then tell me, Princess. Let me hear you."

"Jacob, I…I want your cock."

"That's my girl," he says as he wraps a hand in my hair and pulls my lips down to his. I use one arm to brace myself so I don't fall. I feel the sting of him pulling my hair, my pulse rate jumps in reaction.

"Guide my cock inside of you, Carrie."

I go up on my knees to do as he asks. He hasn't let go of my hair. If anything, he has wrapped it tighter around his hand. It takes me a couple of fumbling tries, but I get him to my entrance and slowly slide down on his dick. There's pain almost instantly, but I bite my lip and ignore it, because even through the pain it feels good. Can you get addicted to sex after one time? I think I might be. When he is all the way inside of me, I freeze. In this position it feels like I'm stretched to my limits. I don't move, I'm not sure I can.

"That's it Princess, get used to having me inside of you. You're so damned beautiful Care Bear and fuck woman, you feel so good. I love the way your pussy squeezes my cock, like it can't get enough."

I'm totally unsure of myself. I've read a lot of books, so I try to remember from them what to do. I don't want to disappoint him, but I draw a blank. Jacob's eyes on me, his…cock inside of me? All I can think is that I want more. I want this *forever*.

I rock on him slowly. *Oh, that feels amazing.* Jacob's face blooms into this lazy smile and his hands go to my hips. He pulls me up and down, showing me the rhythm he wants. On each downward stroke he thrusts up. The pleasure is so intense, I call out his name. I move my hand slowly down his chest. He is perfection. Absolute perfection. There are no other words for it.

He stops my movements with his next words though.

"Play with your tits, Princess. Take each nipple in your fingers and tease them for me."

Under his direction, my ride picks up speed and I get lost in the moment, following each command he gives me without question.

Bring your breasts to my mouth Princess, I need to suck them," he demands.

I do it without question. I am his prisoner. He orders and I give it. I'll do anything he asks at this point. For the first time in my life, I feel like I am…*home*.

It will get better. Jacob will let me in. I need to just give him time. That's the last thought I have before I detonate into a thousand pieces.

My heart cries out…*Jacob, please let me in.*

Chapter 18

DANCER

F UCK. FUCK! FUCK!! FUCK!
What was that? What the hell was that?

I'm lying in bed after the most intense *sex* I've ever had in my life. Carrie fell down against me almost immediately after that last round. She is sleeping wrapped tight around me. It should feel suffocating, it doesn't. It feels like I've reached...hell, I don't even have words. I just know, I wish I could freeze this moment and live *here*—never leaving *here*. *Here* is good.

Still, even *'here'* doesn't feel right deep inside of me. I'm completely satisfied. I have the woman I've dreamed of for years in my arms and still there is fear. My heart is beating out of my chest. I feel like I can't breathe. I am sweating and it feels like I'm going to jump out of my skin. It doesn't make sense. How can I feel so good being with Carrie, but still sense a panic attack waiting for me? I've felt it enough times to know. Panic and I have become bosom buddies.

I need to leave. I need to get out of here. A drink...I need a drink.

I jerk as my phone rings. I stretch to reach down to

my pants on the floor. I find it in my pocket. Carrie moans, the sound is enough to make my cock come to life. How the fuck is that possible? I came so hard the last time I thought the damn thing would have been dead to the world the rest of the night.

"Yeah?" I grumble into the phone. I feel Carrie place a kiss on my chest. I look down to a sea of golden red locks, I feel another feather-light kiss and then she snuggles back down, her breathing evening out. *Shit. Had the other person answered yet?* I've pulled the phone away from my ear to watch Carrie. This woman is so fucking dangerous. "What?" Wondering who the hell is calling.

"I said, I need you at the club."

Dragon.

I may have wanted to take a breather from Carrie, but going to the club is *not* what I had in mind. That place fucks with my head. The men and the loud party atmosphere, I can't handle it. Always before, I'd go to a bar, find a good lay within a few minutes and take her (or them) back to the cheap hotel I was living in. The few times I've been summoned to the club have played hell with my brain. In prison we were always kept in groups, never alone. When the men weren't talking or yelling, the guards were. There was never silence. It only got worse at night. At night you were locked in your tiny cell with another inmate. The room was always so hot and thick with stomach-souring odors. There's no way to describe the actual stink and desperation that clamps over everything in prison.

"Motherfucker, are you listening to me?"

No.

"I can't leave Carrie unprotected," I argue, ignoring the fact that I almost left her alone before Dragon called.

"Bull should be there anytime to watch over Red. You get your ass to me. It's important."

"Fuck no. Bull is not getting around my woman," I yell back before I can stop myself.

"I know you didn't just argue with me. I said Bull will watch over your woman and Dance? He. Will. Watch. Over. Your. Woman."

"Damn it, Dragon," I raise up off the bed. I dislodge Carrie off of me in the process, but I'm fucking pissed at my brother. She moans, but doesn't wake up. She rolls over to her side, the white sheet hangs loosely around her body, leaving her breasts completely exposed. My cock is totally standing at attention now, *shit*. "Bull doesn't need to be anywhere near Carrie, you have to know he's hung up on her."

"He won't go there with a brother's old lady."

"Bullshit...."

"He won't, unless Carrie wants it. So I guess it depends on how you're treating her," Dragon comes back at me. He doesn't realize what a bear he is poking. I cannot handle that shit. The thought of another man putting his hands on Carrie? Someone else getting even a small taste of what I just had? Just the thought makes me tighten my hand on my phone, so much, it is a wonder the damn thing doesn't crumble into dust.

"She's passed out after I popped her cherry and fucked her seven ways to Sunday. I made her scream so loud the neighbors probably called 911. Does that answer your question?"

I hear a gasp from behind me and glance over my shoulder to see Carrie looking as if I had slapped her. Her face is white and those damn green eyes are looking at me with…shame?

"You're a fucking ass, Dance man."

I absolutely am and even more so than he knows right now.

"Bull will watch Carrie and you will get your ass here," Dragon finishes.

"I don't…"

"Wow, I didn't realize."

"Realize what?" I ask trying to watch Carrie as she gets up with the sheet wrapped around her.

"That I woke up this morning in a world where it is fucking okay for you to question me. Get your ass here, or I'll make sure it gets here. I've cut you slack Dance, but do *not* fucking test me on this," he orders, hanging up.

I end the call and turn to watch Carrie walking away.

"Carrie, honey I didn't…"

"Yes you did, you enjoyed telling him," she says quietly, turning to look at me.

"I didn't lie, there's no reason for you to be acting like I did," I grumble, knowing I'm making a bigger fucking mess, but I'm not about to keep apologizing.

"No, you didn't lie."

"Damn it, Princess."

"Don't worry about it, Jacob," she says quietly, turning to go into the bathroom.

"You should be glad you got a man that makes you…"

"I am glad to be with you, Jacob. I just don't think you can say the same. Tell me, Jacob? Will it upset you at all when you succeed in pushing me away? Or is that not important, now that you've had me?"

Her quiet questions punch me in the gut. She doesn't stay to see the hit delivered. She closes the door and leaves it to echo in the silence. I look down and see the small stain of red blood on the sheet. My guilt ramps up.

Fuck. Fuck! Fuck!! FUCK!

Chapter 19

CARRIE

IT IS WEAK, I admit it. I lean against the bathroom door, until I hear Jacob's bike start up and become a distant rumble. I run a bath with hot, hot water and slide inside. I wash every inch of my skin, needing to feel less used. I hold it together, until the hot water becomes less than lukewarm and then, my tears fall.

I don't know how long I cried. It could have been ten minutes—it could have been an hour. I'd probably still be lost, except for the touch on my shoulder. I gasp in surprise. Nicole is looking down at me, with a sad look on her face.

"Let's get you out of here, before you prune up," she says. Proof she has been here for a while, she is holding a big bath towel out to me.

I wrap up in the towel and let her lead me back to the bedroom. She has stripped the bed and put clean sheets on it. I'm a little sad because those sheets smelled like Jacob. I might be hurting, but if I could wrap up in his scent and just pretend it was all okay for the night? Just pretend long enough to sleep? I'd be okay with that.

"I found your pajamas. Dry off and put them on and

I'll brush your hair."

"You don't have to…"

"Shush, you need a friend and I've decided it is going to be me. So suck it up and do as I say. I'll go get you something to drink."

"How do you know?" I question, not able to voice the whole question. I'm not sure I want to face or process what has happened.

"Dragon told me."

"Of course he did, I guess everyone knows now."

"Only me, and shame on you for thinking Dragon would ever do something like that."

"I didn't really. I figured Jacob has already told the world."

I notice she doesn't argue with that. Probably, because she knows I'm right.

"What do you want to drink?" She asks, going to the door.

"Getting drunk sounds appealing right now and don't try to tell me I'm underage," I mumble. I don't need to be told I'm a child. I am adult even if I don't feel equipped to handle this situation with Jacob.

"Brandy it is," she mumbles.

I dry off, and slip on the clothes she laid out. Then, I crawl under the covers. I lay my head on the pillow and mourn the fact that it no longer smells of Jacob. I grab the other one and hold it close to my stomach, hugging it.

I have no idea where to go from here. I'm not ready to give up, but suddenly I'm seeing this may be a bigger job than I first imagined.

"Here, sit up and take a drink of this. We need to

brush your hair."

"I don't want to, I just want to go to sleep," I say honestly.

"Drink and hush," she bosses placing the drink in my hands. I take a sip, grimacing at the obvious dark taste of alcohol.

"Do you want to talk about it?" She asks angling behind me. I guess I'm getting my hair brushed, whether I want it or not. I take another drink.

"No."

"I warned you it wasn't going to be easy," she says while she runs a brush through my curls.

"I think you possibly understated that," I say, my voice dripping with sarcasm.

Nicole makes a sound close to a snort, agreeing with me. It's probably more of an I told you so, because she did. She absolutely did and it is the reason I'm here now and not half way to Georgia, or hell anywhere else. Here is being in Jacob's bed, with my heart ripped out while he tosses out facts about my virginity.

I'm mad at myself because I'm still in his bed. I didn't throw things at him, throw him out or anything! Instead I cried, while he left like hell's fire was nipping at his heels. Worse, I'm still missing him. When did I become such a doormat?

"You're not a doormat."

Shit, I didn't realize I said that out loud.

"I am, but I deserve to be. I'm the reason Jacob killed that man. I'm the reason he was put in jail. I'm the reason he was there and was…attacked."

My voice breaks on the last note. I can't bring myself

to say raped. It keeps screaming in my brain, but I can't give voice to it.

"Carrie…"

"It's true, Nicole," I say, swallowing the last of my drink and reaching over to put it on the table. "It's my fault, all of it."

"Bullshit! Jacob's a grown ass man. He did what he did and you can't take the guilt of that."

"Guilt. God, there's so much guilt. Jacob has so much he can't breathe. I have so much it hurts to breathe. How can that ever work out Nicole? I think you're wrong. I'm not the person to save Jacob. I'm too clueless to help him."

Nicole is silent. She stops brushing my hair and instead I can feel her braiding it. It feels nice, relaxing even. I close my eyes, wishing I could still the thoughts in my brain.

"I wasn't wrong. Dancer's already let you in more than he has anyone else—so I wasn't wrong."

"But?" I ask, because I can hear a but.

"You have to decide if you're strong enough to see this through, because I'm not going to lie, I think this might be small compared to some of the hits you may take."

Am I strong enough?

"Was it worth it for you?" I ask. She's finished with my hair and we're both quiet, like we're afraid to move.

"It is different for me. I love the person involved, but I'm not in love with them. The attacks…they aren't personal so they don't cut as deep as the ones you're taking, Carrie."

"Even when it's good, there are still…things that keep it from being what it should be, Nicole," I confess, like it's a dirty little secret. It hurts that I couldn't hold Jacob while we made love. It cuts that I couldn't hold him close and love him the way I have dreamed of for years.

"I know, baby," She says, only she doesn't—not really.

"I'm so tired," I say for no reason in particular, just that I am. I am bone-deep tired. I think if I managed to shut my brain down and go to sleep, I'd sleep for days, weeks even.

"There's something else I know," Nicole says getting off the bed and picking up the towel I had used.

"What's that?" I ask not really caring. I lay back down against the pillow now that Nicole has left the bed.

"If the roles were reversed and it was me and Dragon? I'd fight so fucking hard to pull him out of the hell he was in. I'd fight with everything I had and I wouldn't give up no matter what. I'd fight with my last dying breath, Carrie."

"Dragon loves you," I answer. If Jacob loved me, I'd never waiver. I don't have the security of that, I don't think I ever will and that's where the problem lies.

"True, but I love Dragon. I love him so much that I'd fight just for the chance that someday he'd be happy. You need to decide if you love Jacob that much, or if everyone and their mothers are right and you're too young to know that kind of love."

"They think I'm too young?" I ask, hurt but annoyed because it seems I've been the topic of conversation among the Savage MC compound.

"Why do you think they moved you away from the

parties and things? They see you as a young kid sister they need to protect. Hell Crusher even lets you call him by a name he hates."

"They don't," I argue, though warmth fills me at the thought of these tough men thinking of me as family.

"Yeah, you're right," she says and damn there goes that feeling of belonging out the window. "Bull absolutely does not think of you as a sister."

Yeah, I'm not going there.

"Turn the light out, I need to sleep," I say rolling over on my side and curling back into Jacob's pillow.

"Just saying, hooking yourself up to Bull's wagon would definitely be easier and he'd be good to you."

"He's not Jacob," I whisper the sad truth, "I don't want anyone but Jacob."

"That's how I knew Dragon was the one for me, Carrie."

I sigh, my brain is on overload.

"Do you know, I'm not that much older than you are?"

I did. I don't say anything.

"I have a brother. No one knows that. He's actually a half-brother, who is ten years older than I am. A brother and we never talk, ever."

"I…" Nicole goes on before I have a chance to say anything.

"He's thirty-five years old and all he can do is drink and make mess after mess. My father always bails him out. Me, they refuse to talk to. Even when I sent word they were going to be grandparents, they wouldn't talk. They're older, my brother is older."

"Nicole…"

"My point Care Bear, is that age is just a number. When I look at you I don't see a young girl who doesn't know her mind. I see a woman who has survived. I see a woman who is in love."

"Care Bear?" I ask, my heart feeling a little lighter.

"Dragon says he heard Dancer call you that. I like it. It fits you."

I don't reply and she must give up, because she turns out the light. I hear the squeak of the door.

"Nicole?"

"Yeah?"

"I won't give up."

"I never thought you would. Take a nap, I'll be out here with Bull if you need me."

"What was all of this?"

"Even strong women need a kick in the pants."

"So you just kicked me?"

"You're welcome," she says and I hear the door close.

I fall asleep with a smile on my lips for some reason.

Chapter 20

DRAGON

I'M PROBABLY MAKING a mistake. Hell, I don't know. I've wrestled with it for a week and I'm still not sure how to handle things. The only thing clear is that Dancer is not getting better. He may have allowed Carrie to get closer to him, but a damned fool could see he is just going through the motions. If I continue to ignore it and do nothing? If I do that and Dancer keeps spiraling? That will be on me. So, I know I have to try and reach him. The thing is, I have no fucking idea how to do that.

When I talked with Nicole in Dance's hospital room and he started having a nightmare, I didn't think anything of it. I thought he was reliving almost drowning. I know he is having trouble adjusting to the outside and I know he has secrets. I had no idea how bad those secrets are.

When he screamed out against unseen men holding him down, my blood ran cold. When he cried out how he would gut them? My heart stopped. When Dance cried? Cried in his motherfucking sleep? I wanted to join in. I didn't. My woman did. She cried and looked at me with such sadness, I wanted to scream. Instead I held her close, buried my face into her neck and tried to absorb her. His words didn't stop, each one more horrific than the next. When Nicole could take no more, I kissed her forehead and squeezed her shoulder. Then, I watched her leave.

It was all I could do not to leave with her. She ran from the room, ran away from the horrible truth. I didn't. I stood there listening to a story unfold that brought me to my fucking knees.

Now this shit is like acid swimming in my system. I need to try and help Dance. I need to be here for him, like I failed to do when he was locked up. I just don't know how. I am at a loss. So, I find myself here. I figure I am fucking up, but I'm afraid not to try. Me...*afraid*. Fuck.

When Dancer makes it into the club the room is eerily quiet. There's no music, no crowds, nothing. It's empty with the exception of me. I'm sitting at a table with a bottle of Jack and two glasses.

"What the fuck is this?" Dancer demands stopping at the door. His hands are pushed so far in his damn jeans, it's a wonder the pockets don't rip.

I don't respond. I figure he knows what is going on. I pour two drinks and kick a chair out in front of me. I watch his hand shake as he rakes it across his beard. He doesn't want this. Hell, *I* don't want this.

"Say what's on your mind," he orders, watching me.

I take my shot and down it quickly. I drop the glass back on the table. The sound echoes in the room.

"Sit."

"I don't feel like doing this shit..."

"SIT THE FUCK DOWN!" I yell, because I knew this wouldn't be easy, but fuck I don't need it to be any harder either.

"Drag, this isn't your concern, this isn't your fight."

"Don't make me tell you again, Dance."

He sits down, refusing to look at me. He downs the drink I poured and then pours another one, downing it just as quick.

My phone is sitting on the table, the ringer is turned off, but it vibrates.

I don't bother looking at the number, already knowing who it is. The boys know what is going down tonight. They know to stay away from the club. A few are outside monitoring for protection, but they know not to come in.

"Hey, Mama."

"Just letting you know I'm here, sweetheart. You were right. Carrie's pretty upset, she is crying in the bath right now."

"Thanks baby, try to stay off your feet and tell Bull if he don't keep you two safe I'll…"

"I'm pregnant Dragon, not struck with some dreaded disease. I'll be fine. Stop worrying, you're starting to sound like a mother hen."

We just found out she is pregnant. It still seems unreal to me. My heart is so full of Nicole; I never realized there would be room for more. Nicole managed to make that possible though. She gives me more even when I don't realize I want or need it.

"Whatever Mama, I'll see you when you get back."

"Love you, Dragon. Forever."

"Forever, Mama."

I hang up and find Dancer just staring at an empty glass in his hand. I take a deep breath and decide to just dive in.

"It can't keep going on like this, Dance."

"Don't know what you mean," he lies and I know he is lying.

"Tell me another one," I respond, filling our glasses again. I just stare at mine, the amber liquid blurring.

"I've got a handle on shit," he lies yet again.

I guess hardball it is.

"You look like death warmed over, your woman is currently in a bathroom crying over your sorry ass and all this is *after* you drove your vehicle into a fucking lake trying to end it all. Doesn't sound at-fucking-all like you've got a handle on shit."

"I believe I said I don't want to talk about this," he growls, moving to stand. "I'm not two, I'm a grown ass man and I do *not* want to do this."

I grab his wrist to hold him in place.

"You move out of this chair and you will regret it. We're going to have this shit out. We're going to have it out now and we're going to work through it. I will *not* lose another brother. I will not lose *you*. Do you hear me, Dance?"

"You've become a meddlesome motherfucker since I've been gone, Dragon," he sighs, but relaxes back into his seat. Only then do I let go and take another drink. Fuck, I'm going to need it.

"You want to tell me why driving your car off a ledge is better than reaching out to your family?"

"I'm not getting why you think this is your business. You weren't there. You haven't lived any of this shit. I have. If I don't want to discuss it, then by god I should have that right."

He's right, I think for a second, but disregard it. If he hadn't tried to end it, he'd be right. If he was coping worth a damn, he'd be right. He's dong none of those things.

"It is my business. You're my business. You're family."

"This family is so fucked up Drag. I'm not sure that's a good thing anymore."

It's a low blow, but I allow it. I still can't figure out how I missed the signs about Irish.

"You can talk or I will, Dance. It makes not one damned bit of difference to me at this point."

"I got nothing to say."

I sigh. I was hoping this would go a different way.

"When you were unconscious at the hospital you had dreams," I watch as my brother's face turns pale white.

"You don't get to go there, Dragon," he says, the words lie heavy in the quiet room. His voice is laced with a cold anger that could chill a man to the bone. "This is my fucking life, and you do not get to go there! You do not get to fucking discuss it and we're not talking about this fucking shit!"

He gets up throwing his glass across the room. I don't know where it lands. I'm too busy watching my brother. Too busy seeing the misery inside of him literally bleed to the surface.

"This does not concern you, Dragon. This has nothing to do with you. This is *my* fucking life and I will deal with this shit the way I want to!" He growls starting towards the door.

"You're not dealing with it, Dance. Man, you aren't even going to the damn therapy appointments the hospital set up."

"You've been fucking checking up on me? What the hell gives you the right?" He yells, turning around to look at me.

"Dance man, I care about you. Hell, we all do. I want to help you."

"You can't help me! You don't know a fucking thing about it! While you were here finding the woman you wanted, I was the one rotting away! I was the one locked behind steel doors, spending my nights staring through bars! I was the one being beat down by the guards! I was the one whose soul was shriveling inside—dying little by little, piece by piece, every fucking, damned day! I was the one who was held down and beaten nearly unconscious while the guards laughed! I was the one they forced! I was the one…SON OF A BITCH! JUST STAY OUT OF IT! It was me, not you, not Crusher, not motherfucking Bull, none of you! It was me! So, don't you fucking try to tell me what the fuck I need to do! You have no clue! NONE!"

He slams out of the room and I let him go. I let him go, because I have no idea what to do. Fuck, maybe I've made it worse.

I have to do something. Anything, because some things can't be unheard, some things can't be undone. Some things eat holes in you. My brother has holes the size of the fucking Grand Canyon eating him alive and I don't have the first idea of how to help him, but I have to try. I have to.

I need to start finding who exactly was involved in those attacks—every last fucking one. I can't use Freak or none of the boys though. This secret is Dance's and I will

NOT add to his pain, but I am going to find every last man involved and then I will make them bleed and beg for death, before I end them. Believe me, I will end them. I will.

Chapter 21

DANCER

I DON'T WANT to say I ran out of there, but I walked fast. I don't look back. I'm mad, not so much at Dragon—more at the world. I knew what was coming and I knew I didn't want to hear what Dragon had to say. I knew I couldn't handle it. I should have turned and left immediately. Why the fuck didn't I leave?

I jump on my bike and point it towards Pussy's. I should go home to Carrie. I should, but I can't. I need to get lost in a bottle. I can't stand her eyes looking at me in sadness and disappointment. I've disappointed her way too much.

My drive there is quick. I drive hard and fast, letting the cold air hit my face. I welcome the sting and the numbness it eventually brings. I curse the tears I feel hitting my face. Men do not cry. Real men! Strong men! I don't feel strong. Hell, I'm not strong. Things like what happened to me, they don't happen to strong men. I scream out into the night air. It doesn't help—not one damn bit.

I grab a seat at the bar and proceed to lose myself. People seem to be giving me a wide berth, I'm glad. Six, is working as a bartender tonight, he nods, but doesn't speak. Does he know too? Did Dragon tell all the men? My hand shakes in fear at the thought. I don't want anyone to know. I can't handle anyone knowing. I want to kill Dragon for knowing. I wrap my hand around the shot glass. I hold it tight to hide the visible signs of the hell I'm going through.

I've never been able to say the word out loud—not once. I've tried, but giving voice to the word is like giving it life—giving it control. I was attacked? That's easy. I was beaten? Still, no problem. Yet, saying aloud the ugly words, the more '*real*' words is impossible. One word keeps repeating over and over in my brain. The mere thought of it feels as if my insides are on fire and I'm going to be devoured by the flames and burned alive. *Rape! I've been... raped!*

Rape is something that happens to the weak. To women who can't protect themselves. It does not happen to men. It sure as hell doesn't happen to strong men, men who are able to take care of themselves. It doesn't happen to men who can protect people they care about.

I was raped!

I leave the glass behind and just grab the bottle, taking a swig out of it. Carrie wants to hitch her wagon to me. She wants me, but how can she want the man I really am? How much would her love turn to disgust if she knew the truth? I should tell her. I should tell her and end this fucking fairytale she's concocted in her head.

I'VE BEEN HERE awhile now. I couldn't tell you how long. I really couldn't. It's a blur. Time ceased to exist half a bottle ago. I want to be back in bed with Carrie. I want to lie next to her and listen to her breathe and forget, if only for a minute. That's another weakness I guess. A real man wouldn't crave escape, he wouldn't need to pretend.

"Dance man, how about I take you home?" I look up to see Crush standing beside me.

"No thanks," I say. My words sound off to me, but I don't really care.

"Man, Carrie's worried about you. Let's get you home and you can sleep it off."

"Carrie, always fucking Carrie," I growl out, reaching for another drink, but the bottle is empty now. When did that happen?

"C'mon Dance, your head is all fucked up. Let's get you home so you can sleep it off. Things will look better in the morning, they always do."

"They don't. Trust me Crusher, sometimes things are much fucking worse in the morning. You got a woman?"

"Not on most days."

"Don't fucking get one, they don't stop until they ruin your life. They bat their eyes and smile at you and think you should just drop to your knees in front of them. Don't fucking get a woman, Crusher."

"Dance, man I happen to like getting on my knees for a woman."

"Then get a pussy. Pussy is free. Pussy is easy. HEY! This man needs pussy! Who's going to help him out?"

Crusher snorts and helps to steady me as I get up. The room sways, but eventually comes to a stop.

"Don't worry, Crusher. You'll get all kinds of pussy now. Women run to a man with a dick because they think they can sink their claws into him. They want to make us into some kind of hero who can do anything. It's crazy."

"C'mon let's get you in the cage."

"Cars are not cages. I have been in a fucking cage, not the same man. It's not the same."

"Yeah brother, you're right. Let's get you in the car."

I stare at the black suburban in front of me. How'd we get outside? Fuck if I know at this point. I see fucking Bull sitting in the passenger side, so I slide in the back when Crusher opens the door. I almost fall out again, but Crusher holds onto my shoulder until I steady myself. I look across from me and Carrie is watching me. I don't know why she's here, but the look on her face is one I do not like. I have disappointed her yet again. Didn't I warn her? I am not a man to hang your hat on. I never have been.

"What's wrong, Princess? Starting to see what I warned you about? Not liking what you see? Tell me Princess, what are you staring at?"

"Nothing, Jacob. Let's just get home."

"Home? We don't have a home. I'm not cut out for a white picket fence and a *home*."

She doesn't reply and it pisses me off. She pisses me off. This whole fucking mess pisses me off.

"I keep telling you I'm not Prince Charming in your story, Princess. I didn't leave one prison, just to be trapped in another."

"Dance man, shut the fuck up," Bull growls from the front passenger seat. Figures that where Carrie was, Bull would try and follow.

"Of course you'd be here. You just can't stay away from her, can you? I got news for you brother, I already got in there. You don't have a chance. She's mine now. I showed her what real men do. Had her screaming in pleasure. She's so loud, I thought the neighbors would call 911. Ain't that right, Carrie?"

Carrie doesn't respond, not that I expected her to. I know I'm being an ass, but I can't stop myself.

"If you weren't drunk off your ass and a pathetic waste, I'd end you. Now shut the fuck up," Bull growls not bothering to look at me. Which again, fucking pisses me off. Who the hell does he think he is?

"Got to tell you man. It was sweet. Thought she was going to break my dick off she was riding it so hard. Bitch loves my cock. I gave her..."

Slap!

The sting of a hand smacking across my face is so hard that my jaw burns like fire. I stop mid-sentence, turning sideways to look at Carrie. She's sitting beside me and I can't really say what the look on her face is. The tears on her cheeks though? That's fucking familiar. My hand goes up to where she slapped me. The skin is hot to the touch. I turn away from her tears. I turn away from the anger I see in those green eyes.

I turn away.

Chapter 22

CARRIE

I CAN TAKE the humiliation. It doesn't mean anything, not in the grand scheme of things. I can take about anything from Jacob, because I know he has this poison in his system. I know that the target of his venom is almost, always me. He blames me. He blames me for his attack, for his pain. I am okay with that, because I blame me too. I do. If I could go back, I would in a heartbeat. If I could take his place, I would. If I could have been the one violated, I would! If Jacob hadn't saved me that night and never rescued me, I'd be okay with that. I would absolutely go back and do that. So, taking shit from Jacob? I am okay with that, because I feel like Dancer's hell is my fault.

Except, I'm not. Not really. Every word he says cuts my heart up. Every time he looks at me with disgust and hate in his eyes I want to cry out at the injustice of it all. I don't. I don't know what to do at this point.

We make it home without Jacob spewing any more of his anger at me. I am grateful. My hand hurts from the force of the blow my hand landed on his face. I make a fist to hold the pain in. He passed out on the ride back and it takes both Alexander and Bull to carry him inside.

They place him on the couch. I shouldn't care, but I get a blanket from the hall closet and drape it over him. He's dead to the world and so far there doesn't seem to be a sign of his usual nightmare. I sit down in the chair across from him, watching as he sleeps. Here like this, he seems a little like the old Jacob—the Jacob I hold close in my heart.

When I woke up earlier to find Nicole and Bull still here I wasn't sure what to think. Then, Nicole told me what Dragon had done tonight and I panicked. I knew instantly that would be trouble. Dragon doing this pushed Jacob into a place he wasn't ready to go. It was like watching an avalanche though, you know what's coming, but there's not a damn thing you can do to stop it. So I just waited.

Eventually, Alexander and Dragon showed up and from Dragon's face, I figured things were worse than I imagined (which was pretty damn bad). I didn't ask and they didn't volunteer. Dragon took Nicole home and the rest of us just waited. Six called before I drove myself too insane and we set out to bring Jacob home.

Now, Bull's gone and Alexander is in the other room supposedly sleeping. I should be. Instead, like a fool I'm sitting here watching Jacob sleep. I think maybe I'm standing guard to keep his nightmares at bay. I realize how stupid that is, but I can't seem to help being stupid when it comes to Jacob.

I watch him silently. I have every angle and indention on his face memorized, but he seems softer in sleep. Like this, I'm reminded of the Jacob I fell in love with. In his dreamless sleep, he looks like the Jacob who found me alone, crying in the parking lot of my school. I had missed the bus and everyone was gone. I'd fallen asleep and apparently none of the staff or students missed me. I fell and skinned-up both my knees and the palms of my hands. Jacob had found me sitting on the concrete crying. He picked me up in his strong arms.

Dry those eyes Care Bear, I got you.

His gruff voice was soft and he used his thumb to wipe my tears away.

That memory morphs into another. This time it was when Jacob showed up at mine and Jazz' prom to make sure we were okay. I hated high school, having never fit in. Jacob danced with the awkward, shy sixteen year old girl and instantly turned a horrible night into one I have always held dear. He took me in his arms and smiled down at me.

I want your first dance to be with me Care Bear, can't have all these boys trying to steal my girl.

I remember the feeling of being in his arms and hearing those words wash over me. I want to go back there—back to the days when Jacob cared about me. I want to go back to the days before he was hurt.

I see glimpses of him. When he calls me Care Bear? When he made love to me there were moments it felt like he was right there with me. I know Nicole told me I would have to fight. I thought I could. I want to. I really do. I just don't know if I can handle more of his hatred.

Sometimes the only thing to do is give up. Either that or hold on, I haven't decided...my brain hasn't told me which to do yet. I'm afraid it never will, because my heart keeps drowning it out. I love him, but maybe there is a limit to what love can truly endure?

I have all kinds of questions, I have no answers. I give up trying to figure it out and decide to go to bed. I go through the motions of taking off my makeup, brushing my teeth and getting ready for bed. My mind is on autopilot. I feel broken.

I don't know how long I've lain in bed. I must have dozed off because I wake up to sounds coming from the bathroom. I lie there hearing the shower shut off. Eventually, I hear water running into the sink. I'm about to go back out again, when I feel the bed shift. Jacob's hand comes around my stomach. I try my best to hold myself solid. I ignore the way the heat from his body tries to invade mine.

"I'm sorry, Care Bear."

Part of me, even now, wants to let it go. I can't.

"Aren't you going to talk to me?" He asks.

"I've nothing to say."

"I've been dealing with shit Carrie, and I got drunk. I shouldn't have."

"I know, I just can't handle being someone you hate. I thought I could, I was wrong. I need for you to go." I'm honest this time. I might understand why he's lashing out at me, but I don't know if I can't handle any more of it, not when there aren't any signs of it changing.

"Baby, I said I'm sorry. Have I messed this up too much, Carrie?"

"I don't even know what this is and I really don't know why you care. You don't even like me, Jacob."

"This is the only time my brain finds any peace. I need you, Care Bear."

"I'm just so tired."

"It's not an excuse, but Dragon brought shit up and I'm just…I need time, Carrie. I need time," Jacob says rolling over on his back looking up at the ceiling. His voice is a mixture of pain and frustration.

"It's fine. Move back in at the club while you figure things out."

"No. I can't stand being at the club it feels like the walls are closing in on me there."

"Okay. Then I'll move out in the morning," I say as my heart breaks inside. I have come to view this house as home. It is stupid to get attached to it, but it seems I only do stupid stuff these days.

Jacob pulls me until I'm lying on my back beside him. He rolls to his side and lets his callused fingers dance gently over my shoulder and along the curve of my collarbone.

"I don't want you to leave Care, I want you to stay with me."

"Jacob…"

"Shh…baby. I was stupid. I took my anger out on you, but I didn't truly mean it."

"I can't keep living like this Jacob, I love you, but I'm not your punching bag either."

"Princess, I'd never hit you."

"Words can hurt worse sometimes."

"I'll try and do better, I…I'm asking you not to leave, Carrie. I'm asking you for another chance."

I deep breathe. It's a hard choice, this is different. This is new. Jacob is asking me to stay with him. Jacob is trying to reach out. Is this a sign that he is healing? Am I being a fool and seeing things that aren't really there? The questions go over in my head and I can't concentrate though because Jacob is kissing the path his fingers made. They are light kisses, not really sexual, but they feel…important. They make me feel important. My eyes begin to close as I decide to give myself over to him. I may be all over the place right now, but I know, in this moment, I need Jacob. I need this connection with him. I need him.

Chapter 23

DANCER

I LET HER sleep for a couple of hours, just listening to her breathe. I'm thankful. She's giving me another chance. I'm not a fool, well about this at least. I know that Carrie not pushing me away is significant. It is huge. I make a vow to try and show Carrie how truly special she is to me. She is. I made a decision to go there with her and I don't want to let her go. This shit with Dragon has messed with my head. I'm all kinds of fucked up. Yet, with Carrie here in my arms the only thing that feels out of control is the beat of my heart. I need a taste of her again. She has a way of making me forget the rest of the world exists and I need that right now. I need her. It's selfish, but I really do.

I place light kisses along her collar bone that I've already traced with my fingers. The taste of her skin sinks inside of me and spreads through my bloodstream. She's like a fever in my system. My teeth graze at the juncture of her neck and shoulder. I bite gently flicking my tongue over the spot a few seconds later.

"Jacob," she moans and her voice further bridges over the holes in my soul that Dragon uncovered.

I kiss along the side of her face. Just small, slow presses of my lips along her hairline until I make it to her ear.

"God Carrie, you're an addiction, baby."

My hand slides under the waist band of her pajamas. The silk of her underwear slides against my fingers teasing me with the pleasure lying underneath. Her hips are rocking slowly, her legs moving restlessly.

"What do you want, baby?" I groan into her ear.

"You...always you," she whispers and again it feels less raw inside. Just by her words, or maybe the fact that I know she means them. She craves me as much as I crave her.

I yank her underwear and pajamas roughly down those fucking sexy, long legs of hers. I figure I might have scared her, but instead she is busy pulling her shirt off. Something about seeing this woman as desperate for me as I am for her soothes the beast inside of me.

"Look at you, Care Bear. God I wish you could see what I see right now. So fucking beautiful and sweet you make my teeth ache. This is going to be fast baby, I'm sorry, but I have to have you. I need to be inside of you."

"Yes, Jacob. Please," she whispers her voice dark, husky and full of need.

I slide my fingers into her depths and I fucking sigh in relief when I find her ready, which is good, because I'm shaking. I don't have the patience to get her there on my own. I am also a motherfucking genius for getting in bed without clothes, because if they had been in my way, I would have shredded them. I bend her legs at the knee and pull them apart, so she is completely open to me—so damned beautiful. I move my cock back and forth against her opening, making sure I tease her swollen clit.

"Carrie baby, look at me."

Slowly those gorgeous emerald green eyes open, looking drugged and breathtaking. Plump, juicy red lips fall open in a gasp. I can see a faint glimpse of that perfect tongue. It calls to me.

"Give it to me baby, let me hear you say it."

She searches my face, the room is quiet except for our harsh breathing.

"I love you, Jacob."

My heart stalls, before picking up speed. I wanted to hear Carrie ask for my cock. That's what I was asking for—not this. Never this. These words… these words fill me with fear. Holy hell. At the same time, a feeling of power surges in me. I'll try to figure it out later, right now I have to have her, I need her.

I plunge inside her depths, without further warning. She's so damned tight. I try not to go to deep, but her hips thrust up and I sink all the way in. I stop moving, afraid I've hurt her. I look down at her face for signs of distress. Instead, I find something out of a dream. Her face is thrown back in pleasure and I could drown in the inky depths of her eyes.

"Wrap your legs around me, Care Bear. Wrap them tight."

She nods her head and does as I ask. I didn't it was possible, but I manage to go deeper. So deep, I'm bottomed out completely inside of her. Never has anything felt this perfect, this right. I know she feels it too, because she moans in reaction.

She has kept her hands wrapped up in the sheet on the bed till this point. I grieve silently. I would love to have her touch on me, but I'm glad she seems to have accepted my rules. I can't take the risk of flashbacks, especially with the memories so close to the surface right now.

I resent the fact I continue to think of this shit, when I am inside my own personal heaven. I hate that these thoughts intrude on the one clean and beautiful thing I've had in my life. I settle over her, bracing myself on one arm, the other tangling in her hair and pulling her lips the small distance to mine.

"Say it," I order against her lips. I don't know why, but I need to hear it again.

"I love you, Jacob," she complies as one of her hands touches the side of my face.

I bite down the order for her to keep her hands down. I can handle this. I can. She loves me, this is different. As long as her touch stays on my face, I'll manage, I just need this. I need this moment. My tongue slides into her mouth and I drink in her words, I drink them down deep.

I can feel my balls tighten with my approaching climax, way too soon. I let go of the hold I have on her hair and tease her clit so she can go with me. It doesn't take long and I'm thankful. My mouth captures her release. She convulses on my cock, pulling me over the edge with her. I come so hard, I feel light headed.

I grab her ass and pull her tight against me as I fall over on my back. I keep my cock buried deep inside of her, while letting her rest on top of me. When she goes to move off of me, I refuse to let her. She settles against me and places a kiss on the side of my neck. I let my fingers slide along the smooth, soft, skin of her back. She holds me close and her hands feel good. I close my eyes and breathe her in. For the space of this minute, I let myself pretend I am different. That the feel of someone else's hands on me is normal and I can enjoy it without fear of the darkness.

"I need to get off," Carrie breathes against my skin her voice sounding exhausted.

"I thought you just did."

I feel her lips spread in a smile against my neck and I like it. I give her too much pain. I like giving her a smile. I want to give her more.

"Get off of you so we can sleep."

"Shh…rest Care Bear, I like you right where you are."

It scares me to admit this, but I give it to her. I give it and ignore the fear.

"I like it too. Goodnight, Jacob. I love you"

"Goodnight, Care." I want to say it back to her. I want to tell her I love her. This time the fear wins and I stay silent.

It takes a few minutes before her breathing evens out. I wish with everything in me that I could join her. I don't. I can't take that risk. I'm okay with staying awake and holding her though. This may be the single, best thing I've felt in my life, so I will savor it and pretend this is my normal. A new normal that I crave, but will never have.

Chapter 24

CARRIE

I'M ALONE IN the bed. It's kind of sad. Jacob woke me up once more in the night. I still didn't get to touch him like I wanted, but it was amazing. I can't deny it, I was scared of the morning light, because last night was the single most perfect night of my life. Well, at least after Jacob got in bed with me. I stretch, my body is sore and well used. The house is quiet, which is odd. Since I've made the move to Kentucky, I don't think Dragon and his men have ever left me alone. I shrug it off. I'm sure he's around somewhere.

I sigh and get up. I'm hungry, so I'm going to have to get my butt moving. I take a quick shower, braiding my wet hair when I get out. It's easier than worrying about blow-drying and fixing it. I don't bother with makeup, because food seems more important right now. I'm starved.

I walk into the living room, expecting to see Jacob asleep on the couch or something, but the room is empty. I try not to let fear grab me. It's silly. Before my parents died I never worried. Living like I have, has made me see shadows where there are none. I go into the kitchen. It's a little after eleven, but surely that's not too late for breakfast. I'll make extra in case Alexander is still here, and him and Jacob are both hungry.

I scramble some eggs, fry bacon and make toast and still…nothing. I figured the smell of food would get their attention. I go outside and look around and there's no one there. The Tahoe is missing too. I look around one last time and go back inside. I'm a little disappointed that Jacob didn't tell me he was leaving, but I suck it up. He gave me more than I was expecting last night. I have to go with that.

"Rome wasn't built in a day," I laugh at myself, opening the door to go back into the kitchen.

"Do you always talk to yourself?" I jerk, looking towards the voice. Sitting at the table is a slightly overweight man with dull, brown hair that has gray weaved throughout. He's sitting calmly at the table, facing the door. He's eating out of the plate I had put down for Jacob, like he doesn't have a care in the world.

I hold onto the door and try to still the beating of my heart. I don't know who he is, but the mere fact that he has shown up the way he has is not a good thing. I look at him and then towards the front door, wondering if I should take off running.

"I wouldn't try that. You can't see it, but there's a gun in my lap and I'll shoot you before you make it outside and besides my man would stop you as soon as you crossed the threshold."

I turn at his words and notice the big, ugly man staring at me, with this leering look that immediately makes my stomach revolt. I fight to keep the bile from rising. The guy comes in and locks the door behind him.

Yeah okay. Now what?

"Come on in Sugar, let's have some of this breakfast you took the time to fix. I do love a woman who knows her way around the kitchen."

I don't want to, like I *really* don't want to? Still, I don't have a choice.

I swallow trying to figure out what to do here, Jacob will be back, I just have to bide my time. Plus, Bull once told me that this whole house was monitored heavily. The cavalry will come, I just need to stall. Heck fire, I have rotten luck.

I take a few steps to the kitchen, but I don't go all the way. That's when he holds up the gun and uses it to motion me into a seat across from him.

I sit down, by that time I have to—my legs feel like jelly.

"Bacon?" He asks, still using the gun to motion. I grab a piece, because I don't know how he'd react if I turn him down.

He stares at me, waiting. I take a bite of the bacon. It tastes like sawdust, but that seems to make him happy, because he places the gun back on the table beside him.

"Tell me Carolina, do you know who I am?"

"No," I have a good idea, but I don't say it. The fact is that he uses a name that I haven't heard since I was old enough to demand no one use it, doesn't exactly fill me with happiness. It doesn't take a rocket scientist to know this is the man who killed my parents. I know it. He knows I know, but saying no seems like the best option right now.

"Carolina, I'm so disappointed. I thought you were smarter than that," he says calmly taking another bite of food.

"Boss, we don't have time for this shit. You promised you'd pay me as soon as you got your hands on this bitch. We need to get out of here before those damn bikers show up. I didn't agree to this damn shit, to get my ass killed," the thug still standing by the door states. He looks antsy. He keeps looking out the window by the door and everything about him screams fear. While this is good, I figure it could also be bad. Having someone with a gun, who is operating on fear and adrenaline, doesn't sound like a good thing.

"Did you make sure we won't be disturbed?"

"I put the idiot out of commission. He never knew what hit him."

"Excellent. "Now my dear," he says putting his fork down. "Let's try this again. Do you know who I am?"

"Not really, no," I answer, worried they've hurt Jacob. Where is the damn cavalry? As for the asshole in front of me, up until this point he has only ever been a shadow to me. I've never seen a face. I've heard Dragon and Alexander refer to him before, but right now I must be too far into panic mode, because I can't even remember the name.

"Boss, damn it! You know this place is under surveillance, even if Shorty did disable the actual alarms before he left. We have to get out of here."

"In due time."

"Due time nothing. If you want to be stupid, fine. Give me my money and you can stay here if you want. I'm not staying to be target practice for the Savage boys."

The man at the table lets off a fake sigh, which is overly loud and heavy. He picks up the gun and aims it at me.

My body instantly breaks out in a cold sweat. I never thought about dying. How strange is that? Even with all the close calls I've had? Even with the way I lost my parents, I've been stupid and never gave myself time to think about dying. I pushed it all to the back of my mind. When there is a gun pointed at you, staring you straight in the face, there is no denying it. There just isn't. When I die, will anyone miss me? Will anyone mourn me? There's so much more I wanted in life. I'll never have that now. I'll never get another minute with Jacob. I'll never be able to try to help him further. I'll never have his lips on mine again. I'll never feel his hands touch me. Just the thought of never having that hurts physically.

I hear the click of the hammer from the gun and I figure that's it. I can't stop the tears that fall. I wait for the shot. The bacon in my hand drops to the table, my eyes on those of my killer.

I watch as his finger presses against the trigger, as if it is in slow motion. At the last second he moves the gun up and to the right. I can feel the breeze of a bullet as it whizzes past me. I jump and scream at the sound of the blast. My ears ring so loud, I can barely hear the laughter of the madman. His face is blurry from the tears in my eyes and they only increase with the near death experience I've just survived. I take the back of my hand and try to wipe away the tears. I'm mad they are there, but I can't stop them. I turn to see that he has shot the man behind me. The man falls immediately, his white t-shirt becomes soaked with blood. It's so dark, thick and horrific that I can't seem to look away. When I finally do, it is to see hollow eyes staring back at me. Dead. I knew he would be, but something about those eyes, so lifeless and stark, seems wrong.

"That was such fun, but alas a gun is not to be your end, Sugar." He tells me once he stops his laughter. He tosses me a napkin from the table and I pick it up, trying to dry my eyes.

I hate crying in front of him. I hate that my hands are shaking even more, because I know he is enjoying that. I take a breath. Jacob will save me. I try to ignore the coppery odor of blood and death that have invaded the room. I go back to my original plan. I have to give Jacob enough time to rescue me. I know he will, I just have to keep this monster talking and delay whatever plan he has.

"Jacob will be back any minute. You won't get away with this."

"Oh but I will. He left you in the care of another to run errands for his boss. I hope he does come back soon though. To be honest I'm actually waiting on him. I just needed to make sure I had you first to hold over him."

"Why would you…"

My voice freezes as he moves his jacket to the side and reveals a bomb. Well, I'm pretty sure it is. It looks weird compared to the way they are portrayed in the movies, but there is a small digital timer counting backwards on it. It looks like a stop watch. There are no glowing large numbers counting down my doom. No, these numbers are small and hard to see because of my tears. I strain to see. I have just a little over sixteen minutes.

"Why?" I ask again. "Why would you do this? What am I to you?"

"To me nothing, but you mean something to Mr. Blake. You mean something to him and he took away everything from me. Killing you is not the complete revenge I wished for," he pauses, seems to think it over, and shrugs. "That damn club has frozen my assets and I have nothing. That's just another reason I had to kill my friend over there. Thanks to the Savage Brothers I couldn't pay anyone, even if I wanted to. No, that damn club has me by the balls. I know it's just a matter of time before they find me. I'm a marked man. I figure if I'm going to die, I shall get revenge for my son's death in the bargain. So you see dear Carolina, you're all mine. Whatever shall we do?"

Chapter 25

DANCER

SIX CAME BY to pick me up on his way into work at Pussy's. I left Crusher in charge of Carrie.

Carrie. Just her name makes things better. I hated leaving her, even temporarily. I came close to waking her up, but I hadn't let her sleep much last night. That thought makes a smile spread on my face. Last night was near perfect. The only thing that marred the perfection was that I hadn't slept. I am dragging ass, but I can't take the chance of having a nightmare and talking in my sleep like I did with Dragon. I don't know how to tackle this problem. Never sleeping is not a long term solution. Maybe I can have one of the boys watch Carrie through the day and nap at the club in my old room? The thought doesn't make me happy, but I don't know any other way to do it.

Six pulls into the parking lot and we say our goodbyes. I don't know the man that well. I like him well enough I guess. It's kind of screwed up, but I miss Irish. Part of me is glad I wasn't around when shit went down. I don't know how Dragon handled having to end a brother, someone we had fought beside and bled with. Irish and his betrayal is a dark cloud over the club, even now.

I get on my bike, ready to head back to the house. Maybe I can talk Carrie into getting away for the day with me. I like having her on the back of my bike. It still bugs me that she's been on the back of Bull's. A man is careful about who he lets on his ride. The club has pretty much adopted Carrie, but the fact that Bull cares for her puts another spin on it. I can't help it, I do *not* like it. Carrie is mine. Last night cemented that. I can keep her happy. I just have to be careful about what I let her see. I don't know how to hide some shit from her, but I'll figure it out as I go along.

I go to start my bike when my phone vibrates.

Dragon. I don't want to talk to him. It's been a good fucking day. I don't want his shit to ruin it. Still, I answer. If he starts his crap, I'll hang up.

"Yeah man."

"We got trouble, man. Freak was checking cameras for the safe house before running some routine maintenance on our system and there were two men sneaking around the garage."

"What the hell do you mean sneaking around? What about the alarms?"

"We backed the cameras up, seems there is a third man with them. He disabled the fucking alarms."

"What the fuck! You said that place was solid!" I growl, panic at the thought of Carrie being in danger pounding through my system.

"I don't fucking know how they knew where the alarms were, I just know he disabled the entire fucking system. I'll make heads roll about that later. For now we got bigger fucking fish to fry, you feel me?"

"Fuck, please tell me Crush got the sons of bitches."

"Crush was in the garage and the two men split up and surrounded it. They both went in, and when they came back out there was no sign of Crusher."

"Fuck!" I yell.

"We're on our way, but you need to get Six and get your ass out there. You're closer. Watch your back, we'll be there as soon as we can."

"You call Six, he's already in the club. I'm not waiting. I'm heading out now."

Dragon's arguing when I hang up the phone. I don't know what he said and I don't care. I need to get to Carrie. I break every traffic law coming and going to get back to the house. I have one gun and I've been keeping it locked up in the house. I haven't looked at it since the night I accidentally hurt Carrie. I don't carry one, because ex-cons aren't allowed that privilege. I'm not about to tempt fate just yet. Still, I know that Drag keeps a safe with emergency weapons hid in the garden shed out back. I turn my bike off and leave it at the bottom of the long drive. I don't want to take the chance that I will be discovered before I make my move. I should check on Crush, but Carrie is my first concern. I can't think past her.

I sprint to the shed, trying to stay away from direct view of the windows in the house, not an easy task. I manage somehow and make it to the shed. I breathe a sigh of relief when I find the old, bent up safe hid behind the wall of hoes, shovels, and rakes. Inside are three, thirty-eights and a box of ammo. I grab one, loading it quickly. I stuff about ten or fifteen bullets in my pocket. I'm hoping to find all of the motherfuckers together, but who the hell knows. I don't have the best of luck.

With a deep breath, I take off for the back of the house. I'm betting that he will have Carrie either in the living room or kitchen. With that in mind, I know I don't want to use the front door. Damn place doesn't have a back door and that's fucked up. I search what I know about the house and quickly decide to get in through Carrie's bathroom window. It's at the back of the house and the farthest away from the kitchen. I pray I can get in quietly. I need surprise on my side. I sure as hell don't have much else.

I make it to the window and it's locked. I figured it would be. I reach in my pocket and pull out my knife. I suppose carrying a pocket knife might be bad for an ex-con too, but I'm thankful I never worried about it. I angle the longest part of the knife's blade where the upper and lower window meets. I attempt to trip the lock. I try ten fucking times. TEN! Way too many when my woman could be inside dying. I close my eyes, take a breath and try to steady myself. Then I try again. Finally! On the second attempt I manage to slide the lever over and it unlocks. I raise the window as quietly as I can.

Once I get it open enough to slide in, I stop and listen. When I don't hear anyone coming towards the room, I take that as a good sign. I slide my knife back in my pocket, heft myself onto the window ledge, and pull myself up. I manage to push through the opening, but I scrape my side on the corner of a wooden chest that's beside the window. *Fuck! That hurt.* I can feel the sticky wet drip of blood on my skin. I don't bother to inspect it.

I have no time.

I carefully make my way through the hall. I can hear talking in the kitchen. The voices aren't overly loud, so I can't really hear what they're saying, until I get closer. I hide behind the half wall that divides the kitchen and living room.

I smell the odor of gun powder mixed with the coppery scent of blood in the room and my heart stalls. I almost lose it, until I hear Carrie's voice. She's alive.

"You don't have to do this."

"Oh don't be so naïve. We're beyond these dramatics by now, Carolina."

There's a man's body lying on the floor, on his back. His face is turned towards the kitchen, but I see enough to know that the man is dead. I turn my attention back to my woman. I can hear the terror in her voice. I want to go straight in right now, but I know I can't. When I stand up, I have to have my gun ready and aim. I won't get a second chance. So, I need to be careful. It kills me, but I remain where I'm at.

"Why did you kill them?" Carrie says her voice quiet and full of sadness.

"Kill who? Go on now, don't leave me hanging now," he says and I can hear the sick delight in his voice. I'm going to enjoy killing this motherfucker.

"Never mind, I know."

"Enlighten me."

"You killed my parents to get even with me," she whispers and the guilt in her voice physically hurts me. I pray she can hold on for just a few more minutes.

"Bingo. You're smarter than you look. Which is sad

really. That means you have brains and can cook. Such a waste."

"You're sick."

I hope she doesn't cause him to lash out at her. I need her to hold on and stay safe for me. I hold my breath and peek out over the corner where the wall stops.

An older man is sitting at the table facing my way with Carrie's back to me. He's got a gun in his hand, motioning it around while he's talking.

"Tell me, were your parents proud of you? Were you close?"

"What?"

"My son and I were very close. He was all I had in the world and he was taken away from me. Taken away, because of you."

Fuck...this would be the unknown Phoenix...Dragon said he felt like things would happen soon. I wish he had been wrong.

"He tried to rape me!" Carrie defended. Just hearing that word kicks me in the gut and makes my hands shake. Now is not the time for a panic attack. I beat that shit back down. I hate feeling like this.

I hear a loud sound of a hand connecting with flesh. I peek around the corner and see that Phoenix has laid the gun down and smacked my woman. The hit was so violent, her head is thrown back and her chair scrapes backwards against the floor, almost tipping over. I don't even think about it. I should. I would have liked to make him hurt more, for the hell he has put Carrie through—to make him suffer for touching her. I don't, I stand up and aim my gun.

He looks at me in shock, but before he can even get a word out, I shoot the motherfucker in the head. He goes backward with a crash as Carrie screams. I walk further in the room, my gun still trained on the man. When I step to the chair Carrie is sitting in I feel her arms going around me. Her face buries into my side, muffling her cries.

I look down at my enemy. Blood is leaking from his head and it looks dark against his pale skin. His eyes are open. He's not coming back. Still, I shoot the remaining five shots into his head. There's probably nothing deader than dead, but it can't hurt trying for it. Every time I shoot, Carrie jumps. I wrap my free arm around her and hold her to me. When the chamber is empty I put the gun on the table and wrap both arms around her, pulling her up to me.

"Shhh… I got you, Care Bear. I got you."

Chapter 26

CARRIE

I GOT YOU Care Bear, I got you.

The words echo in my head and Jacob holds me. I'm shaking like a leaf on a tree as he subtly shuffles me so I'm hugging his front now instead of his side. I wrap my arms tight around him. I know he's protecting me from seeing the body. I don't really want to see it, so that's fine with me. I hold him tighter and breathe in his scent. I want to forget everything that just happened, but something is stopping me.

"Jacob?"

"Yeah, Care Bear."

"He said he was going to kill me."

"I know baby, but you don't have to worry anymore. He won't hurt you ever again."

"I know but he…"

"I told you baby, you don't have to…"

"Jacob! He has a bomb at least I think it's a bomb," I exclaim and I can hear the wild panic in my voice.

"Carrie…"

"Under his coat, Jacob! We have to get out of here!"

Jacob lets go of me to investigate. I look over his

shoulder when he bends down. I don't want to look at the dead guy, but I have to know if that is really a bomb. Jacob moves the coat back and the small timer device now has only a minute showing. Jacob grabs my hand, and pulls me to the door.

"Run!" I stumble to catch up because of the force he uses to get us through the door.

"Alexand…"

"Drag said Crush was in the garage! GO CARRIE!" He yells and I take off running as soon as I clear the door. Jacob must have decided I didn't move fast enough, because he picks me up in his arms and takes off running.

We've almost made it to the garage when an explosion rocks and vibrates around us. Jacob is propelled downward from the force of the blast and we hit the ground. He braces himself so I'm not crushed beneath him. Even more, he uses his body to shield me. This is a man. This is the type of man you love for life. This is a good man. Please God, let me keep him.

My ears ring and sound becomes distorted either because of the loud noise of the blast, the gunshot or maybe both combined. Jacob is asking me if I'm okay, but it sounds like his voice is in a dark hole and being filtered before it gets to me. I can barely make it out.

Dragon and several others come running toward us. I look at the house and the entire right side is in flames. The roof is caved in over the area we just left.

"Bull! Where's Bull?" Dragon growls when he makes it to us.

"Bull? What are you talking about? You only mentioned Crusher being in the garage?" Dancer responds, motioning over to where Poncho, the club doctor and a couple of the other boys are.

"Dani said Crush called Bull this morning and asked him to come watch Carrie while he did some things. We went back and checked the cameras. They picked up Bull getting here right after you left. It looked like they met outside and Bull went in the house while Crusher went on in the garage."

"No one was here when I woke up," I respond, feeling a sense of dread come over me. Could the man already have killed Bull?

"I didn't see anyone in the house either," Jacob adds. "Only rooms I didn't check were the hall bath and the second bedroom."

We all look back at the house engulfed in flames and I get physically sick to my stomach. The thought of Bull trapped in there...

"Fuck, let's go around back. Maybe we can get in through a window," Dragon orders.

"The bathroom window in Carrie's room is already open, it'd be our best bet, plus it's furthest from the main blaze."

Jacob stands up and he and Dragon start running towards the other side of the house.

"Be careful!" I yell, but I don't think he hears me. I start to follow them, maybe I can help them somehow. I feel a hand on my shoulder and look up to see Freak.

"Where are you going?" Freak asks.

"I need to be close by in case they need help getting Bull out."

"Dragon and Dance can handle it and Gunner and Frog are there too. You stay here where it's safe. If you get closer to the house, you'll just distract them."

I don't necessarily agree, but I give up trying to go after them. I don't want to do anything that might distract Jacob and get him hurt.

In the distance I can hear sirens.

Freak leads me over to the garage. I look back at the house not wanting to leave Jacob. I want to see him the minute he gets free…

"We're getting company, is Crush going to be okay?" Freak asks.

"Shit! There would have been less questions if we could have taken care of Crush at my place," Doc says.

I turn around to see a very pale Alexander, a white bandage stained with red blood on his chest, up close to his shoulder. Dani is standing close by and there are tears in her eyes. It could be nothing, but it seems like more. I finally decide it is my imagination, since she makes no move to touch him.

"Shot in his chest, but you could tell the man either didn't know what he was doing, or was in a hurry. If Crush hadn't hit his head on the fall down he wouldn't have been out of commission. It went straight through, so there was a lot of blood, but it was clean."

"Shouldn't you be glad an ambulance is here to take him to the hospital?" I ask confused. The others say nothing.

Alexander gives me a weak smile. "I'll be okay, Red. I've had worse."

I don't think I believe him, but I'm too worried about Jacob, Dragon and Bull to say anything else.

Please God, let them be okay.

Chapter 27

DANCER

I MAKE IT back to the window. I can't see fire in the room itself, so I jump in without wasting time. I hear Dragon fall in behind me. There's smoke, lots of fucking smoke, but no real flames. It seems the blaze has been limited to the site of the homemade bomb. Thank fuck it was a homemade bomb and small. It took out half of the kitchen and started a fire, but had the man been a professional, there would have been nothing left.

You can't see a damned foot in front of you for the smoke and haze. I'm holding my breath and I've got my arm up over my mouth and nose, but soon I could be in real trouble.

I feel my way through Carrie's bedroom and out into the hall. I can hear Dragon behind me, but I can't stop to check on him. I have to hurry. If Bull is in here, there's a limited time to get to him. He'll die of smoke inhalation. Hell, I can already feel the burning in my lungs. I make it to the hall bath first.

"Bull!!!" I call out, but can't find him anywhere, even with the low visibility, had he been in there I would have.

That only leaves one room. Holding onto the wall I

make my way to the spare bedroom. The door is locked. I use my shoulder and ram it, Dragon joins in and it breaks away from the frame and opens up. Lying on the bed is Bull. He's unconscious, that much is clear. Still, even through the smoke I can see the blood. A fucking lot of blood coming from his head! I don't have time to inspect him further, I grab him in a fireman's hold and start back the way I came. Dragon leads the way to our escape route, none too soon. The heat is closing in on us and you can hear the crack of wood all around. We need out of here before the whole damn place collapses on us.

"Damn Bull, you are a big motherfucker," I say to no one in particular, as I struggle to carry this hulk of a man.

We make it back to the bathroom much quicker, but by now the flames have spread and they are reaching out towards us like deadly hands. The creaking of weakening beams becomes louder.

Dragon helps me carefully get Bull out the window, handing him out to Gunner and Frog. He then insists I go out the window first and since we're both coughing like little bitches, I don't argue. He plows out just seconds behind me and we drag our tired asses from around the house and back to the garage.

I see Carrie the minute I turn the corner and she runs straight at me. She's a damn mess, but at the same time so achingly perfect. She is the answer to every dream I've ever had.

I grunt as she connects with my body at full force. She wraps her arms around me and I grab hold of her ass and lift her up. A second later her legs are locked at the back of my ass.

"I was so worried," she whispers against my lips. I push into her mouth kissing her hard. My throat is burning and dry but I do not give one damn. I need this. Our lips break away slowly and I give her one more chaste lip touch before pulling away completely.

"Care Bear. I'm okay."

"I love you, Jacob."

The words give me the familiar kick in my gut and a speeding heart. They also bring me a feeling of joy. I can't stop myself from kissing her again—this time with everything I've got inside of me. Our tongues dance and mate and then war with each other, fighting for dominance. Even the taste of smoke can't stop the flavor of Carrie from coming through. This woman is better than a drug. She's like pure air and I need her to survive.

"Bull?" She asks and I shake my head, because I don't know.

I'm jealous which is fucked up seven ways to Sunday. My brother is in bad shape, even I could tell that through the smoke. Yet, here I am jealous because my woman is worried about him. Hell, I'm worried about him. I grab her by the back of the neck and turn her face towards me.

"Give me the words."

She looks thoroughly confused and I understand, because I am too. Still, she takes her hand and moves it along the side of my face. With her other hand, she places it over my heart and applies gentle pressure. The warmth of it is enough to calm the heavy beating.

"I love you, Jacob."

"Sir, we need to check you over," I look over my shoulder and there's a paramedic standing behind me.

"I'm fine, see to my brother."

I don't want to be bothered. I want to stay with Carrie. It's weak and totally the wrong time to be feeling shit, but crowds trigger panic attacks. I do not want to have one of those surrounded by strangers and having my brothers here would make that shit worse. I hold on tightly to Carrie's hand. Can she tell how it shakes? I look at her face, but she just smiles. I pray I've kept it hid.

"The other wagon has your buddy," the paramedic explains referring to the other ambulance. "Please sir it's my job, you inhaled a lot of smoke. Let me just check out your lungs. I also see some blood, it won't take long."

I'm about to tell him to fuck off when Carrie's hand goes to my side. Is it wrong to get turned on with all the shit going on around us? I swear I can feel my dick harden as her hand moves along my side and her fingers tease against the edge of my jeans.

"Jacob, you've been hurt!"

I look down as she pulls my shirt up. It's a jagged cut down my side. It's nothing, but my woman is worried about *me* and I'm an ass enough to eat that shit up. So, I let her guide me to the ambulance. I sit on the base of the bumper step, while the paramedic does his business.

I've barely settled before the guy pushes an oxygen mask in my face as a 'precaution' whatever in the hell that means. Then, Carrie leaves me to go check on Bull.

Motherfucker!

I'm left with a piece of plastic held over my mouth and nose, watching her cry over another man.

I want Bull to survive. I love the man, I want him to be okay and I know he is in scary ass shape. That said, right now in this moment, I want him to get better so I can kill him.

I look over at Dragon and he's pretty much being poked at like me. We look at each other for a second and nod. Shoving the masks back, we head over to Bull with the paramedics yelling behind us.

We make it to the wagon where they have Bull inside working on him. Shit, it looks like someone bashed his head with a baseball bat. That's the only thought I can form before it hits me that they are performing CPR on my brother. What the fuck? I knew he was bad, I had no idea he wasn't fucking breathing.

One paramedic is applying chest compressions, while another is squeezing a balloon like thing with a mask attached over his face. There's still another one holding up paddles.

"CLEAR!"

One of them hollers and the others back away while the paddles are put over the heart and he's hit with electricity. His body jerks. We all look at a monitor willing it to move. There's just a green line and it's barely moving. They assume their first positions again and you can hear the electricity surging from the paddles, as the other paramedic turns the knob increasing the charge.

"CLEAR!" She calls again.

I feel Carrie curl into my side and I hold her close. We wait while Bull is hit again. The beep of the machine is faint as a heartbeat is found, but it seems like thunder and the line on the screen appears steadier.

"Let's get him to the main road. Medi-vac is waiting for transport to send him down to UT," one of the paramedics orders.

"You're flying him out?" Dragon asks and my heart stops in my throat.

"Sir, your friend has major head trauma and went into respiratory failure. UT is the closest trauma center around equipped to deal with head trauma like his."

"I'm going with him," Dragon says starting to get in the ambulance.

"Sorry sir, I can't allow that. You can drive down to Knoxville," she pulls out a card from her pocket and hands it to Dragon. "You can call that number, give them your friend's info and they can give you updates. Now we've got to go."

She bangs on the ambulance doors with a strong thud and slams them shut. We watch the ambulance take off, each one of us in shock. I don't think any of us thought we could lose Bull until we watched the paramedics struggle to keep a heartbeat.

Carrie looks up at me with soot and dirt marring her face. You can see streaks left behind by the tracks of her tears.

"Will he make it?" She asks her voice weak.

"Damn straight he'll make it," Dragon growls, running towards his SUV. I see Frog and Gunner pile in with him. Crusher was taken to the hospital earlier. I need to check on him too. I need to get to Tennessee…. Fuck.

"Let's go to the club, get cleaned up and go check on Bull."

"Okay, Jacob."

We walk towards the group hand in hand. Even with all the shit that has gone down, I can almost smile at the feeling that settles inside of me. My hand tightens over hers as we move forward…together.

Chapter 28

CARRIE

I'M EXHAUSTED AND I don't even know how Jacob is functioning. He couldn't have slept much the night before and it's midnight now. We're all piled in the waiting room for trauma surgery. We had gone to the club. Jacob and I quickly showered (and by that I mean we showered together and since I had never done that before, I wished we had more time, but we didn't). We got dressed and headed out just in time to load up in the SUV with Dragon and Nicole. Crusher was still in the local hospital and in no shape to travel, though he was raising the roof because no one would let him. Dani was watching over him closely and again I thought I saw something between them.

We got here around three in the afternoon and we've been here ever since. Dr. Lyn, who is apparently the chief resident and director of the trauma-care floor, directed us to this small waiting room. We got to see Bull once, but he didn't know we were around. He went in for surgery about an hour ago. They're putting a gage in to help relieve pressure on his brain. There's swelling, bruising and several spots bleeding. With each minute that passes by, the pit in my stomach seems to grow. The old adage about no news being good news, I am totally not buying it. Anything would be better than the not knowing. The door opens and we all look up expectantly.

"Kane family?" Dr. Lyn asks as she comes into the waiting area. All four of us stand up.

"I assisted in Dorian's surgery. We successfully put in the gage to monitor the swelling and pressure on his brain. Considering everything, the bleeding we found was not substantial."

"Will he be okay?" Dragon asks the question we all want the answer to.

"We're hopeful. The swelling on the cranium is measured on a scale. Mr. Kane's swelling measures in at fifteen. While that is something to worry about, the real danger area is around twenty. He's on a ventilator and we're going to keep him in a medically induced coma for the next day or so to keep him calm. We'll start to slowly bring him out of it after that. Hopefully then we can run some tests and try to ascertain the extent of the damage inflicted."

"Can we see him?"

"I'm sorry that can't happen right now. Mr. Kane is medically sedated but we can't risk that something might agitate him."

"Will you have one of the staff update us if there are any changes?" Nicole asks, while Dragon walks off to stand facing the wall away from us.

"I can, but I suggest you leave a number where we can reach you with the nursing station and get some rest. There's nothing else you can do tonight."

Nicole nods and the doctor gives a tight smile and

walks away. I turn into Jacob's arms while I look over at Dragon. Nicole puts her hands on Dragon's back. He's got his head bent down and he slaps his fist on the wall. I wince at the force of the hit.

"I can't lose another brother Mama."

"I know. Sweetheart, let's go back to the hotel and get some rest so we can be here for Bull tomorrow."

Jacob's hands tighten against my back and I look up at him. I see the worry and fear on his face and do my best to give him a reassuring smile. I'm sure it falls short. We give our information to the nurses and make our way back to the SUV. We head to the hotel that Nicole booked before we arrived.

I'M SITTING ON the bed wearing one of the silk negligees that Dani gave me. All of my clothes were destroyed. Thankfully Dani and I are pretty much the same size. It is way too sexy and not something I would pick out on my own. I miss my pajamas. It is a deep purple color which I love though. Plus, it feels good against my skin. It has thin spaghetti straps with the delicate silk trimmed in the prettiest lace. The top is loose and falls about mid-thigh. The bottom is a barely there strand of silk that seems small even for a thong. I quickly put lotion on while Jacob is busy in the bathroom. If I can get this done and under the covers I won't feel so self-conscious around him. I'm not used to being dressed like this and dressed like this in front of Jacob is intimidating.

I don't quite make it. I feel the bed shift with weight behind me. Jacob's arms come around me, as he pulls me close. His hands come up and brush my breasts teasingly before cupping them, while he buries his head into my neck.

"Care Bear, you are so fucking beautiful."

I lean back into him, my eyes close savoring this moment and holding it close. This moment, this exact moment and the feeling that Jacob pulls from me, is why I've held onto my love for him.

"Mmmm...I like this side of you, Jacob."

"I like this get up you have on. You look good enough to eat."

His voice is husky with need and that combined with his touch makes me instantly wet and ready.

"You should sleep," I say because he should and I'm worried about him, but even I can hear the lack of conviction in my voice.

"After," he says moving the strap away from my shoulder, his lips grazing the same path.

"After?" I gasp as he bites into the juncture of my neck and shoulder, sucking the same area. Will he leave his mark on me? I want that.

"After I fuck you and make you beg to come."

"I...Oh god..." I moan as he pulls the top off of me.

I try to turn towards him, wanting more, but he doesn't let me.

"Oh no, I got plans for you. Now if you don't want me to rip off that thong you're barely wearing take it off."

I lift up and he guides them off my hips and down my legs.

"Keep your back to me baby, and climb up on my lap."

"Like this?" I ask feeling unsure. I crawl backwards to straddle him.

"Oh fuck yeah."

He grabs my hips and holds me still before I can settle back on his lap. I feel his hand move between my folds and then his fingers push inside of me. I gasp at the intimate contact. He moves in further. I'm so wet his fingers slide smoothly.

"My Princess is all ready for me aren't you?"

"Yes…" I groan when his fingers slowly leave my depths, only to begin teasing my clit. "Jacob!" I call out. I feel his teeth bite into the right cheek of my ass. His tongue flicks over the bite.

"What is it, sweetheart?"

"Stop torturing me…" I whimper.

"How am I torturing you? Is it because I'm teasing your clit?" He asks pushing hard against the swollen nub. At the same time, he uses his other hand to thrust two fingers inside of me. My knees are shaking from the force of the sensations attacking me, so much so I'm not sure how much longer they will hold me up.

"That's it Carrie, ride my hand. Do you need fucked, sweetheart?"

"Yes….please, Jacob."

"Tell me, Carrie. Come on baby, tell me you want my cock."

"I need your cock, Jacob. I need it so bad."

"Reach down and wrap that sweet little hand of yours around my cock and slide down on me."

My hands are trembling, but I reach down and grab his cock in my hand. It's soft and hard at the same time. I stroke it slowly, because I can't stop myself.

"Fuck yeah. Stroke my cock." Jacob groans, his hands have moved to my breasts, holding them, kneading them and teasing all at the same time. He's kissing along my back and it all feels so good my brain goes hazy.

"Jacob... I need..."

"I know what you need. Hold my cock still and slide down on me, Carrie. Slide down slowly."

I do as he instructs, lowering on his staff, slow...feeling everything, as he sinks deeper and deeper inside of me. Every inch stretches me and satisfies something I didn't know I was craving.

"Perfect..." I gasp.

Jacob hums his agreement against my ear. I feel one of his hands tangle into my hair and pull so that my head bows back to rest against his shoulder.

"You were made for me, Carrie."

"I know," I admit it freely, because I was. I've known it since I was five years old.

"Rotate your hips and rock baby, get used to my cock moving inside you."

I do as he instructs, careful at first, since I'm unsure. It feels so good though I find myself grinding against his lap and tightening my inner muscles against his erection. He lets me experiment to the point I am about to come. Just when my moves become erratic and I can't contain the moan of pleasure he grabs my hips and keeps me from moving.

"No!" I call out desperate to finish the fire I've started.

"Not yet, sweetheart. Remember how I taught you to ride the other night."

"Yes," I whisper as he pinches my nipples. His breath on my skin is just another instrument of torture.

"Ride me like that, Carrie. Fuck yourself with my cock."

"God, yes," I say as I start riding him using the movements he taught me. Movements that I know will bring us both pleasure.

"I wish you could see how gorgeous you are right now, sweetheart. Taking your pleasure, and demanding it. You're so fucking wet it's like being inside of heaven. You're my heaven. The closest thing to a miracle I'll ever see."

"Jacob!" I yell desperate for more than I'm getting and I don't know what I'm doing wrong.

"Are you ready to come now, sweetheart?"

"Help me," I gasp my breath short and ragged. "I can't…it's not enough…Jacob, I need…"

"What do you need? Tell me, Carrie."

"I need you to fuck me!" I growl near mindless with the need for completion.

He rises behind me holding my hips tight as he tilts us so that we are propelled forward. I brace myself on my hands and knees and slowly slide from his. All the while, Jacob makes sure we stay connected. This new position takes what little breath I have away. Before I can gain it again, he is withdrawing and slamming back into me. The force of the blow moves me on the mattress. It takes a few tries to get the rhythm, but I grab it and soon I'm pushing back to meet his thrusts. It's so intense, so primal that it feels like he's getting larger, and stretching me even more. I wonder if I might die trying to take all of him. His hands are biting into my hips and the pressure is harsh, painful and everything I want all rolled up together. I will be bruised tomorrow from the force of his hold and I like it. Every time I see it I can remember how wild he was with me, how much he lost himself in our lovemaking.

"Touch your clit, Carrie. Rub your fingers over it baby, and stop fighting it. I want to hear you scream as I fill you so full of cum it's dripping down your legs. Do it."

I hear his words and I want to do as he orders, but I'm so lost in the need he has created, I can't get my mind and body to work together. His hand wraps once more in my hair and he pulls it to get my attention.

"I said fucking touch that clit now. Do it, Carrie."

I groan, but my hand moves down as he orders. I'm already so close it just takes a couple of teasing touches and I'm ready to climax. Jacob isn't satisfied though. He pinches my nipples hard. My body jumps and tightens up on his cock all at once.

"Pinch your clit, Carrie. Hard."

My hands are shaking and with the force that he's using to fuck me, it's hard to manage it all. Somehow I do though, at the same time he pinches and twists my nipples and thrusts so deep inside of me I can almost taste him.

I detonate giving a scream that echoes with his cry of release.

Perfection.

Chapter 29

DANCER

SIX WEEKS. THAT'S how long it's been since all hell broke loose. It's also the closest thing to happiness I ever imagined I would have. My days are spent working at the club garage. I've always had a knack for working on vehicles and the busy work keeps me from going insane. Nights are spent in bed with Carrie and fucking her every way I can think of. She might have been shy when we first started, but each time we're together she becomes more vocal. It's fucking phenomenal.

The whole thing with Francis (aka Phoenix) took a lot out of all of us. Crusher has recovered from his gun shot. The bullet somehow managed to go straight through and missed anything vital. He lost a lot of blood at the time, but that probably saved his life. We figure the goon working for *Francis* saw the blood and decided Crush was dead, not bothering to finish the job.

Bull is another story. Bull was released from the trauma center a couple of days ago, but he was sent to a rehab center in Nashville that is part of the Vanderbilt Hospital Complex. The hit on the head combined with the oxygen deprivation he endured (however briefly) took a toll on his body. He doesn't talk much, not that he ever did—but now it is even less. Something happened with his vocal chords and talking pains him physically, but more than that, he has a stammer. His right side is weak as a result of the damage and for someone like Bull that's probably the hardest thing to accept. We got him settled and offered to have one of us stay down there with him, but he wouldn't hear of it. In fact he told us to go fuck ourselves. No one else understood, but on this I totally understood where my brother was coming from. Unless we had been there, our words were useless and pathetic. Dragon is planning on going down and spending the weekend there next week. Carrie and I might go, though to be honest? Fucking bastard that I am? I don't like Carrie being around him one bit. For all I know, she has a thing for trying to heal the broken and she'll switch her interest in me over to my brother.

The other thing I'm dealing with is this house of cards I'm building with Carrie. I'm not sleeping. I take a nap through the day so I can function. Carrie believes I sleep when she does. I haven't been able to manage that. Ever since Dragon confronted me about my dreams, I have this big knot of fear inside of me. I don't want anyone else to know about the …about my attack. No one, but especially not Carrie, I can't handle her knowing. The thought literally makes me break out in a cold sweat.

She also thinks I'm going to therapy twice a week. I hide out in a hotel on old State Route 25 and sleep for a couple of hours instead. I'm not about to share those memories with anyone, but especially some jerk in a suit who knows shit about the real world.

I'm not stupid. I know that eventually the cards will fall. I'll face that day when it comes. In the meantime, I'm doing everything I can to fix it so Carrie won't leave me when she discovers the truth. I need her to be so deep in this thing with me, she won't ever think of leaving.

At times, I'm almost like I was before I went to jail. I know that's because Carrie is in my life. She shines light in the darkness and fills up some of the emptiness which threatens to swallow me whole. I need her to function.

At least Dragon and the club have become less tense with the threat gone. Seems the fucking idiot panicked when Dragon had Freak made sure his assets were tied up. So his big scheme was to blow up Carrie, me and himself all at once to get revenge for his son's death. Funny, how the mighty fall when they don't have money to back their asses up.

These thoughts filter through my brain as I pull into the house that Carrie and I have been living in. Dragon offered it to us after I let him know I wouldn't be living at the club. He didn't question me about it. I think he was afraid to rock the boat after our last blow up.

Carrie told me it is the one that Nicole and Dani rented when they first got to town. I like it. It's bigger than the safe house, closer to the club and it suits Carrie. She's happy. I see it in the way she smiles and that's all that matters. I need her happy. If she's happy, she's less likely to leave, so this house is essential to my plan.

I walk in the back door that leads into a kitchen. The house is quiet, which is unusual. Carrie normally has music blasting while she's getting supper together. Maybe she's taking a nap. All of the excitement has worn her out and she's having trouble catching back up. It doesn't help that I wake her up all night long to fuck her senseless. That thought makes me smile as I enter the living room. Carrie is asleep on the couch, looking like an angel. No she is an angel. My angel. She's saving me and doesn't even know it.

I bend down to kiss her lips, pulling away to watch her slowly wake up.

"Hey, Care Bear."

Her eyes open slowly, those sparkling emeralds drawing me in yet again.

"I love you," she whispers and it hits me sweet like it always does. She says it more often these days. The first time she said it, I can remember a feeling of panic and now...now if she doesn't say it, I panic. I need those three words from her to know she is still mine.

I kiss her lips soaking in the words.

"You okay, Care Bear?"

"I wasn't feeling good. I'm okay though," She says her hand caressing the side of my face. She moves her fingers along the stubble of my beard. I keep it trimmed small, because she seems to like it, so I refuse to shave.

"Carrie, you've been sick for a week. You better get to the doctor."

"I made an appointment."

I fight down the fear at the thought of Carrie being sick. Things have been going too smooth. I've been able to keep the nightmares hid from her, I'm behaving almost normal and I have her. That's more than I dreamed, so I know I shouldn't get too comfortable.

"How about you and I hop on my bike and go get some food, maybe pick up some takeout and drive down to the marina?"

She studies me for a second and gives me a soft smile. Those might be my favorite of the smiles she gives. They are sleepy and full of feeling.

"I'd like that."

"Good, let's get out of here."

WE DRIVE DOWN to the Tasty Freeze Dairy Bar and order a couple burgers and fries. I get a couple of canned sodas and put it all in the bags on the back of my bike. I like having Carrie on my bike. We fit and move like one, as if we've been riding together for years. It feels...*right*.

We drive down to the marina and find an empty picnic table looking out over the boats and water.

"It really is beautiful here," Carrie says placing our food out on the table. I put the sodas down and grab a seat across from her.

"I like to come here and think. It helps to clear my mind. It makes me feel closer to Jazz. You two used to love to play here and feed the ducks and fish."

I see a look in Carrie's eyes and I know she's remembering the night I tried to end it all, but she doesn't push me about it. She's my safe zone, at least that's how she makes me feel.

"I remember, but I have a confession."

"What's that? I say and take a bite of my burger.

I watch as she twirls a French fry in the ketchup seeming to think about her words. Then she looks up at me with this impish smile on her face.

"We hated fishing. We only wanted to spend the day with you," she laughs popping the fry in her mouth.

I stop mid-bite, watching her and can tell that she is completely serious.

"You used to harass me for hours to take you fishing."

She swallows down her food and grins.

"You'd follow me around and whine until I crumbled."

"You really were so easy, Jacob. Putty in our little five and six year old hands," She says with a grin, taking another bite.

"I can't believe you. I even bought you those matching Barbie fishing rods!"

She pauses, staring off into space like she's thinking about something, "Actually I think it was a Sleeping Beauty fishing rod."

"Same thing," I dismiss.

"Totally not, though to be honest I would have rather had the Spiderman."

"Get out of town."

"Nope, I am not a girly girl."

"Princess, this is the first time I can remember you not having a dress on in forever, you most certainly are a girly-girl—whatever the hell that is."

"Well maybe about some things, but not most."

"Name one," I dare here watching her eat. How can a woman eating be sexy? Seems impossible, but somehow Carrie pulls it off.

"Well, I went through a scene from a bad James Bond film and didn't fall completely apart," she says, continuing to eat.

"Bad James Bond film?"

She puts her burger down and licks the ketchup off her lips and starts counting holding up a finger for each new item.

"I was held at gun point. I withstood flying bullets, people dying, a house explosion, fire, having someone I care about get hurt...see? Not girly-girl or I'd be in a corner crying somewhere. Well either that, or a padded cell."

I nod in agreement, thinking over her words. I feel a twinge of jealousy when she mentions caring about Bull, hell maybe she means Crusher. I hate that it bothers me, but it does.

I look down pretending to eat, avoiding eye contact.

"Oh no. What's that look for Jacob Blake?"

"Nothing," I answer, not about to admit it. I concentrate instead on my food.

"You don't get to do that now."

I look up and she's focused on me and the look on her face says she's not going to let this pass.

"Just thinking maybe you would have been happier if you ended up with Crush or Bull," I try and shrug it off, dropping my food on the table. My appetite is gone. I sack up my garbage, refusing to look her in the face. A greasy, wadded up paper hits me in the face. I look over at her.

"What was that for?"

"For being stupid," She says and her eyes are sparking with anger. She gets up and starts walking away.

"Where in the hell are you going?"

"Anywhere away from you," She tosses back at me,

but she doesn't bother to turn around or stop. I get up and take off after her.

"Carrie, damn it."

She's walking along the concrete pathway by the lake.

"We're on my bike! Are you planning on walking all the way home?" I yell aggravated.

"If I have to! Who knows maybe someone will pick me up along the side of the road and we'll fall madly in love! I'm stupid like that. I can fall in love with man after man. Heck! Sometimes I fall in love with three a day!"

She's screaming and it's a nice evening, so the marina is not empty. People are staring at her likes she's crazy. There's nothing about our situation funny, but I can't help the smile that breaks out on my face. I increase my pace and catch her, grab her arm and turn her around to me. The smile on my face dies when I see the tears in her eyes and how pale her face looks.

"I'm sorry Care Bear, it was a stupid thing to say."

She pushes the hair away from her face and tugs until I let her go. I bury my hands in my pockets to keep from picking her up and carrying her away.

"I won't do this with you anymore, Jacob. I can't. If you don't understand by now how much I love you? How much I've bent over backwards for you and swallowed your hateful words? Damn it! If you don't get it by now, you're never going to and I'm tired of banging my head against a brick wall! It hurts! I don't understand what else I'm supposed to do so that you finally get it!"

"Get what, Care Bear?"

"That I love you! You and only you, Jacob Blake! I am not five years old, with a case of puppy love for the older boy! I am here now! I know you're riddled with problems and God knows there's nothing perfect about you! I get it! I live with it every day and I'm still here!"

I listen to her words. My heart picks up in beat. I want to believe in her...I think I'm starting to.

"You got to know that doesn't sound like you love me. It doesn't even sound like you like me, Princess."

She stops her tirade and turns her head to the side like she thinks I am insane and hell maybe I am.

"I told you I'm not a girly-girl."

"No, you're mine," I tell her and I almost believe it.

Chapter 30

CARRIE

I AM LYING in bed as the front door closes. Jacob's headed to the club. He thinks I'm clueless to the secrets he's keeping. I'm not. I know he's not sleeping when he's in our bed. Worse, the therapist called the house a couple of weeks ago wondering if Jacob had found other services. He had missed his scheduled appointments and failed to respond to their calls and letters. He's been lying to me, saying he's going to therapy.

I need to talk to him about all of this. I've been afraid to rock the boat, so I've let it go. I let a lot of things go. Most notably the fact that I am pregnant. I went to the doctor yesterday. I thought I had a vitamin problem because I'm just so tired all the time. I'm not. I'm pregnant. I. Am. Pregnant.

Yeah I keep telling myself that over and over and it's still not totally sinking in. My hand moves over my stomach which is still flat of course, but I swear I can almost feel a warmth that has never been there before. I have Jacob's baby inside of me. Jacob's baby! I don't know anything about being a mom. I don't even have my mom to lean on to show me the ropes. I'm scared.

I lock down that thought before it blossoms. I've done that since my parents died. I can't think about it, not right now. I can't handle it! I'll tackle it all later. That's been my motto. At first it was, I'll deal with it all after Dragon finds the man who hurt us. Now it's after I get everything better with Jacob. I know it's not healthy. I do. I just can't seem to stop myself.

Like right now. I'm terrified of how Jacob will react. I should have told him the truth yesterday. I couldn't bring myself to. I love him. I love him completely. These last six weeks have been the best in my life, even with all the other stuff going on around us. I don't want to lose him and I'm terrified this might do it. Jacob hasn't mentioned the future. I know he wants me with him. I feel like I'm helping him. He's more open with me than I imagined he would be. He doesn't say, but I know he wants to hear me tell him I love him. He gets this look in his eyes when I give him the words. I can't explain it, but it feels like for a minute or two I might bring him peace and I want that. I want to do that for him.

I get up, shower and let thoughts run through my brain while I wash my hair. I could go to the garage and surprise Jacob. The Tahoe is out there. Jacob insists I keep one to get around during the day. I should buy a car. I have all this money just sitting in an account that I haven't really touched. It was my parents but using the money somehow makes their deaths seem real. Which is stupid, you can't get any more real than dead. Still, that's what I think about every time I start to spend it.

I should take lessons from Nicole or Dani when dealing with this stuff. I want to be Jacob's for life, not just for now. I didn't think that was possible, but it's been months since we first made love and it has been six weeks since we've been completely together, so I'm starting to hope. That's nothing to sneeze at right? Surely in all that time I've come to mean something to Jacob. A man like that doesn't just come home to one woman—the same woman, unless she's special. I may be new to all this, but I have read a lot and I've seen how Nicole and Dragon are with each other and even Six and Vida (it's getting harder and harder to think of her as Lips).

I should take a page out of Nicole's book. She wouldn't hide this and worry about how Dragon would react. She would face it all head on. I need to do that. If I am going to be the woman of a Savage MC member I need to start facing things and not hiding from them.

Decision made, I finish my shower and head downstairs to find something to eat. I grab a quick piece of toast and juice. I'm not a breakfast person, but that seems like something an expectant mother should do. I go a step further and make a basket of tuna salad sandwiches, chips and pickles for lunch. Not gourmet, but it works and Jacob and I can spend lunch together.

The only moment of indecision I have is dressing. Jacob made a comment about my jeans yesterday. I think he liked them and I do love being on his bike. Still, dresses are who I am and they are comfortable. Plus, I don't know, maybe it's good to have something loose against my stomach? I have no idea. I make a note to stop by the bookstore in town on the way and grab that pregnancy book the doctor recommended.

I finally decide to put on my sage green sundress with

the little pink roses on it. Jacob likes it. Well, he liked taking it off of me the last time I wore it.

I make it to the club around noon and head straight for the garage that Jacob has been working in. Freak is standing out front talking with Nikki and Frog.

"Hey, Red. What are you doing here looking so gorgeous? Dancer ever drops the ball baby you're going to have to give me a chance," Frog says with this big smile. I shake my head at his words, but laugh when Freak slaps him on the back of the head.

"Ignore him Red, he forgot his brains in his ass. You lookin' for Dance?"

"Yeah I thought I might steal him away for lunch."

"He just took a break from work. You can catch him in the club though."

I smile, trying to hold on to the courage that brought me here. Nikki might have seen I was wavering, even if she didn't know what was going on, because she grabs my hand.

"We'll go in together. I need to check with Nicole on something."

Freak pulls her back to him before we can leave and slams his lips against hers in a kiss that is so intense and carnal you can feel the heat just from watching it.

"Behave yourself, stud," Nikki breathes against his lips when they break apart.

"Remember my promise, woman."

Nikki licks her lips, but doesn't say anything else. I bite my tongue to keep from asking what the promise was!

Then she grabs my hand and pulls me along to the club.

"Things seem to be going good with Freak."

"Girl, you have no idea. I'll tell you some time though, just bring a fan," she says with a laugh, wiggling her eyebrows in mock suggestion. We're both laughing as we open the doors.

It takes a minute for my eyes to adjust from the bright sunshine to the darkness of the room. When it does, the laughter clogs in my throat.

Jacob is sitting at the bar with Tash, a club Twinkie in his lap. They're laughing. Her hand is playing with his hair while she drags a finger down the side of his face teasing his lips. She's dressed like the Twinkies always are, almost naked. Today though her white, see-through shirt and clearly no bra or panties, seems worse. It is worse, because she's in the lap of my man. She's in his lap and he's not pushing her away. Instead his hand is on her thigh. Sure the shirt is between his touch and her skin, but he is holding her thigh! He is letting her sit in his lap! He is…laughing with her! I thought I was the only one who made him laugh! I thought I was…the only one.

Something inside of me screams, no and then I hear his words. I hear him talking about something that should be private. I hear him talking about me, about us. I hear him and just like that my new found will to face things head on and be stronger crumbles around me.

Chapter 31

DANCER

(Just before Carrie's arrival)

I'M EXHAUSTED AND I keep messing shit up. I've been trying to get a fucking spring in a fucking carburetor for the last fucking hour! I can rebuild those son of a bitches with my eyes closed I've done so many of them and yet, I'm so tired I can't concentrate. I don't want to be here. The men are talking and laughing so loud my head feels like it is being bombarded. There's people everywhere and it's unreasonable, it's completely unreasonable, because truly it's the same bunch who are always here and not even as many as normal. Still, it is making my skin feel as if it is trying to crawl off my body. The faces and the voices all mix into one blurring roar in my head. It's like they are all on a carousel that spins around so fast and quick that I just catch images of them flashing in my head. Then they spin again with a whirl. Their combined voices are like a strange sadistic music and blends until all I can hear is gibberish. Gibberish but with mocking laughter in the background. My heart drums a million beats a minute and jars my body with its force.

Panic attack. I'm having a fucking panic attack in broad daylight. Each person that comes up to me is hidden by unseen arms, unseen hands reaching out to grab me. Reaching out to grab me and pull me down into the darkness. My hands shake, a cold sweat breaks out over my skin. I'm dizzy. I'm going to fucking lose it in front of my brothers. NO! I CAN'T!! I throw the parts down on the work bench and stomp out of the garage.

I want to fucking run. I want to run so fucking far that I can feel nothing but the burn of the air in my lungs. I can't do that either. If I run they will all know, they will know and it will all crumble around me and I'll lose Carrie. I make it to the back of the garage and lean against the block wall, slowly falling to my ass. I bring my knees up and put my head down and breathe deep.

This one might have been the worse yet. My hands are trembling. Hell, my whole body is shaking. I have been doing so well. I cope so much better when Carrie is with me. I'm a grown ass man, and I need a woman around to hold my hand. It pisses me off. I do not want to be weak. A weak man can't take care of himself. He can't defend himself. I do not want to be this person. I need to be different for Carrie. I just don't know if that is possible.

I get a little control and decide on a couple of drinks before going to my old room to nap. I need Carrie. I need her so bad, it's all I can do not to jump on my bike and head back to the house. Instead I pull myself up and go into the bar.

I down one shot after another. I'm on the fifth when Tash, a club Twinkie, comes over and slides on my lap. She feels wrong. She smells wrong.

"Dancer baby, I thought being in the joint might have changed you."

My heart stalls. Is there talk? Does she know something? Did Dragon tell the men?

"What do you mean?" I ask my voice gruff. My hand grabs her leg tight. She doesn't seem to notice. Hell, she probably thinks I want her there. Really I'm trying to keep the room from spinning and fighting back the traces of the panic attack that is still in my system.

"I was starting to think we had lost you to the land of soccer dads and minivans. Figured we wouldn't see you around here until you had a ring through your nose and a couple of kids screaming for attention," Tash laughs her fingers moving along the side of my face and moving close to my lip.

My emotions are all over the place. An image of Carrie with babies at her feet… but not just any babies, my babies flash in my head. Then I feel the sweat still popped out on my neck and the pounding beat of my heart from the earlier panic attack and immediately get jerked back into reality. I am not father material. I can't even protect myself, how can I protect kids? Hell, I almost got Carrie killed if you get down to it.

"Fuck, if there is one thing I'm not cut out for girl, it's being a dad. You won't ever catch me with my balls cut off for some woman. You know me better than that shit. The only van you might catch me in, is one rockin' if you get my meaning," I say, giving a half-hearted attempt to laugh it all off.

She laughs and the noise is shrill and annoying. She bends down like she's going to kiss me. Fuck, I don't want that. I don't want her anywhere near me. Her perfume is about to make me gag. I'm about to pull away when my world stops turning.

"You dildo, juggling, thunder cunt! What the hell Tash? Did you **NOT** learn to stay away from a brother who is spoken for?" Freak's woman, Nikki demands. That isn't what destroys me though. No, what does that is Carrie's quiet gasp.

Fuck! I stand up, not caring one fucking bit that Tash falls to the ground. In the background Nikki and Tash start yelling, but it is Carrie standing in front of me that I concentrate on. I have to fix this. I need to fix this. I can't lose Carrie.

"Carrie sweetheart, I can…it's not what you think, Care Bear."

She flinches like I hit her.

"Don't. Oh, God Jacob, please don't. Don't you dare use that name on me, not now."

She turns around and pushes through the front door before I can tell my fucking feet to move. I catch up with her seconds later outside.

"Carrie, I swear, nothing was happening. It wouldn't. I have you, I don't…"

"That's just it, Jacob," she says turning around, facing me and the sight of her tears is so hard to take, I almost wish she had kept her back to me. How many tears have I caused her? Why do I always hurt her? "You don't have me. You've been pretending with me. I'm not what you want, not at all."

"Bullshit. I've been showing you for months that you're what I want."

"Really, Jacob?"

"Damn it, you've been there in our house. You know! You get more of me than I've ever willingly given anyone."

"Why do you refuse to sleep with me?"

"We fuck like bu…."

"I'm not talking sex Jacob, I mean sleep. Why can't you sleep with me?"

"Now you're talking crazy, Carrie. We sleep beside each other every night. C'mon baby, let's go home," I counter, her face looking even more shaken with my answer. I know I'm lying, but there's no way she can. I need to get her home, calm her down. I can't lose her. I start walking her towards her car.

Chapter 32
CARRIE

SOMETIMES I THINK if you lie to someone enough you can break them. It's like you're delicate hand-blown glass and all the lies you've swallowed bends you until you shatter, completely shatter. When Jacob stands in front of me and says he sleeps beside me every night, I shatter. At that moment I am a walking corpse. The hurt is too big to measure, the pain is too substantial and the fear, the fear of life without Jacob, without having a half of me, is too consuming.

Oddly enough, I believe him about Tash. I don't know that probably makes me a fool. What we've been sharing is too beautiful. I can't see him giving that to anyone else. Is that what every woman says though who gets cheated on? I have no idea, but I feel in my heart he's telling the truth. He looks me in the eye when he talks about her. He couldn't when he vowed he slept by me every night. Even in my current state, I can see that.

So I'm weak. I let him take me back to the vehicle. I let him usher me into the passenger seat. I let him drive me home. I let all this happen and don't say one word. I watch as he grabs the basket of food and carries it inside with us when we get home. I watch all of it, like it's not really happening to me. It happens in slow motion in my brain, and I can't bring myself to say one word.

Jacob leads me into the bathroom and sits me on the toilet. I watch as he runs water, adding my favorite bubble bath. I've still not spoken. He keeps talking and it sounds like it's coming at me from far off in the distance.

I'm like a marionette and he's controlling the strings. I say nothing when he begins to undress me, just lifting my hands and doing as he says. I don't even understand it. I should be mad, I should be screaming at him. I can't. Something is broken inside of me. With his final lie to me, something severed. I don't know how he hasn't noticed.

He helps me get into the tub and the hot water does feel good. I close my eyes and let the heat invade my body and ignore the one lone tear that falls down my face. I feel Jacob get in behind me. His legs come around each side of mine and he wraps his arm around my waist and brings me back into him so my back is against his front. He urges my head to fall back against his chest and despite the heat of the water bringing me somewhat back to life, I go. I lay my head there and wait for his heat and that of the water to work magic and heal me. I'm so deadly cold. Yet, it is so deep inside I know nothing will penetrate it.

I lie against him, listening to his heartbeat and notice that he has stopped talking. He has turned the water off. Now there is just silence. How long has there been silence?

"Carrie, you have to believe me, baby. I wasn't going to let her touch me. I wouldn't do that to you. I just… my head is fucked up, Care Bea…"

I stiffen when he starts to use my nickname and he must have felt it. It seems I'm not so robotic after all.

"My head is fucked up Princess, it is just things… there's things you don't know Carrie, things I can't share—not yet. Things that sneak up on me without me even realizing it. She said shit…and it's not an excuse, sweetheart. It's not, but I promise you I wasn't doing what it looked like. You would have seen that a few minutes later, I promise."

"You haven't been going to therapy."

"Carrie, I…"

"They called Jacob," I stop him before he lies again, because that is what is wrong. When we talk about what is really wrong with him? When we talk about what is causing all the trouble? That is when he lies.

"I can't talk about it, Carrie. Especially with some college idiot, with some initials after his name, who has no idea what I am feeling or what I am going through. There are things Princess that if you haven't lived it, there is no way you can help someone else.

"Then find a support group, there are those around, Jacob."

"I can't Carrie, I can't talk to strangers about…I can't, not even for you."

"Then talk to me, give it to me."

"Damn it Carrie, I can't tell you! I can't go there, not right now—hell maybe not ever, you don't know, Carrie. You can't know…"

"I do know. I know it all, Jacob."

He stops and his body goes hard like stone behind me.

"The night I came into your room, before

you…before… You were dreaming. I heard, Jacob. I know," I say quietly, praying I'm not doing this wrong.

I have been attending a Kentucky Rape Crisis Outreach support group with Nicole. We hadn't told anyone, though I figure Dragon knows—I didn't ask. I've only been to four meetings though and we're mostly dealing with the effects rape has on friends and family members. What if I'm handling this all wrong? I don't want to make things worse. I feel like I'm walking on eggshells.

"I can't talk about this with you, Carrie. Don't ask me to."

My heart sinks. "I know you blame me Jacob, I blame myself too. I understand and that's the reason I should probably leave. How can you want to be with someone who is responsible for…?"

He stops me and his hand caresses my face and turns it towards him.

"Stop that, Carrie. I don't blame you. I was angry sweetheart, so angry when I got out and I focused that anger on you, but what happened is not your fault. It is not your fault at all and I don't want you blaming yourself."

"Jacob…"

"Let's go to bed, Carrie. Let's just hold each other for a while. Then we'll get up and eat and spend the night holding each other. I'll sleep with you tonight. Let's ignore the world around us and concentrate just on the two of us."

"Jacob, I don't…"

"We'll start small, let's take a nap. Let me hold you in our bed. We both need that. Okay?"

I don't remember agreeing, but he must have taken my silence for doing so. He lifts me out of the bathtub. Standing me on the rug, he takes a towel and wraps it around me, after first securing one on his hip. He lifts me again, taking me into the bedroom. He proceeds to take the towel from me and dries me off. He kisses my forehead, my eyes, my lips, and then my shoulders, before finally placing me in the bed and pulling me close. We lie there in the dark, as if we're both afraid to say anything that might destroy the tenuous truce we have in this moment.

"Don't leave me, Carrie. I need you," he says into the quiet, a good fifteen minutes or more later.

At one time those words would have been more than enough to get me to stay. They totally would have worked. I didn't realize he thought I was leaving, but I can't deny I am thinking hard on it. I love Jacob. I love him with all my heart, but how can you be with someone who refuses to help himself? Still I might try it, just because the past month and a half have been so wonderful I might try it…just….

"Do you really not want kids, Jacob?"

His body tenses up again and his arm that he has wrapped around my chest tightens until the point of pain, but I say nothing.

"I can't be a father, Carrie. I'm not…capable…I'm just not cut out for it. I could make you happy though, sweetheart. I know I can, if you give me another chance. We'll be happy together, just the two of us, for the rest of our lives, just the two of us."

His words are like a physical blow, even if the last

sentence is a sweet temptation. Can I do that? Can I trade the life growing inside of me for a shot of forever with Jacob? I don't think I can, which means letting go of the one man who has always had my heart.

It's over.

Those words echo in my soul.

Chapter 33

DANCER

SHE DIDN'T SAY she loved me. I have come to count on those three words over the last month and a half we have been together. Those words work to give me strength to make it through the day. Carrie is my lifeline. Yet, I think I've fucked up so much this time that I'm losing her. I hold her so close it's almost like my body is absorbing hers, but there is this wall between us now, separating us. I did that. I put that wall there with my stupid weakness. I should have protected and cherished what Carrie gave me and I fucked it up.

I live with fear every damn hour, of every damn day. I live with it. I beat down the urge to run and crawl in a fucking hole and hide constantly. This is my life. Panic attacks and my heart beating in fear? This is my life. Feeling dirty and ashamed and weak…feeling so fucking weak and useless? This is my life.

It's always there. ALWAYS! Yet, with Carrie it is smaller, it is less apparent, it's like I have whole blocks of the day when I can be almost normal. She is my light, and I didn't protect it. I didn't fully appreciate it. If I lose her I'll be completely lost.

Which means right now fear is near to suffocating me and is more intense, bigger than anything I've ever felt before in my life—including the night I was attacked. The fear I have now, is a fear that goes bone deep. The fear of losing someone I love. I love Carrie. I. Love. Her. Yes, I realize the irony of acknowledging I love her, just when I have pushed her so far away she's not giving it back to me. I need to fix it, I'm not sure how.

I had Carrie drop me off at the club this morning, since my bike was here. I've been here for three hours, and I can't concentrate on anything. I need to be with her. I have to fight for her and show her she matters more than anything else. I may not be great, but I know with her I can be okay. I can make her happy.

With that in mind, I throw my tools down and get to my bike. It's time I prove to Carrie that I can be better for her. Her vehicle is not at the house. I will not panic. She probably is just doing errands in town. I can catch her there and we can have lunch together and maybe go home for dessert. I didn't make love to her last night and I need her. Over the past month we haven't missed a night of making love, most of the time two and three times a night. I hunger for her and the way it feels when I'm that close to her.

This could be a bad idea though. I have no idea where she is. London might still give a small town feel, but there are elements of a bigger city in it, with too many places she could be. I start with her favorite. The Curl up and Dye hair salon she gets her hair fixed at is a bust, the local grocery she prefers, the bank, the library, the bookstore— all a bust. I'm about to give up when I decide to drive downtown to the local diner she likes.

Downtown London is probably my favorite area besides the marina and lake. It's a busy place with shopping, offices, diners, schools and clinics all put together to give someone everything they need without having to really visit the outer areas, which are overcrowded with large shopping outlets. The buildings are kept up nicely and all have an architectural feel of the past. It is modern, but also a step back in time. It doesn't stress me out like most crowded areas do.

I'm approaching Weaver's which is a London, Kentucky classic and Carrie's favorite place to eat downtown when I see her vehicle parked outside the Wellness Center and Clinic. I remember she told me she had made an appointment. Why didn't I ask when it was? I would have gone with her. I know she has been sick for a while maybe she was worse this morning?

I park and walk inside scanning the lobby for her. I'm about to give up and wait for her outside, when a door opens across from reception and Carrie walks out with a nurse. She hasn't spotted me, but I can tell she is upset. I walk over to her afraid this might be something more than a cold.

"Ms. Grace here's your prescription for prenatal vitamins and the pamphlets you should look at. The clerk out front will schedule your follow-up appointment."

"Thank you, I appreciate it," Carrie says.

"We'll see you next visit. Please call if you need anything before then."

"Prenatal...?" I ask, not even realizing I spoke out loud. The room fades away with the exception of the nurse's words and Carrie's face as she turns around and sees me standing in front of her.

"Jacob? What…what are you doing here?" She asks once the nurse goes back through the door.

"Prenatal? Did she say Prenatal Vitamins? Carrie, are you pregnant?" I ask and even I can hear the panic in my voice.

Carrie's face drains of what little color she had. I watch as her eyes water, but she takes a breath and composes herself.

"Jacob, what are you doing here? Shouldn't you be working? How did you find me?"

She asks all those questions, but she doesn't look at me. She instead starts walking to the door. I turn her back around to me instead.

"Carrie, are you pregnant?" I'm pretty sure if my heart doesn't stop beating this hard I will have a stroke.

"Jacob please, there are too many people here to do this right now. Let's go…"

"I don't give a fuck who is here. I'm asking you, are you pregnant?"

"Yes."

Yes.

It floors me. Shit. Carrie's pregnant. It's not like it should be a big surprise, I've been fucking the hell out of her and not once—not one damn time did I ever think about using a condom. I never went ungloved before Carrie. With her, I didn't even think about it. I knew I was the first to ever be inside of her and I didn't want anything between us, she was special. She is special. It was an unconscious decision. It was…fuck, why didn't I think about it? Me a dad? What could I ever offer a kid? How could I take care of a kid? What kind of kid would want me as a role model? Most days, I can't even look in the damn mirror. How will a kid ever want to look at me? What happens when he or she learns about their old man and what happened to him?

"Fuck."

The word comes out without me meaning it to. I seem to have a problem with that lately, but holy hell my world was just shook on its axis.

Carrie hears me and she flinches as if the word slaps her. I know it does, and I want to bite it back. Instead, I make it worse.

"I'm not ready for this Carrie, I'm not sure I'll ever be ready."

"I've taken so much crap off of you," her quiet voice echoes in the room.

I know there are other people around, but for me all that exists is Carrie. There's so much pain in her sentence. I hear it and look at my woman, really look at her. She is standing in a yellow sundress with small daisies all over it. Her long auburn hair has been braided in some kind of complicated style and swirled on her head and it makes a man long to undo it. She's gorgeous, even now with the faint glimpse of tears in her eyes. Yet, she looks miserable. I've done that.

"I've taken so much crap. I begged you to love me, to be with me and I shouldn't have. If you couldn't see that I was worth it, that I was…."

"Princess…"

"I've kept my mouth shut and I've let you blame and

unload on me, because I felt responsible for it all. So I just kept going along, saying it was okay. It's okay because I love Jacob and he has to work through so much, but I love him and he cares for me and I want to be with him and this is what couples do. They work through issues and problems and they come out on the other side stronger."

"Princess…" I try again, but she doesn't let me.

"I might be young and naïve like everyone keeps throwing at me, but I *loved* you Jacob. I loved you and I just knew if I held on and gave you all I could, it would be okay. That's what couples do. They comfort each other. They are there for each other and they hold the fuck on TOGETHER!"

Carrie doesn't curse. She goes out of her way to not curse. She doesn't even yell. Except for the day at the marina, she's hardly ever spoken back to any one in her life. Yet, here she is doing both, doing both in a crowded clinic with people we know, however distantly, staring at us. This is when I know I am in complete trouble. I have kept my head in my ass for too long. I've been so wrapped up in my misery, wrapped up in what was all about me, what was good for me, what I wanted and needed, that I left Carrie swinging out there on her own. I see it clearly and I am in trouble, but at the same time I keep hearing the same word and panic swaps me.

Baby. I'm going to be a dad. How the fuck can I take care of a baby when I need Carrie to even make it through a day? What happens if I have a panic attack when I'm alone with him? What happens if I crack and even Carrie can't help me? A baby! How can I do this?

"They do Carrie, baby they absolutely do hold on

and…"

"Except you didn't, Jacob. I did. It was always me, but really, you never held on with me. You never held on *for* me."

"I did Carrie, I'm here," I say, but I am lying.

"No, you didn't, Jacob. You held on for *you*."

"Carrie, sweetheart…"

"I'm twenty years old. I discover I'm pregnant so I go to tell my boyfriend that I am and find a whore on his lap. All that and yet, I still talk myself into HOLDING ON! I listen to my boyfriend feed me excuse after excuse and I lie in our bed and talk myself into HOLDING ON! I go to the doctor to get information about ending a life inside of me. A life I dearly love already, knowing I couldn't do it, knowing there was no way, but sitting and listening to the doctor calmly explain the option, all because I was trying to HOLD THE FUCK ON!"

There are several people letting out collective gasps in the room. I can't pay attention though, because her words are like bullets and each one strikes a deadly hit in my heart. She throws a pamphlet at my chest and I reach up and grab it in reaction. The rest of the paper fades into the background except for the hateful word staring back at me ABORTION. I did that. I drove Carrie to even hearing about this.

"Carrie…"

"I'm done."

"What?" I ask and now the terror in my voice is thick. It chokes me.

"I'm done," she walks around me and I'm too shook up to stop her.

"Carrie wait!" I yell walking out with her.

She has the door open to the SUV by the time I make it to her. She leans against the opened driver's door. The tears aren't just glimmering in her eyes anymore. They are falling fast and hard, but she doesn't even blink.

"I'm done, Jacob. I'm not enough. I've never been enough and now? Now I'm fucking done."

"You love me we can…"

"Right now I don't even like you, Jacob Blake. We're finished."

She hops up in the SUV and I should be stopping her, I should be throwing the door open and taking her in my arms and stopping her, but I am frozen. Everything is replaying in my head. I see the hurt, the anger and the pain in Carrie's eyes. I watch her back out of her parking spot.

We're finished.

I may be standing on a busy street with the sun beating down, but right now I am standing in the cold. I am standing in complete darkness. Carrie took the light.

Chapter 34
CARRIE

I CAN'T GO home. There is nothing there for me anyway. Most of the clothes were given to me, the few items I've replaced are unimportant. It is my turn to quit hiding, because in my own small way I have been just as bad as Jacob. I've been hiding from the death of my parents. I can't do that anymore.

I need distance—time and distance. I've always heard those fix everything. Incidentally, I'm pretty sure that is a lie.

So I drive to the local Greyhound station, say goodbye to my life in Kentucky and hop a bus back to Tennessee. I visit my parents' graves. I cry. I replace my wardrobe with their money. I finally accept it is my money now. It can't be more real than looking at tombstones.

I do all of that, feeling half alive. Before I know it, a couple of weeks have gone by. Jacob knows where I'm at. I know because he's called. He calls a lot. I usually let the machine answer. I talked to him once. I told him again that we were done. I didn't let him talk. I was afraid to. As much as I insist that we are done, I have this small hope that somehow Jacob will fight for me—fight for us. He hasn't. I'm glad—at least that's what I tell myself.

Jacob's mom has come by. She doesn't know I'm pregnant, but apparently Jacob has asked her to check on me and make sure I'm okay. That's kind of sweet, but I can't weaken. I've had enough.

I'm so tired lately. My doctor assures me that this is normal, but most afternoons it is all I can do hold my eyes open. It's only one in the afternoon now and I'm lying in bed. I'm almost out when the phone rings. Maybe that explains why I reach over and pick up the receiver, I know who it is. I know and honestly, I want to hear his voice.

"Hello."

"How are you?" Nicole asks and I ignore the disappointment that falls over me.

"I'm okay," I lie. "Getting settled in."

"Stop lying to me," she responds and I smile. I've missed Nicole.

"I miss him."

"I know, Care," she says and I figure she does because that one sentence is filled with sadness.

"I was hoping he'd follow me and tell me…"

"I know that too. I'm sorry."

"How's he doing?" I ask because I can't stop myself.

"Avoiding everyone and getting drunk a lot."

"Does he ask about me at all?" Damn, I wish I was strong enough to not ask that question.

"I don't think he knows we talk, but he's not really talking with any of us."

"How's the baby?" We ask each other at the same time and Nicole laughs, I can only manage a half way smile.

"I'm starting to show. It's a small bump, but it's there.

I go next week to find the sex of the baby. How about you?"

"Nothing to show here, but I'm so tired and it's probably too soon but this morning the smell of bacon made me hurl."

"Ohhh…Bacon…I need some of that."

"I take it no sickness?" I ask and this time it was a real smile on my face, mostly anyways.

"Hell no! I'm just hungry all the time. I swear by the time I have little Dragon I'm going to weigh five hundred pounds."

"Well Dragon does love your ass…"

"Yeah well, there will sure be plenty of it for him to love at this rate. Are you taking care of yourself? I'm worried about you being alone right now," she responds and although her concern makes me feel better, I wish it was coming from Jacob.

"I'm okay. Don't worry about me."

"Yeah, that's not going to happen girl. I better get though I'll call you again tomorrow. There's a party here tonight and Dragon's flipping his shit because Skull and his boys will be here. You should see the outfit he wants me to wear."

I definitely smile now because Nicole has told me how jealous Dragon is, especially of Skull.

"What is it?"

"Oh my lord woman, it's like this dress from the eighties that has poufy shoulders and buttons all the way to the wrist and buttons up at the neck! The neck, Carrie!"

I laugh out loud.

"Well some of those dresses can be pretty?" I try to

console her, but the response comes out as a question, because I know it will get worse.

I was right.

"Carrie! It comes down to my ankles! MY ANKLES!"

"Well…"

"WOMAN! It has flowers on it! Before you start, it's not flowers like you wear! We're talking full-fledged pink and dusty rose flowers that are like bigger than a dinner plate all over the damn thing! My grandmother would have refused to wear this dress."

"So, I take it you're not wearing it?"

"Not on your life. I'm wearing the sleaziest outfit I could find and I raided Lip's closet, so there you go."

"Dragon will go off the deep end."

"Probably, but I'll get sex out of it and get to watch him explode so hey."

"Love you, Nicole."

"Right back at you girl, don't you forget it. We'll talk soon."

"Okay," I stare at the phone in my hand once she hangs up.

I miss her. I miss all of them to be honest. It hurt to hear that Jacob hasn't been asking about me. I didn't expect him to, but really it would have been nice. As I put the phone down, my stomach drops. Party? The picture of Jacob with Tash on his lap comes to mind and I want to scream.

I go grab the pint of chocolate ice cream I have in the freezer instead.

Chapter 35

DANCER

TWO WEEKS. IT'S been two weeks since I've laid eyes on Carrie. It's been almost as long as that since I've heard her voice. I call every night. Fuck sometimes twice a night. She's only picked up once. It turns out you can walk around dead on the inside. I am. Nothing seems to matter anymore. It's all empty without my woman. I asked my mom to check on her. I finally broke down and called her the other night, desperate to know someone was trying to take care of Carrie. Mom's not exactly happy with me either, so that conversation did nothing to lessen the guilt eating me alive since Carrie left.

I want to fucking scream and go and get her. I don't. She deserves someone to make her happy, someone who can get his life together. That's obviously not me.

I say obviously because it's another night alone without her and I'm at the club, drunk off my ass and the party hasn't even started yet. It's not due to start for another couple of hours. Dragon is throwing a party to announce Nicole being pregnant with his baby. They've apparently set a wedding date too. La' de' fucking da.

I look over at them. He's got her on his lap, their

hands overlapping on her stomach. She's got a small bump there. It's barely noticeable and you'd probably not see it now except for what she is wearing.

Actually I'm kind of surprised that Dragon let his woman dress like that. She's got a lot of skin showing and if that skirt got any shorter I could see her ass. As it is, you can still catch a glimpse here and there. No way in hell I'd let Carrie wear anything like that.

I stare at their hands and watch as Dragon leans down to place a kiss on her stomach. The bitterness twists in my gut. What would it be like to be a whole man? To be able to claim your woman and your baby to the world, knowing you could protect them, be there for them and not fail them…

My baby.

I'm so screwed up in the head. I don't know how I feel. I want Carrie. I think I could be almost whole with Carrie. I could be normal…mostly. A baby? A baby changes everything. I never had a father, not really. Even after I left the streets there wasn't much time to enjoy having a father before I was the one working and providing and taking care of the family. But hell, I couldn't even get through a regular work day without having a panic attack and that's when things were good. Now without Carrie the only way I can face the sun is to be buried in a bottle. That's weak. Being…raped is weak. As always, the word echoes through me and I down the rest of my drink trying to bury it. I pour another shot as I watch Dragon kiss his woman and then follow Crusher and Freak outside. They don't ask me to join them. It doesn't surprise me. I haven't felt like part of their group since I got sent up. Maybe I should leave? Head out somewhere warm, Florida maybe or Arizona. Start fresh far away from the dark memories that haunt me, I could do it. It might be better. A new life, a new world and eventually this pain of missing Carrie and not being part of her life would lessen.

"Hey, baby. You look lonesome."

I look up to see Tash. I look at her—really look at her. There's nothing wrong with being a Twinkie. Lips is a great example of a good woman. Tash though…she's ugly, and I'm not talking about the outside. Inside she's ugly—like me. She's got the same rotting insides as I do. This is what I deserve. Carrie, the baby…that's not the life for me. I should have never touched her—never let myself dream.

"Sure baby climb on board," I tell her, patting my lap. She slides on and my dick…lays there. Her perfume feels as if it's going to choke me. Carrie doesn't wear perfume. Her scent is a mixture of the lotion and shampoo she uses. It's clean, sweet and…too good for me.

She starts licking on my neck like some damn dog in heat. Is this what I have to look forward to in life? I down another shot to dull the feel of her.

"Keep your fucking hands away from my head, Tash," I bark when she starts to pull my face to her. I can't handle that shit. I couldn't handle certain things with Carrie, but the feel of this bitch's hands pulling my head down… fuck I want to vomit. Instead, I down another drink. My hands are shaking. Images flash in my mind. I was unconscious during most of my attack but every now and then I remember the smell, the voices, and the laughter as another... SHIT! Why the fuck are the memories getting more intense and coming so often?

I look back at Nicole, her face is blurry as hell. I see her laughing, her hand on her stomach. My mind pictures Carrie in that same pose, laughing and being happy—with me. The thought of her makes my dick jerk, which considering the bottle I've ingested is a miracle. Tash is undoing my pants. What does it matter? Not a damn thing, unless you count the fact that my dick just shriveled up at the thought.

I'm about to push the bitch off of me when I feel her hand graze the head of my cock. I can feel bile rise in my throat. I haven't been able to let anyone touch my dick, but me. I grieved it. I wanted Carrie to suck me off. I longed for it. Yet, just the thought of giving someone control...

I take another drink. The bottle is empty now. I'm going to grab another and get the fuck away from Tash and pray the liquor does its job.

"You disgust me," Nicole says from beside me.

I jerk around to face her, swaying but I manage to stay on the stool. She's looking at me with so much revulsion it pisses me the hell off. She wasn't lying. Fuck I was pretty sick of myself. Still I don't appreciate this bitch calling me out in front of everyone.

"Who the hell do you think you are?" I ask, knowing if Dragon walks in, he will hand me my ass on a platter.

"I am apparently the only one here with enough nerve to tell you what a fuck up, you're being. I know you got shit going on in your head Dancer, but don't you think it's time to grow the hell up? You're home now quit hurting people who give a damn about you and be a fucking man!"

"Woman, I'm not going to tell your ass again. Get the hell out of my business."

"Carrie is my business."

"I don't owe that cunt a damn thing. She wanted my cock and she got it. End-of-story!"

Even saying this shit hurts me, but I can't give in. Carrie left me. She gave up on me. She finally discovered what I already know. She's too good for me.

"You're such a pig. She loves you. Dragon does too."

Her words cut open the part inside of me that isn't dead. Dragon and Carrie are probably the only two people in my life who have ever cared about me besides Jazz. That thought hurts so deep, I lash out.

"The bitch asked for my cock, she got it. Who I give my dick to, is none of your fucking concern. That is unless you want to take a ride on the train too?"

"Don't make me gag! You stay drunk off your ass! You take a good woman's virginity, who just so happens to love you and you just kick her to the curb for a woman whose pussy has been used so many times it's wider than the grand fucking canyon? What is wrong with you?"

"What'd you say about me bitch?" Tash joins in.

"Do you really want me to show you how the fuck I feel about you again Tash? If you do, bring it on. I'll do your ugly ass a favor and break your nose the other way this time and get rid of that nasty crooked shit you got going on," Nicole responds.

"Are you going to let her talk to me like that?" Tash asks.

I hold my head down and rub the bridge of my nose.

Fuck a duck, I can't handle this.

"Bitch please, your legs get spread more than peanut butter," Nicole snaps at Tash and I want to laugh.

"Well I never!" Tash whines back and her voice is so grating I cringe.

"There are three words no one ever thought they'd hear out of your mouth. I guess God still gives out miracles."

"I doubt you know anything about God," Tash snaps in response to Nicole.

"I know you've been on your knees more than Billy Graham, does that count?"

"Bitch..."

"WILL YOU TWO SHUT THE HELL UP? I'm fucking tired of it. Nicole, get your cunt ass back to Dragon and get the fuck away from me!"

The room goes completely quiet. It had died down before, but this quiet is more.

"I can't believe you, but yeah I'll leave you alone. Carrie and the baby are better off without your sorry ass anyway."

I get out of my chair pushing Tash off of me. I need out of here. It feels like I'm fucking choking on the air.

"Only time I need to hear or see your damn mouth is if you want to suck my cock. I hear you're good at that shit..."

I growl dismissing Nicole, intent on getting the fuck out of here.

"What the fuck did you just say to my woman, Dance?" Dragon yells out from across the room.

I shove Nicole out of my way, I have to leave. The

room is swimming and my heart is pounding double time. I can't let anyone see me like that. I can't....

Dragon grabs the edge of a table and propels it half way across the room. Before I even blink, he's in front of me and his fist is coming at my face.

It's one punch and I'm down. I couldn't stand after a punch like that, even sober. I lay on the floor trying for some reason to hold onto consciousness.

I look up and focus on Dragon. He is looking down at me and again it's just another person with disgust in their eyes. I try to shake off the effects of the upper cut and all of the alcohol swimming in my system, I can't.

I let out a painful breath and bend double as Dragon's steel toed boot connects with my stomach. Before I can react further, not that I could have at that point, Dragon slams his size twelve boot into my nuts.

The pain is so intense I turn to the side and puke some of the liquid poison I'm swimming in. My pulse pounds and thrums in my ears. Dragon grabs me by the neck of my shirt and now I can see the pain in his eyes as well as the disgust.

"I know you got shit gutting you, Dance. I see it and it kills me that I can't help, but Motherfucker if you ever talk to my woman like that again? If you ever put your hands on her in any fucking way, I will end you. Do you hear me? I will put a bullet in your fucking brain, and end you. I'll give you what you've wanted since you got out."

Dragon lets me go and my head hits the floor and rolls into my own vomit. My vision is blurry, but I could see Crusher, Freak and Gunner standing beside Dragon and the pity in their eyes makes me want to fucking scream. I close my eyes to avoid it instead.

"Dragon, sweetheart let it go."

I open my eyes when I feel a towel on the side of my head. Nicole is wiping the side of my face. She is trying to help me, even after I had shot my mouth off towards her.

"Mama, get up from there, you shouldn't be bending down in your condition," Dragon says.

My eyes lock on Nicole's blue ones. I'm not sure what is there. There's pity, but something else. I want to ask, but I don't. She gives me a weak smile and lets her man pull her away from me.

"Get your shit together, Dance. You want revenge? I'll help you. Whatever you need brother you got it, but get your fucking shit together. We're brothers. I'm here for you. No judgment. You feel me?"

I don't answer. I hear him I just can't stop looking at the way my brother is holding Nicole. I watch as she stretches her head up and kisses him on the lips and slowly pulls away.

She gets to the hall at the back of the club, stops and looks at me. She gives me a weak smile. I pull my eyes from her and look back at my brothers. They're all standing in a semi-circle looking down on the fucking mess I have become. I know what they want from me, I'm just not sure I can give it.

I'm lying here in vomit with my pants undone, with my brothers watching. Is this rock bottom?

Chapter 36

DANCER

THE FEEL OF cold water rushing over me greets me. I sputter into consciousness. Dragon is standing over my bed in the club, a dripping empty bucket in his hand.

"What the fuck, man?" I yell jumping out of the bed, using my hand to wipe the water out of my eyes. I moan at the pain the sudden movement costs me. I sway but manage to stay on my feet.

"Time to get off your ass, Dance. We got shit to do."

He throws a towel at me, I wipe my face off and then put the towel on the bed and sit down to get my bearings. Sadly, most of the water hit me not the bed.

"What kind of shit?"

He throws down a flyer and I look at it.

Hope Harbor, A Sexual Trauma Recovery Center

"Oh, fuck no!"

"Oh, fuck yes," Dragon returns.

"You don't know what the…"

"I don't, exactly. I'll give you that, but I know what it's like to be used for sex when I had no idea what sex was."

"Damn it, Drag…"

"Look at me, motherfucker. Do I look weak to you?"

I stop and look at him.

"I was traded around the streets as a kid for sex. A fucking kid! I survived. I am my own fucking man and I fucking fight to keep that. I fucking fight to keep my woman and…"

"It's not the same! I went off half-cocked!" I scream standing up, the state of my hangover lost in the crap that Dragon seems intent on bringing to the surface.

"So? You kept Carrie from being…"

"If it had been you, it would have turned out different! You would have kept your cool! You would have saved your woman and covered your ass and none of the other shit would have happened! You even told me that shit!"

"I fucking lied!" Dragon yells back and I freeze.

"If it had been Nicole attacked in that fucking alley. If it had been Nicole some motherfucker had his hands on, I would have gutted him like a motherfucking fish and I would have danced on his corpse. Fuck I might have even made a necklace out of his entrails."

I listen and my hand comes up to rub the stubble on my face. I almost want to smile.

"You're a sick bastard."

"Never claimed different."

I sit back down.

"If it had been you Drag, you would have been able to protect yourself better. You would have stopped them…'

"Bullshit. You were one man. One man, who they grabbed, shanked from behind like the fucking pussies they were and then beat you into unconsciousness—all before they took from you what they did. Hell Dance, even with all that you still managed to put two of the guards in the hospital."

I swallow as I look down at the floor. I can't look up at Dragon. I'm not ready.

"They didn't take from me, Dragon. They didn't steal a watch off of me. They didn't rob me of money. They raped me."

It's a whisper. A broken whisper and I hate that there are tears, but there are. So, I keep my head down.

"They did, but they did *not* break you, Dance. You're still here and you got a good woman who loves you. You got a baby on the way. You got a family who needs you and brothers that would fucking die for you. Do NOT let these pussies take that shit from you, man. Don't let it happen. If they do that, if you let them do that, then you're **weak**. Right now brother, there's not a motherfucking thing weak about you."

"How do you know?"

"Your dreams in the hospital, then I did some digging."

"The brothers?"

"Might guess, but have no idea. I did this, I called in a marker."

"You really think some new age recovery center can help me?"

"I think it's worth a shot. I think it will help you get your woman and kid back."

I swallow and chance a look at him. I breathe easier when he is looking down at me and I don't see pity. I see... belief. I grab the paper again.

Hope Harbor. I sure could fucking use some hope.

"I want them all to die. I want to send them to hell. I doubt Hope Harbor can do that for me."

"No, that's where I come in."

I look up at him and he has another sheet of paper. He slides it in the pocket of his jeans.

"You get better. If you want to help you're welcome to, but I will make the fuckers pay. I made a promise."

"A promise?" I ask trying to ignore the panic at the thought of the men on that paper.

"Red told me to make it hurt. I intend to."

My eyes freeze on Dragon's.

"She did?"

Dragon nods.

"I need help, Drag. I…I can't do it on my own."

"Then let's get you help and get your woman home where she belongs."

"She might not want to come home."

"Then you'll just have to convince her."

"You think I can do that?" I ask, but I feel lighter than I have in forever.

"It'll take a lot of work," Dragon shrugs, but he is smiling too.

"A lot of work," I echo.

"Anything good in life is."

"Let's get me healthy then," I respond and when I stand in front of Dragon he cups my shoulder in support.

Chapter 37

CARRIE

GOD, I MISS him.
I thought with time it would get better, but it hasn't. It's been four weeks. A whole month now since I have seen Jacob and every day the need for him gets worse. What is wrong with me?

I've gotten settled. I have a routine, but that's what it is. A routine. The highlight of my week is when Nicole calls me. She told me that Dancer has been attending therapy for the last two weeks. She feels like he's trying to get better. I'm glad. I really am, but there's a part of me wondering why he couldn't do that when we were together. A bigger part of me is hurt because he hasn't tried to contact me. Did I mean so little? Now that he's trying to get better, am I no longer important to him? Did I finally convince him it was over? That thought chills me.

These questions have haunted me constantly for the last three days—ever since Nicole's last call where she told me that Dancer had moved back into the house he and I had shared.

My hand goes down to my stomach and I rub it gently. I'm not showing yet, but I can feel changes. I will be having an ultrasound soon. I want Jacob to be there. I sigh. People in hell want ice water I guess.

The phone rings and my hand automatically grabs it on the first ring, not bothering to check the caller I.D— just praying I know who it is.

"Hello?"

"Carrie."

The word is more breathed than said. I feel it and it warms me.

"Hello, Jacob."

"Don't hang up on me Care Bear, please don't hang up on me."

"I should."

"I know sweetheart, but I'm begging you not to."

I say nothing in return, but I don't hang up.

"I've missed you, Care Bear. The house feels empty without you."

"You'll get used to it," I say praying I'm wrong.

"How are you? How's our angel?"

"Angel?" I ask looking down at my hand that is cupping my stomach.

"I've decided we're having a girl."

"We are?" I ask, not sure if him saying *we're* having a baby, or the fact he says it's a girl touches me more.

"Yeah, the world needs more beautiful women like her mommy."

"Jacob…"

"Shhh… baby. I've not heard your voice in over ten days. I just want to lie here on the bed and hear you, please?"

"Shouldn't you be at work?" I ask, my eyes closing.

"Therapy today in Glasgow, so I didn't feel like going in. You didn't answer, how are you?"

"I'm okay, getting settled. I went to the cemetery and visited with my parents. It's a nice plot they would like it. It's peaceful.

"That's good baby. I'm sorry I wasn't there with you.

"I would have liked that."

Nicole said you were going to therapy. How is, I mean, you know, is that going okay?"

"It's rough going, but I'll make it."

"Are you eating okay? The book says you shouldn't eat fish Carrie, I know you like it but…"

"The book?"

"I bought some pregnancy books. I wanted to know what you are going through."

"I…I don't know what to say to that."

"Say you won't eat fish, Care Bear."

I smile.

"I won't, Jacob. What else did you buy?"

"I bought a book for the baby. This lady at the book store told me it's good if the baby hears our voices. She suggested it."

"She did?"

"Yeah, she said her sons read to all of her grandkids like that. She swears they came out of the stomach looking for their dad's voices. I kind of like that idea."

I listen to him talk, I like the way he sounds kind of sheepish. It's a good sound.

"What book did you get?"

"*Goodnight Moon.*"

"You could read it to me now."

"I'd like that. Do you have a speakerphone?"

"Yeah why?"

"Turn it on so the munchkin can hear it too."

Munchkin? I can't help but grin.

"Okay Jacob," I say while I click the speaker button.

I listen to him read and notice the subtle differences in him. He seems at ease, he seems…tender.

As he finishes, I pick the phone back up and turn off the speaker.

"That was nice Jacob, thank you."

"Do you think the baby liked it? I've tried to find a book about motorcycles. There's not that many. I'm going to make one up for our girl."

"You're a confusing man, Jacob Blake."

"You should try being me. I'm trying to get better, Carrie. I promise. I'm trying, Care Bear."

"And therapy?" I ask, needing to know more.

"I hate it. I hate every minute of it, but I'm trying."

"Jacob…"

"Can I call you tomorrow night?"

This is it. The moment of truth.

"I'd like that, but kind of early? I get tired easily these days, so I crash with the chickens."

"Eight?"

"Okay. Talk to you then."

"Sweet dreams, Care Bear."

"Sweet dreams, Jacob."

Chapter 38

DANCER

I'VE BEEN TALKING to Carrie on the phone every evening now for two weeks. Two weeks and I'm going insane. I'm doing my best not to rush her, but damn it all to Hell, something has to give. Listening to her sweet voice is driving me insane. I need to touch her, I need to hold her. I need to be with her. I haven't held her, been inside of her or kissed her in over a month and a half. I can't keep going like this.

So today starts operation, 'Win Back My Woman'.

I decide to start small. I send her George. A giant teddy bear I bought the day of my first therapy meeting.

I have been online checking the tracking numbers all day. She got the present an hour ago. She hasn't called. I'm disappointed, but there's not much more I can do. It takes all I got, but I don't call her that night.

Day two, I send her flowers. Daisies. The type that were on her dress the last time I saw her. I'd be lying if I said it didn't hurt when she doesn't call.

Day three, I text her saying I miss her and attach a picture. It is of the crib I purchased and spent all night putting together. No word.

Day four, I'm about to give up hope. One small word from her, that's all I need. Well okay, that's not all. It would be a damn good start though. Today I send her a picture of the hummingbird feeder she hung up outside. There are two hummingbirds around it and I thought she'd like to see it. I also send her another text.

I miss you. Please call me.

I stare at my phone for an hour, for nothing.

Day five, I send her chocolate covered strawberries. They are her favorites.

I hear nothing. I've hurt her too bad. I've lost her.

Day six, I'm not even bothering to get out of bed. I'm depressed, I'm horny as hell and I just don't see the point anymore. I'd rather stay in bed, stroke my cock and think about Carrie, than get up and miss her.

Life is just too empty without her. I'm missing everything from her smile, her laugh, to the way she lights up my world. I miss her voice, how she says my name. I miss her body—especially her body.

Fuck, if I close my eyes, I can picture her straddling me. Her creamy, milk white skin with a faint dusting of freckles. Her breasts filling my hands, her nipples large and glistening because I've sucked on them. I moan out loud picturing her.

My hand moves down to stroke my cock. I squeeze it tight, as I imagine slipping inside my woman's wet, tight pussy. Her body rocks up and down on my cock. Her nails dig into my abdomen. Her head is thrown back in pleasure, all the while riding me harder and harder.

I can almost hear her voice, begging me to make her

come. I stroke myself faster, pre-cum bathes the head of my cock and drizzles slowly downward. My balls tighten, and just as I get ready to blow I can hear her voice.

I love you, Jacob. I love you.

I explode. My cum shoots on my chest, my stomach and my hand, as I call out her name. After the initial rush, I look at myself disgusted. It doesn't satisfy me. If anything I feel emptier and even more alone.

I drag my ass up, towel off, grab a beer and lay back down. I might be doing better with some things, but right now I hate myself for running off the one great thing I've ever had in my life.

I haven't been drunk lately—not since Dragon kicked my ass. I'm thinking today might be a good day to get shitfaced. It's going to take something a hell of a lot more powerful than beer though. There's nothing in the house and I don't have the energy to go out.

I'm probably just a bigger fucking fool at this point, but after my third fucking beer I give up and text her.

I need you, Care Bear. Give me another chance.

Another beer later, I close my phone. I'm almost back to sleep. I used to dread going to sleep because of dreams. Now, I willingly surrender, hoping to dream of being with Carrie. I need to see her so bad, even if sleep just brings one glance at my woman, it is worth it. I'm almost asleep, when the phone rings.

"Yeah."

"Hi, Jacob."

"Care Bear. God sweetheart, I've missed you."

"I...I miss you too."

"Are you doing okay? Did you get the stuff I sent you? Are you getting plenty of rest?"

"Yeah…"

We're both silent. Shit. It feels like she's so far away from me and I'm not talking just physically. Is this what I've done?

"Are you still going to therapy?" She asks, and I close my eyes.

"Yeah, twice a week."

"That's good, Jacob. I'm proud of you."

"How's the baby?"

"You do realize I'm barely past two months pregnant right?" She questions, but I hear laughter.

"Your point? I ask.

She doesn't answer, but she laughs harder. It is a beautiful sound.

"How is our little angel, Care Bear?"

"It's a boy."

"You know? You had one of those sonograms done?" I ask, disappointed because Dragon and Nicole have and I wanted to be there for our baby's.

"No, I just know it is."

"We'll see, I'm still saying it's a beautiful girl who looks like her mom."

"I was hoping you'd like to read…to the baby."

I close my eyes and breathe easy for the first time in days.

"Always," I whisper, because my throat is clogged with emotion. "You got it on speaker?" I hear the button click and then her voice comes back to me.

"I do now."

"Once upon a time in a land far, far away there was a Princess named Carolina, with long, flowing locks the color of a fall sky at sunset."

"That doesn't sound like a story about the moon."

"I've decided to expand my horizons. Now hush, our munchkin wants to hear this story."

"Okay."

"Princess Carolina grew to be kind and strong, with a heart so full that she gave off a golden light full of love..."

"Golden light? Where's my badass biker?"

"He was stupid and lost his woman," I answer honestly.

"Jacob..."

"People would come from all across the world to gaze upon Princess Carolina's beauty. They would bring her gifts and flowers, but most of all they would bring people to her that needed help. One day a friend of Princess Carolina's told her of a dark and evil creature named Troll."

"Troll?" She asks, but I hear the smile.

"Troll. Now, Troll had done some bad things and was doomed into the dark forest for years. He was all on his own, with no one to care about him."

"Jacob..."

"Troll was mad and angry at the world, however he took one look at the Princess and wanted to be her friend..."

"Her friend?"

"It's a children's story Care Bear, some things munchkin will never discover until she's a hundred and I'm dead and gone."

That's when I hear her laugh fully and I let go of a breath I didn't even know I was holding. I breathe. Oh god, I breathe.

"I don't think it works that way Jacob, but please continue."

"Now where was I? Oh yeah, so Troll took one look at the beautiful Princess Carolina and wanted to be her friend. Still, to do so would mean bringing her deep into the forest with him and he couldn't do that to her. If he let her into the forest, then her beauty and light would disappear and the people needed her light. She made the world better. So, he turned her away and hurt her heart.

Troll was very sad and his world just got darker and darker. One day it became so dark that Troll went to sleep. It was a deep, deep sleep and none of the Troll's friends could wake him. When Princess Carolina heard of the news, she decided to come to the Troll one more time—in hopes of saving him."

"Jacob...."

I hear the tears in her voice. I hope this means she understands what I'm trying to say.

"When she gets there Troll's friends he had pushed away, are gathered around him crying. They all have given up hope. Princess Carolina looks down where the Troll is sleeping. She sees through his ugly hideous form, to the man underneath. She bends down and places a kiss on his lips. Slowly the Troll begins to warm, as Princess Carolina's light shines through him and releases him from the darkness.

The Troll wakes, so thankful that the Princess has saved him. He vows to love her forever and ever. Then she takes him away from the dark forest, to a beautiful castle full of love and laughter. They become a family and have a little baby Princess named Jasmine."

"Jasmine?" She's crying now, but I can hear happiness. It's a sound in Carrie's voice you can't mistake.

"Shhh...sweetheart, I'm at the most important part," I say and this time there are tears in my eyes.

"What's that?" She asks.

"They lived happily ever after."

I hear her breathing hard and I lie there hoping.

"Jacob?"

"Yeah Care Bear?"

"Come get us."

Thank fuck.

"I'll be there in a few hours."

I BREAK EVERY traffic law coming and going, but I make it to Carrie's parents' home in record time. I've barely turned the car off before I jump out and run up to the front door. Carrie opens it before I knock and I just drink her in. She's lost weight. Her face is pale, but she has never been more beautiful.

"Hey Care Bear."

"My Biker Troll."

I smile, "I've missed you, sweetheart."

I open my arms and she walks into them. I wrap them around her.

"I've missed you too," she whispers against my neck. I

pull away slightly, looking at her. She's so beautiful. There are tears shining in her eyes and they slowly leak to the surface, but it is okay. I know these are happy tears and I kiss them away. I bend down to graze my lips against hers, I mean it to be just a touch, but after all this time away from her? I can't help but make it deeper.

My tongue pushes into her mouth, teasing, dancing with hers and I drink down her taste like a dying man savoring his last meal. I kiss her until neither of us have the air to continue. Then I just hold her close and place a kiss on her forehead.

"I'm sorry Care Bear, I know that's not enough, but I'm so fucking sorry."

"Just take me and munchkin home Jacob."

With those words? I feel alive again.

Chapter 39
CARRIE

IT'S LATE, BUT I'm not sleepy. I'm lying in Jacob's arms in our bed. He brought me home immediately. We made love, had a very late dinner and now I'm lying in his arms. I should be exhausted, but I can't shut my brain down. It is impossible. When you've lived your whole life for one dream and that dream is in your arms? When you get that dream after thinking it was gone forever? You can't sleep. You're afraid to sleep.

Jacob pulls my hand up, looking at it. His thumb presses into my palm, his fingers brush against mine.

"What are you thinking?" I ask, watching as he continues playing with my hand, curling my fingers and his together.

"I'm better Carrie, losing you woke me up, but…"

"But?"

"You have to know, I'm not magically healed. I still… shit Carrie…panic is just a breath away. I'm terrified of you touching me sometimes. I have this anger inside of me and there are times I just want to scream. I can't promise that you won't, that I…"

He turns to get out of the bed and I stop him, curling

tighter into him.

"Jacob. I've known about your attack since before the first time we made love. Don't you think I get it? We'll get through it together."

"Carrie, I wasn't attacked…I was…"

"You were forced," I interrupt him, my heart breaking. "You didn't do anything, Jacob."

"You can't pretty it up, Carrie. This…there is no way to make this pretty. I was raped."

The last word is broken and whispered so quietly it breaks my heart.

"It happens, Jacob. I… it happens."

I feel helpless and ill equipped to battle this. I want to have this magic word to heal him and there's nothing. I have nothing.

"It doesn't happen, not to a man. How can you want me, Carrie? I wasn't even strong enough to defend myself. How can I protect you or our baby?"

"Stop it, just stop it. You were held down and stabbed and you fought with everything you had in you."

"How do you…"

"The dreams Jacob, the dreams and that scar on your side. Most of all I know, because *I know you*. Rape is a crime. You were a victim, not weak. You're one of the strongest men I know."

"Carrie…"

"When I was five years old crying and hurt in the school parking lot all by myself, who picked me up, doctored my leg, held me and told me he had me? Who told me it would be okay? Who Jacob?"

"Sweetheart, you were…"

"When I was the one who was almost raped Jacob, who stopped it? Who stopped it and held me close and told me he had me and it would be okay?"

"Carrie...."

"If I had been raped Jacob, would you have thought me weak? Would you have been unable to care about me?"

"Fuck, no. I love you, Care Bear."

I let the tears fall at his words, but I ignore them, this is too important.

"When I had a gun pointed at me and thought I was going to die. Who saved me, Jacob? Who made it all okay? Who?"

He doesn't say anything, but he looks at me differently.

"When there was a bomb and we didn't have time to get away, who not only got us out but covered me with his body and protected me? Who made it all okay?"

"Carr..."

"Who Jacob?"

"What about all the times I failed you. When I hurt you? When I failed..."

"WILL YOU STOP? When it counts Jacob, always, when it has counted you have been there for me. I would trust you over anyone I have ever known to watch over our child. Let the rest go. We'll work through it, together."

"Together?" He asks and I hear the hope in his question.

"It's all going to be okay, Jacob," I say earnestly.

"And we'll live happily ever after," He whispers, his voice full of warmth.

His lips come down softly against mine. He kisses me gently, reverently and slowly. His tongue slides into my mouth as his hand brushes the side of my face. The kiss is full of emotion, full of tenderness and most of all, full of promise.

"I love you, Carolina Grace."

"I love you, Jacob *Dancer* Blake."

"Just Jacob to you baby, just to you."

"Okay that's it," I say slapping his chest. "Stop being sweet. I need my badass Biker now."

"Is that right?" He asks on a laugh, pulling me over top of him.

"Yeah, I'm a biker's old lady now, so there are certain things expected."

"What's that?"

I give him what I hope is a saucy look, full of challenge.

"Cock. Old Ladies need lots of throbbing, hard cock."

His head goes back with laughter and his dark eyes shine up at me with happiness.

"I'll see what I can do, Care Bear. I'll see what I can do."

Chapter 40

DANCER

I HOLD CARRIE close. The last round of lovemaking wore her out. Me too, but it's a good feeling. I find myself studying her hand again. For so long I feared being touched, still do. Yet, now there's something different…something special in the feel of Carrie's hand. I haven't let her touch me everywhere, but I've let her do more than I ever dreamed possible and she's right. It's a start. I can face the future with her by my side.

I watch her sleep. She has a smile on those beautiful lips and I take pride in knowing that I put it there. I gave her that smile. I vow to give her more of those.

My hand slides down to Carrie's stomach, resting gently where our baby is. I told her I believe it's a girl. The truth is, I don't care. Girl or boy as long as it is healthy and Carrie is okay, I will be the happiest man on the planet.

I let the darkness surround me. I listen to the delicate whispers of her breath. I let that soothe me. I let that be my focus as sleep takes hold of me. I let Carrie be what she has always been, my anchor and the reason I exist.

Sleep claims me and tonight, I don't dream of the darkness. I don't dream of pain and misery. This dream is completely different. I am standing in a hospital room, I watch as a nurse wraps mine and Carrie's baby in a blanket. She puts a beanie cap on this perfect, little head. A head covered with light strands of hair, the color of her mom's. The nurse looks at me, but my eyes won't leave that of my beautiful daughter.

"Mr. Blake? Would you like to hold your baby?"

"What?" I ask, trying to pay attention, but still hypnotized by this little creature.

"I asked if you'd like to hold your baby, Daddy."

Daddy. That one word shatters the darkness and heals my soul. That one word gives me…Peace.

And they lived happily ever after.

Read on for a teaser for what happens next with the Savage Brothers MC

Excerpt
CLAIMING CRUSHER
Coming in 2015

I PUSH MY chair back tilting it and bringing my feet up, I rest them on my desk. My eyes follow the perfect crease in my three thousand dollar Armani suit. You have to pay for perfection, demand it really. From where I am sitting I can see my secretary buttoning up her black, silk blouse.

A shame really, because it will ultimately cover up the marks I left moments earlier on her body. I had come oh so close to choking the life out of her. She blacked out this time. Just the memory of it causes my dick to jump and I wonder how quick I can finish this call. Will I have time to take her again, before my next meeting? Maybe I'll force her to suck me off and hide under my desk. If she's a good little dog, I'll give her what she wants later. She's always begging for it. As dangerous as I am, she still craves more. It's good, it's an aphrodisiac knowing she's getting off on it—but only because it makes me push it further. I have to, because if not, I don't get to see the fear in her eyes and motherfucker, I crave the fear.

"Hurry Donald, I have someone waiting on me."

At my words, my secretary turns and looks at me, her brown eyes flash in understanding.

I take my feet down, slide my seat back another couple of inches and motion under my desk. She walks towards me, but I shake my head no. She stops instantly, such a good little pet.

Naked. I mouth the word. She nods her understanding and begins undressing.

"Mr. Kavanagh, we've found her."

I freeze. The little bitch has been missing for four fucking years.

"Where?" I demand, waving my secretary off. My dick being jammed down her throat is the last thing on my mind now. She picks up her clothes and quickly exits, having seen this mood enough to know to run for cover.

"She's in a small town in Eastern Kentucky."

"No fucking way."

"Yes sir, do we apprehend her and bring her to you?"

I consider this as it would be the easiest and ultimately the cleanest alternative. But alas, I do not do clean nor easy.

"No. Watch her, evaluate the situation. I want pictures tonight. I will decide after that."

"Yes sir, there might be one slight issue."

My hand tightens on the receiver. I will not have anything stand in my way now. It will not happen.

"That is?" I prompt.

"She seems to have taken up with a gang."

"A gang? That does not sound like Melinda. Perhaps your incompetence is showing again, Donald."

"No sir, the hair is different, but this is definitely Mrs.

Kavanagh."

"A gang?"

"A motorcycle gang, I believe they call themselves the Savage Brothers."

A motorcycle gang? Well, well. My Melinda never ceases to amaze, too bad I'm going to kill her.

"I expect a detailed report tonight. Do not disappoint, Donald."

"Yes, sir."

I hang the phone up and turn my seat around to stare at the landscape of the downtown Manhattan skyline. The different shapes and sizes of the skyscrapers jut and point in a strange pattern which is strangely beautiful. The water in the distance is calm and the blue reflects and shines in the sun. My hands grip tight on the arms of my leather, cushioned chair.

Finally Melinda is in my grasp. I vow she will not get away this time.

Thank you for purchasing Saving Dancer Book 2 of the Savage Brothers MC. I hope you enjoyed it. A Wedding Novella will be out soon entitled *Loving Nicole* and look for more of *Claiming Crusher* in the summer of 2015.

TURN THE PAGE FOR AN EXCITING EXCERPT FROM THE AMAZING MAYRA STRATHAM'S NEW BOOK ***ETCHED IN STONE***

April

Excerpt of Etched in Stone, Book 2 of Six Degrees Series by Mayra Statham

Chapter One
Liz

Two Months Later
Edwards Automotive Charity Breast Cancer Gala

EVERY PART OF my body aches. My shoulders are burning from hand rolling the various types of dough for different pastries. My feet are aching from being on them since three this morning. It doesn't help that I stuffed them into incredibly sexy peep-toe pink sling backs that Lucy let me borrow, because they went perfect with my dress.

My hands feel heavy and are probably swollen, but as I gaze at the table in front of me, all I can do is let the feeling of accomplishment flow freely through me. All the aches and pains are completely worth it as I look at the extravagant dessert table in front of me.

It's incredibly satisfying to see the fruits of your labor. Being able to mix simple ingredients, like flour and sugar with your own hands and somehow magically they become beautiful pieces of edible art.

The table is beautiful, exquisite really. Better than I

dreamed possible.

I admire the long beautiful table draped in expensive cream tablecloths that probably cost more than what I'm wearing, excluding Lucy's shoes. It made my beauties even more beautiful, they were definitely worth the investment. Tess, my business partner and friend, thought I was nuts spending that much on tablecloths.

Sweet sophistication!

My edible art is sitting and waiting on beautifully colored cake stands arranged at different heights with accent trays in shades of pink and cream. The cream puffs sit in the center of the table, gorgeous and fresh. While some have powdered sugar sifted on top, others are drizzled with chocolate to add a little more sweetness. Some have a dollop of cream and a piece of a locally grown strawberry sitting on top. The cupcakes, I agree with Tess, she had been right to add the iridescent powder that made them sparkle under the soft lighting in the elegant Beverly Hills Hotel's Crystal Room. Rectangular trays hold a variety of cannoli. Mini strawberry cheesecakes float at different elevations on the expensive pink tinted crystal cake stands. The two employees that will be manning the table are already standing by, dressed in pastry chef uniforms, white and pristine. They are the perfect finishing touch.

I watch Tess chat with Laney, the owner of Ritz Events. Who also happens to be the Gala's event coordinator and they are both smiling. A huge wave of relief sweeps through me, it is obvious that Laney is extremely happy with the dessert table. Our bakery, Izzy Tizzy's, is making a name for itself in Southern California.

I love that, at our bakery, we cater to everyone. We

appeal to the stay at home mom seeking a moment of refuge, Hollywood celebrities, even to the workers from the industrial side of town picking up their morning breakfast and coffee. However, the obscene price we are paid by the rich and famous makes me nervous. Even after a full year of being in business, I constantly worry that my creations aren't good enough for the clientele we serve.

Tess and I have Sabrina Miller to thank for a large portion of our higher end clientele. Sabrina, one of Laney's event planners, referred business to us from the moment she found our shop. There isn't a week that by that she doesn't send a new customer to us by. Some come in; others call to place an order, always telling us that Sabrina sent them. We even hired two new bakers, allowing Tess and I an actual day off. There are times when we joke about Sabrina being our business fairy Godmother and one day, we will figure out a way to thank her for everything she has done, not only for us, but our shop as well.

Lost in my own thoughts, I don't realize someone has approached me until a warm finger taps my shoulder. Even the fabric doesn't stop me from feeling the heat flowing into my body. The warmth lingers on my shoulder as I turn around with a smile on my face. Ready to answer questions, as early guests had already started coming up to me, asking for my business card. I was, however, not prepared to face the most incredibly handsome man I'd ever seen in my life! My smile wobbled at the same time my breath caught in the middle of my throat, as I took him in completely.

He's tall. From where I stand, even in heels, he has at least eight inches over me. Well over six feet, and I only really noticed because of the way I had to arch my neck to look up at him.

He has light, creamy skin that contrasts attractively against his jet black hair. Slightly overgrown and wavy you would think it was naturally curly. My fingers itch to touch his hair.

His face is a masterpiece. Squared jaw with a cleft in the center, a clean shaven face highlights the flawlessness of his skin and makes me want to feel it, bare against my own flesh. His strong nose is completely masculine, with a slight bump on the ridge that makes me wonder if at some time in his life he'd broken it in a fight or by accident. Either way, it added a sense of ruggedness and of the bad boy hiding beneath the obviously expensive tuxedo he was wearing.

Every single thing about this man makes him stunning, but it is his eyes that make my heart stutter. The outside of his irises are dark, like rich, thick, black ink. His eyes are light pools of grey mixed with a slight hint of sage green, making them unusual. All I can think about is how I want to memorize his eyes, so that I can duplicate them in paint, they are that striking. But it wasn't only the color of his eyes; it's what is behind them, a light that shines through. A brightness children have when they are about to make a wish right before they blow out the candles on their birthday cake.

At the bittersweet thought, I can't help the smile that washes over me. In an instant, a smile replaces his serious expression as he looks me in the eyes. The way he looks at me with that genuine smile on his face, makes me breathless. Like some nitwit heroine from one of the romance novels Lucy tries to push on me. I don't have words to describe how handsome he really is, with just a smile, he literally makes my knees weak.

"Hi." I say soundly slightly breathy in a bad Marilyn Monroe kind of way. I immediately want to run away. I'm such a nerd!

"Hey." His deep voice rumbles. I feel a quiver go down my spine and out my toes.

Down my spine and out my toes? What the hell is wrong with me?

We stare at one another. I wouldn't have been able to look away if my life depended on it. He is more than the stereotypical pretty-boy that L.A. offers. God knows this place has more than enough of those running all over Hollywood. No. He's the perfect example of masculine beauty. To put it simply, he really is THAT beautiful!

"Are you from Izzy Tizzy's?" He asks, his voice deeper than I would have thought possible. I nod since my mind decides at this particular moment, to stop functioning.

"Any chance that I can ask you a couple of questions about having a birthday cake made?" He asks looking completely amused. I silently curse and remind myself, that there was no way that a guy like this would be interested in a girl like me.

"Of course," I croak out and clear my throat, trying to smile.

"How much time in advance do you need for a birthday cake order?" He asks, a single dark eyebrow going up slightly.

He wants to order a birthday cake. I want to sigh. Of course, Hottie McMysterious would want to order a cake, probably for his ... glancing at his bare ring finger... for his girlfriend.

"We usually require at least forty-eight hours in advance for preparation, but we can rush one in twenty-four. Unless you were looking for something elaborate, then I'd stick to forty-eight." I answer as if I'm on autopilot. At least I can try to sell him something.

"What do you consider elaborate?" He asks, one side of his mouth slightly tipping up gives him a cocky look.

"Six tiered fondant with hand piping or life-size creations." I answer quickly and his eyes go wide, his lips go from a smirk to a smile.

"Okay. Any chance I can have your card?"

"Sure." I walk to the table and grab a business card, not noticing as he steps closer.

As I turn around, his chest is now an inch or two from my face. I try to step back but of course I don't lift my leg high enough, my heel catches on the carpet and I begin to stumble. My mind running with horrible images of falling dead center into the table that holds all the sweets that took forever to create and making a complete fool of myself in front of not only the sexy stranger but some of the rich and powerful of southern California. But instead of falling, his strong hands quickly go to my shoulders, bringing my body back close to his. Keeping his hands on me, as I make sure my feet are now solidly on the floor, saving me from falling on the table.

"Sorry." "Thank you" We both mumble, his hands holding on to my forearms, bringing my body a step closer to his as he steadies us. Everything happened in mere seconds, so quickly no one probably even noticed. Not that I am going to look around to see if someone had. But as quickly as it had happened, I felt every second in slow motion.

His grey eyes are melting into my eyes. He is a snake charmer, and I've been charmed.

All this without even knowing his name!

Straightening my back at the thought, making my face serious, I extend my arms handing him the card.

"Here's my card." I blurt nervously.

"Liz!" Tess calls and I look behind me to see Tess waving me over as she stands next to Laney. I raise a finger, asking her for a moment.

"Did you have any other questions?" I ask, part of me hoping he had an hours' worth of questions, the embarrassed side of me hoping he was ready to walk away.

He stands in front of me, one of his hands still touching my elbow softly. Fingertips lightly grazing my elbow, heat is radiating all through me, as my brain quickly turns to mush from looking at him.

My snake charmer.

"Your name is Liz?" He asks in a tone that means something, I don't know, and I smile. Not that I'm going to let myself think a man like the one in front of me would want to know my name for any other reason than to know who to refer to when he orders his very lucky girlfriend, her birthday cake.

"Yeah," I mumble smiling, trying to ignore the sad feeling of not having a chance with the guy in front of me. He nods, his hand leaves my elbow, and I immediately miss his touch. He looks down at the card in his hand and smiles at me.

"I'll call about that cake," He says and walks away leaving me completely intrigued over a guy for the first time in I don't know how long.

Parker Stone

She is so damn beautiful.

Her olive skin hints at her Hispanic background, the skin that I want to touch and kiss. Her eyes, fuck her eyes are round, and dark, almost black as night. They are framed by thick, natural, black lashes. She renders me stupid. I grin at the thought, amazed that I have found her again.

What are the chances?

I saw her two months ago at my friend's wedding, delivering a cake, and I had acted like a gawky, nerdy teenage boy staring at the homecoming queen. I've never had that happen. Not in high school or college. Talking to women has always come easy to me like it was second nature, but with her, my mind blanks. She'd been a vision then, and by the time I had worked up the courage to talk to her, she'd left, vanishing into thin air so quickly, I almost thought I'd somehow imagined her.

Like an angel.

Seeing her, standing in front of the huge dessert bar tonight, I didn't hesitate to go and talk to her. I probably made a complete idiot of myself, asking lame questions about a freaking birthday cake, but I don't care. I had to talk to her. I will order ten fake birthday cakes if I have to. I finally heard her voice. I even held her close, the softness of her body and the sweet scent that surrounded her, made me feel alive more than I ever had before.

My angel finally has a name, Liz.

Breaking Dragon's Playlist

Breaking Dragon Final

open.spotify.com/user/12149197675/playlist/1JWfJFpsf4odID9kgVULIV

Saving Dancer's Playlist

Saving Dancer Final

open.spotify.com/user/12149197675/playlist/1uMJhzmhkKYLeWWW7aBZZX

Acknowledgments

I hope you enjoyed Dancer's story. His story was especially important to me. As a survivor of sexual violence, I was determined to show not the violence itself, but more of an understanding of the recovery, the pain and desperation and how sometimes, it is more debilitating than the actual act itself (at least it was for me).

It is not something you fully recover from with time. It always haunts you, but there is hope and there is a light. The organizations mentioned in this book do not endorse this book, they have nothing to do with this book and were mentioned to further the story. I fully acknowledge this. Yet, they are great organizations that truly help victims.

Every 107 seconds another victim of sexual violence joins already frightening high numbers. 68% percent of all assaults are never reported and almost 98% percent of rapists will never spend a day in prison. Those are staggering numbers, because when it happened to me I felt alone, dirty and ashamed. We aren't alone. We should never feel desperate to end the pain, but always, ALWAYS look for the light.

Jordan

Groups available for guidance:
Rape Crisis Outreach (rapecrisis.com)
National Sexual Violence Resource Center (nsvrc.org)
*Statistics courtesy of RAINN (rainn.org/statistics)

Links

Facebook:
www.facebook.com/JordanMarieAuthor

TSU:
www.tsu.co/Jordan_Marie

Pinterest:
www.pinterest.com/jordanmarieauth

Twitter:
twitter.com/Author_JordanM

Goodreads:
www.goodreads.com/author/show/9860469.Jordan_Marie

Newsletter:
http://eepurl.com/barBKv

Webpage:
jordanmarieauthor.weebly.com

Printed in Great Britain
by Amazon.co.uk, Ltd.,
Marston Gate.